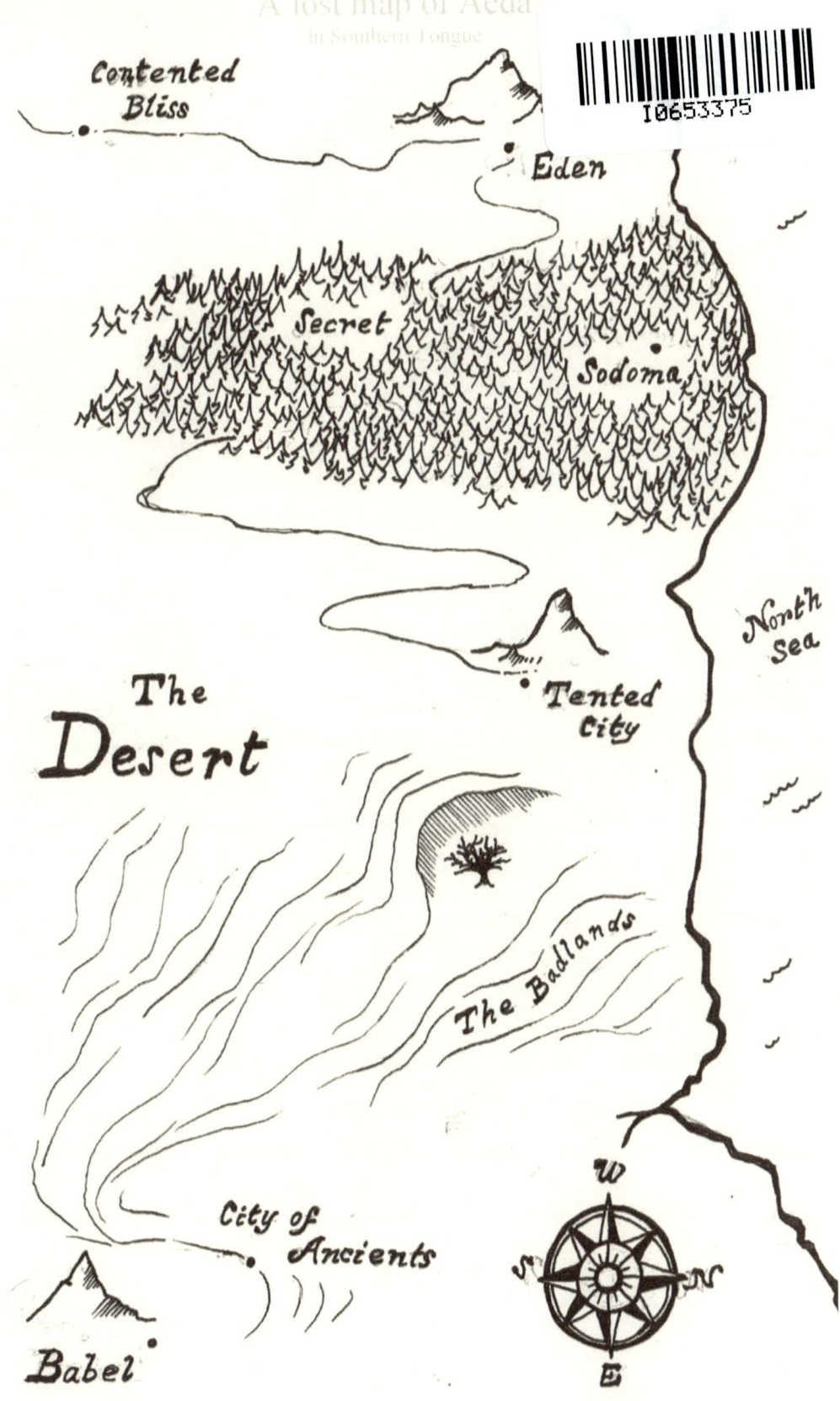

A lost map of Aeda
in Southern Tongue

Contented
Bliss

Eden

Secret

Sodoma

North
Sea

The
Desert

Tented
City

The Badlands

City of
Ancients

Babel

W
N
S
E

THE DESERT

THEY WILL NOT ENDURE

BY
E DANE ROGERS

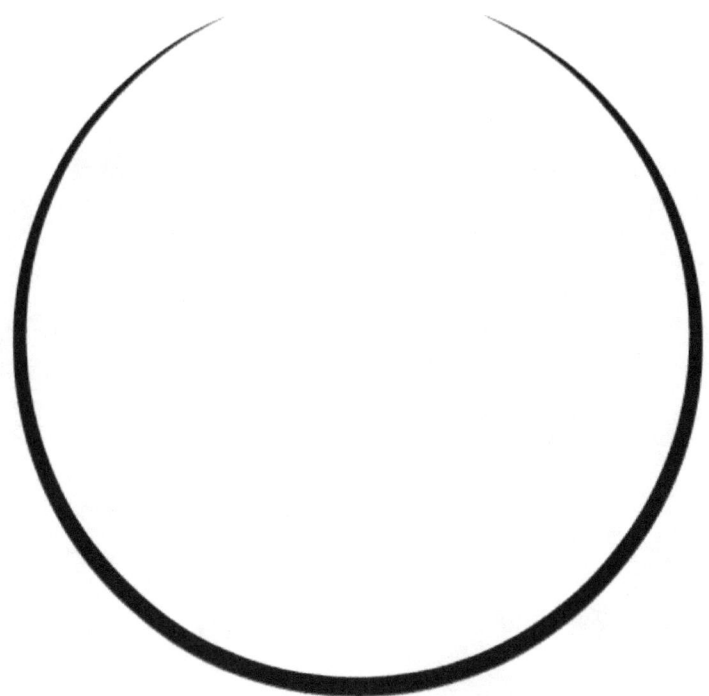

1

THE DESERT

THE BOOKS OF AEDA

~ A Novel ~

BY
E DANE ROGERS

RENDER UNTO THEM THEIR DESERT

PSALM 28:4

TABLE OF CONTENTS

E Dane Rogers

ACKNOWLEDGEMENT

This project consumed more time, effort and help than I assumed when I began to put this story to paper in early 2015. The process and experiences that made this story what it is spanned many experiences and many regions, from the Pacific Northwest, to the Midwest, to Ecuador, Korea and Italy. More important than the places themselves are the people in those places who gave of themselves to nurture this project.

A huge thank-you is due my wonderful aunts, Allison Raduziner and Crystal Wrabetz, for their diligence in editing, proof reading, advice on storyline and flow of writing style. There is no one I would have rather gone through this monotonous process with than these wonderful women.

Secondly, my artists. Ashleigh Darby and Mallory Rogers lent more than just their thoughts, but their creativity to the project. Ashleigh was a joy to work with, and although her acrylic pieces did not make the final cut, most all the chapters begin with a design created by her talented fingers. Mallory's fine eye caught the perfect moment in time and place to represent this story in picture. The cover photo is hers. Pictured is her friend, Satoshi. Thank you!

A few more pieces were added to the project to make it complete, save the men-of-old who gave their profound words to the inspiration of the story and its search for morality, which were the generous gifts of friends. Cathy Wootton and Julie Rust were kind enough to read it, lending encouragement, doctrinal direction and the occasional grammatical correction! Thank you, my sisters-in-Christ. Stephen Bickley, my pastor at Providence Community Church in Victoria, B.C., wrote a beautiful forward to the book which I will cherish for years to come.

My inspirers are more copious than those who knowingly gave of themselves for this project. It's best I not mention their names as they have painted the tapestry of my life and my story; I have no right to them but for the memories and experiences we've shared. I suffice to say that for some, as they read this story, certain characters may be more real to them than others. For me, every character is one I've spoken to outside this imagined desert landscape.

On that note, I must also thank those who I can name, being that they were inspiring to me through advice and encouragement. First, of course, my mother, Dayna Jessen-Rogers, from whom I got any semblance of creativity that may have found its way onto the pages of the Desert. Secondly, my grandmother, Shirley Rogers, who eagerly awaits reading a copy! My friends have all been willing to lend an ear to the development of storyline, characters and conveying my thoughts. Victoria Shin is perhaps my most frequent victim who is always eager to hear the recent developments in the writing process.

Finally, not a page of this story would have been possible had its parallel consumed me in reality. It is only by the Grace of God that this story has the ending it did, for its every twist and turn follows my juvenile rebellion against *He who died that I might live.*

FORWARD

Nothing strikes our hearts with fear like brutal acts of terror. They seem random and unpredictable, but we know they are planned with care and executed without remorse. Their perpetrators are quick to emerge from the shadows to claim responsibility and shout the justice of their cause.

But what if there exists *another* kind of terror, which assaults the very soul with consequences that extend even beyond death? Assailants who burn with hatred toward us, and whose only cause is our hopeless misery and everlasting destruction? What if these terrorists need no masks or hoods because they are *invisible* malevolent spirits, who target unwary victims taught to believe only in what they can see? Shakespeare's Hamlet laments that *"The flesh is heir to a thousand natural shocks."* But how can we face far worse shocks that are *supernatural?*

In *the Desert*, E Dane Rogers tells a hair-raising story of a reckless and willful journey to hell and back, made by one who has betrayed all his values and everyone he truly cares about. The story traces a boy who embraces every alluring indulgence and pleasure only to see how swiftly they turn vicious and vile. In his agony he finds himself among *the walking dead*, with an excruciating awareness of how evil first deceives, then defiles, and finally *destroys.* In shocking pain and brutal torment, he looks for a way back. But can he ever escape the spine-tingling, soul-destroying *emptiness* of his own choosing?

This is a book you won't *enjoy* but it's one that may protect you from your own worst enemy, the sensate-self who lives only in the moment and knows nothing of consequences. This story will remind you that every temptation is an outrageous lie. It will point you to the One who leads you *not* into temptation, and who alone can deliver you from the Evil One.

- Stephen Bickley, Pastor of Providence Community Church, Victoria

PREFACE

From Milton's *Paradise Lost*. 1903 ed.

"Say first—for Heaven hides nothing from thy
view,
Nor the deep tract of Hell—say first what cause
Moved our grand Parents, in that happy state,
Favoured of Heaven so highly, to fall off
From their Creator, and transgress his will
For one restraint, lords of the World besides.
Who first seduced them to that foul revolt?
            The infernal Serpent ; he it was whose guile,
Stirred up with envy and revenge, deceived
The mother of mankind, what time his pride
Had cast him out from Heaven, with all his host
Of rebel Angels, by whose aid, aspiring
To set himself in glory above his peers,
He trusted to have equaled the Most High,
If he opposed, and, with ambitious aim
Against the throne and monarchy of God,
Raised impious war in Heaven and battle proud,
With vain attempt. Him the Almighty Power
Hurled headlong flaming from the ethereal sky,
With hideous ruin and combustion, down
To the bottomless perdition, there to dwell
In adamantine chains and penal fire,
Who durst defy the Omnipotent to arms."

E Dane Rogers

PROLOGUE

THE FALL

"… había de recordar aquella tarde remota en que su padre
lo llevó a conocer el hielo… "

-Gabriel García Márquez, *Cien Años de Soledad*

*"He remembered that remote afternoon that his father betook
himself to know the ice…"*

1

I held my ear close to the wall. The stone felt cold against my cheek. The whispers were louder than usual. Mom would say they are the waves crashing against the breakwater; but I know differently. Waves don't have voices. I moved my body closer, concentrating on the syllables, trying to distinguish one word from another.

I was not very old this stormy night. My sixth birthday would come a few months later in the season when the wind blew from the North. I had lived in this city for my entire life. I knew nowhere else. My mother was a foreigner; she would tell me stories of a beautiful land in the north. She said she had come here when the dam was built to cut off the river from the ocean. It was supposed to be a wonderful plan to bring regulation to the wilderness of the world, but instead, death and drought followed, and she was trapped in a foreign country. The city was named Qontaas, which meant To content oneself. The people built their walls against the breakwaters in hopes of fresh water, but the water was stagnant, not having its freedom to flow through the land. It became a mystery. The water grew sour. It gave no life, only death to those who tried to quench their thirst with its poisons.

It wasn't long before Mother met Father and moved to the western wall of Qontaas in the region of Bleis. Here she found a new family in which to align herself. However, she had a love for the language of her birth country. She would sing us lullabies in her native tongue. It was something that she would have lost long ago if it weren't fused with the very red-blood that filled her veins.

3

It was this language that caused the fight between my parents. All memory from whence she had come was a threat to Qontaas, and my father was a patriot. Mother was forbidden from teaching us her language. She did so in secret.

My father was a well-tempered man. This was the first time I had seen him so angry. I rushed to my room — nothing more than four stone walls of a dingy gray sort of rock which had been polished to make it beautiful, but I did not see the use.

While examining this wall with my fingers, trying to find contentment in the shouts and screams below, I heard the Voices for the first time. They had most likely always been there. There was no reason that today was any different than any other day. Only, today they chose to make themselves audible; or, perhaps, something inside of me made them audible.

My ear grew numb against the wall; the cold lake had risen well above the level of my wall and it became frigid like the north wind. The Voices were coming from somewhere in the deep waters beyond. Their strange incantations captured my mind. The faint sound of my parents' arguing soon grew quiet to their captivating power.

As the voices grew louder, I grew colder. The language seemed to be of rasps and hums that made it strangely beautiful. It gave me a mood of deep purple which festered in my mind. It was that odd sort of depression that I loved to give in to. I found beauty in its melancholy. It wrapped me in its cold arms and threatened not to let me loose until it had had its way with my soul.

A low rush of water sounded deep in my mind and put me into a subtle trance. I could feel my body being taken by its ferocity. I lay back, enjoying this new feeling of inner peace as my house crumbled around me.

I did not wake until my mother's hand yanked at my shoulder uncomfortably. I yelled, but she did not seem to care. My siblings were in her arms. She rushed out the door, dragging me behind. I turned to look in my room as the walls began to show fracture lines. For a moment, as the wall finally gave way, I thought that I saw a face through the darkness of the ocean. Before I had a chance to focus we were up the stairs to the roof.

I hadn't ever been on these stairs. There was no need to go outside. We had our community within the stone walls of Contentment and that was good enough. In fact, I had hardly noticed this staircase before. I knew that it was there, but it always seemed to disappear into the wall like a dull picture that hung on the same wall for far too long until it fades into near nonexistence.

The stairs were narrow. I didn't see how we would all fit. I looked back for my father but did not see him. He was a pillar of strength to me; he would be coming behind us shortly. I trusted my mother and followed her up the stairs.

The light grew dimmer as each step brought us closer to what seemed to be nowhere. I closed my eyes because the darkness was too much for them. It was a strange sensation, like when one become so cold that he feels burned. But this feeling was far worse. In darkness one cannot see the end of their suffering; it is presently eternal. Each step became thinner and higher until I felt that I could go no further. When we finally emerged out of the rocky fortress of Contentment, I thought the stairs might be a better place to be.

A storm raged mercilessly in the west; our cove was nearly consumed by the storm surge which was no friend to any man in its way. The storm grew as I watched; winds far exceeded that with which anything built by human hands can reckon. Such simple powers of nature stand firm before the mightiest fortresses of man. Before I had much time to reconsider, I was rushed away by Mother. I had never seen her run so quickly. Tears streamed down her face. I wished to assume they were tears from the icy wind that blew against us, but there was a look in her eye that told me I was wrong.

We ran for hours. I tried to stop only twice. After the second time, I realized that Mother was not about to stop, nor leave one of us behind. I fought through the pain and kept my feet moving to the same rhythm as hers.

We reached the edge of the storm around the time my energy was depleted. I pleaded to stop and rest, but Mother's response was unwavering.

"We do not stop until we no longer sit in the storm's path of destruction."

And so, we continued our unexpected journey until we left the terrible shore and walked only on cold-packed dirt. The dirt felt good on my blistering feet. We reached the edge of a thick of trees. Mother turned to face us. She put a finger to her lips and pressed firmly while giving us a commanding look which we dared not disobey. We became quiet even to our own thoughts.

We moved ever so quietly through the brush. Mother stopped and hesitated for a moment at every noise before silently waving us on.

My brother was much younger, and so, cannot be blamed for what he did, but somewhere near the center of the forest he began to cry out for Father.

Mother stopped dead in her tracks, lips pursed. She knew a danger which we did not. She hugged him closely as her tears began to stream from her eyes yet again. This time there was no denying their internal origin. She took my younger brother by the hand and gestured quickly to my older sister to run. She flew north, in the direction we were facing, and we followed, moments behind in Mother's grasp. The woods began to take on a heavier atmosphere as if the air had suddenly lost its oxygen. I was out of breath in moments.

The noises of the waking forest gave me a new terror that put enough breath in my lungs to keep up with my mother. Mere moments later we were through the woods and the screeching, howling noises of the forest behind us died down at the edge of the woods. I looked over my shoulder and saw a pair of eyes in the thicket. They shone orange and the Voices began to speak to me again.

There was an old gate leading into a meadow in front of us. It was warm and welcoming. To either side, the laws of the land were posted. I read some as I passed; they seemed easy enough to keep. I didn't finish reading before I entered the gates behind my mother.

The air was fresh here and I breathed in the warmth. I had not seen such a beautiful place in all my life. I lay down in the grass just as Mother had, and I slept.

My sleep was restless; not how I had expected it to be after an exhausting flight. I awoke, surprised to see the sun hovering lethargically in the sky, having won its battle with the dark storm. Mother was curled up with two of my siblings, crying.

I went to her and stroked her hair. She hid her face and her bawling grew louder. Soon, people began to run in our direction from around the meadow. I hadn't seen anyone before. They were surprisingly close to have come so quickly.

They picked us up, each one of us, and carried us into the land. Once we arrived at a tent that had been pitched, over the first hill, inside of the gate, we were told to rest. Mother recounted all that had happened to an elder of the community.

I stayed awake and listened.

My father was dead.

As their fighting grew louder, the walls of our house grew restless and caved in around them. But what was frightening about the water was not its killing power, but what fell in with the waves. A nest of goçips had made their home in our walls, eating the algae and rot that soured the waters of Contentment. The structure was weakened and when the walls gave way, their siren calls called my father into their clutches and into the depths of the rushing ocean. He had apparently put no thought to the fact that he himself could not breathe beneath the surface of the water.

My mother gave into her tears again. I lay catatonic. I did not truly know how I felt. Empty, perhaps. There was no strength left in my life. I slept soundly. I had no reason to be awake, so I gave myself completely to sleep. And so, the waters began to change, first disrupting Contentment.

I was awakened again in the morning by a sweet aroma that I had never smelled before. I remember having dreamt, but not what the dream was about. I lost all other thoughts but for this sweet odor.

I stretched and rolled over, opening my eyes to look in the direction of the smell. A table was set with bread, honey and milk. The food seemed to glow. There had been too much exertion on my young body the day before. I needed good food, and this was beyond compare.

It was not long into breakfast that we learned the people who lived here had been waiting for Mother's return for many years. This was her country. A journey was planned for us and we were given our instructions. We were to travel to Mount Saia on the northern shore of Aeda to obtain our citizenship in the land. I looked in the direction which the elder pointed. The mountain hung in the clouds, snowcapped and glowing in the sunlight. Nothing I had ever seen before had been so beautiful. Mother's tears were a different type of tears. She accepted the journey on her knees.

So much had happened to her in only one day; the death and betrayal of her husband to the siren calls of the goçips that he stayed to die in hopes of their accompaniment. The treacherous journey through the storm and the woods and now a journey ahead of her that was yet to begin. I felt sorry for her. Why couldn't she just rest here? But she accepted the journey as if she could think of no more necessary a thing to do. We followed.

PT 1

The Fall

The gleaming sun arrests my heart and sings
Of nations come and gone, yet I remain.
The heavens shine upon my face like kings;
Their mighty strength within makes my heart vain!

My ocean dark and daring can't abide
Within a border, neither wall nor bay,
But pushes back such feeble tries to hide
The tempest deep inside that won't obey.

But darker yet; my weary days are come,
For in my hubris I dethroned the King—
How can I be alive and yet so numb?

Then what I sought was just to feel death's sting.
For when my throne of ir'n and clay
comes down, my sin will be consumed by day.

EDR

I

LYRIC

Alone, I sit upon my sacred throne—
A dingy, dirty, frail, gray, grass-stained stone.
A beastly smile tears my face in two
As thoughts-of-self begin my mind to woo.

Entombed within a nightmare-state so vile,
Each thought so full of Secret bile,
Each passerby can see I'm not my own.
Eclipsed by lust, I am corrupted to the bone!

Defile me not, O Desert, cold and wild!
Deceived, beguiled, but lo! no more a child,
Decay besets my inner-self to rot—
Delicious food I am for Beasts. Fear not!

A King is watching; He will call me back.
A King who loves me; he will call me home.

EDR

other, my siblings and I were in the eighth year of our journey. The days had become tedious. Mount Saia rested sturdily in our view, day in and day out. We had directions, but we never seemed closer than the previous day—at least I thought not—everyone seemed to have a different interpretation as to our proximity to the mountain. But surely our true ascent was still ahead.

We met many people and learned many things about Aeda along the way. I could imagine no more beautiful a home than this. The paths were lined with the greenest grass and fruit hung from every tree. Our days would generally consist of walking, reading, singing and playing—yet the journey pressed on. Food was never an issue; all that was around us was edible and sweet. Its freshness rivaled all the food that I had ever eaten; each day it seemed to grow more delicious! This had become our home. It was strange to look back on life before Aeda, on the stone walls, the nauseating emptiness of the city as people walked about, blindly doing what they needed, forgetting the lives of those around them. I was glad not to return there. But I mourned still my homeland, knowing that I would never again on this earth see Contentment for it had been washed away by the dark waters of the stagnant ocean.

The law there was also strange. I remember when I entered the gates of Aeda, because of my presuppositions of Law, I had believed them somewhat backwards; however, I soon learned a new logic that is not tainted by the desires of man. But at times the dicta of this law made my stomach sick. It seemed that this logic told me to die to live.

15

We had to travel to Saia to see Paradise. Anyone could see from looking at the towering summit of Saia that it was not a simple trek. This law is the law of the King of Aeda and it is unchangeable by its citizens.

Now, I see the fallacy of Contentment's only law: To live truly to one's self. But I did not know why this had grown strange to me. It was hard to live in the land of Aeda and not find the outside world—for this was the only land within a boarder—to be a contradiction of itself.

There was one secret that I held onto from my past which I told no one. I feared it. The Voices from the lake still spoke to me in my sleep—their siren sounds lured me into a euphoric sleep to which I could escape when the trekking became difficult. Often in my trances I would wander back many days' worth of travel.

We were nowhere near the lake. I would wake up in a start to look for the source of the noises, but it became apparent that they lived inside of me. I chose to keep this to myself for two reasons: firstly, I feared what people would think of such a ridiculous problem, and secondly, I feared letting go of that last piece of my first home, this little piece of obscurity that had found a root in my brain. Instead, I nurtured it with more care than my own body.

Aeda spoke a language contrary to my homeland. The Voices, however, did not speak my native language or the language of Aeda, which I now knew better than the other.

In eight years, I had not deciphered their speech, but I listened as intently as someone obsessed. I followed my mother with a blank look on my face; a world growing in my mind that was foreign, yet it gave me a true place to call my own.

16

While I mulled over a few syllables whispered to me in the night, my mother stopped abruptly at a fork in the road. Usually we did not stop at this type of break. We would follow the smaller road because our instructions said to do so. However, these pathways were equal in size. It was neither too small nor too large. Each way appeared to have similar difficulties. It did not matter to me which we took. I let my family decide without my input.

"Although they are the same size," pondered my mother as she rubbed her chin between her index finger and thumb, "the eastward path is more tread with deeper groves. We should take the path less traveled."

So, we ended our rest and started down the path that she had selected for us. Just inside the path, I understood the first of this mysterious language in my head: *She's wrong.*

I froze. I had not misunderstood. I watched my family fading into the distance, not noticing that I had stopped. I slowly walked backwards until I again faced both paths. *She's wrong.* Again. I listened and took the eastern path, not consciously thinking of leaving my family. For the first time, the terrible peaks of Saia were not within my sight. I followed the path. It was more comfortable than any path I had yet walked. It was comfortable, good and easier. The Voices in my head seemed to want what was good for me.

I followed the directions of the Voices until they left me by a Fence. I forgot my family. Not that they were forgettable people, only that I was a forgetful child with no room but for one thought in my head at any given time. These Voices from the lake took over my every consideration. There was an uncanny familiarity about this place. I found a nice place to sit; a gray stone which did not look natural next to the white stones of Aeda. Someone had obviously placed it there, so I sat upon it, seeing that it was large enough to support me.

My back was on the splintered face of a Fence which was all that kept me and the people of Aeda from the woods and wilderness beyond. It poked and prodded uncomfortably, but it was the Fence none the less; I felt content to be there.

I named my stone Religion and I was proud of this name. Religion gave me an odd amount of pleasure for such a simple object. It resembled the stones of my home that had been in Contentment. I did not bother with its inspection much beyond discovering that its surface was familiar to me, and its perma-chill much like that of my childhood bedroom. I felt it beneath me. I was higher than any other that crossed my path when I sat upon it, though it was a flat stone, lacking much in depth.

I sat alone here for some time and watched the days turn over to weeks which then fell to months in time's never-ending battle. Due to my solidarity, I had become obsessed with the idea that all, besides myself, had become lost. Surely, having not taken many steps on my own, I could not have wandered off nearly so far as those who walked aimlessly in the wilderness; I was in Aeda, after all. From this vantage point I could see a different view of Mount Saia. The cliffs from this angle were sloped. I thought I had come too far to return and find my family. I took comfort knowing that their journey might be simple. I had found my way, however, and I was not about to change it.

I continued to look on in silence. Saia is the only look-out for Paradise. It sits anciently in the foreground of the entire known world. I quickly wondered if I would

18

ever climb it. The Voices picked up speed and calmed me. Of course, I would; I followed the right path.

I boasted of my knowledge when any man came to pass me. They all seemed somewhat lost; no one there knew their way but me. They hurried on busily, not bothering with my obnoxiousness. When I thought about it, none who passed me had yet passed the place that I sat. Of course, they did not know as much as I knew. I could see a way ahead and a way back from the path which they traveled, lost and needing my experienced direction.

Few tried to beckon me to the hills which rested within the inner region of Aeda where they had made their homes. I would wave and lend a smile, but I gave no travel to the land which separated us. The words of those who said I was in danger did not please me, so my thoughts did not linger on them, nor did I travel in their direction.

I spent my time with my hands behind my back, fingers picking delicately at the wooden boards of the Fence. None could see anything but the smile on my face. But my deed was mysterious. My fingers prying for death, body acting alone in search of the grave, face lacquered with a smile which could fool a jackal into giving me its kill. I gave my all to the destruction of my protection. I became convinced that the boundaries of Aeda were constricting, not protective. I tore down the Fence in secret.

Occasionally, a passerby would come up close and pause to speak with me; I feared that they would tell me to leave my little rock and venture out with them. I didn't want any to see the hole in the Fence which I had created for myself. For this reason, I kept my eyes on both the north and the south as it ran along the Fence.

I would find, on the rare occasion, someone who melded well with the thoughts of my heart. I tried to keep him in conversation for as long as he would stay. We would discuss the ventures of the path and the beauty of it, but we never venture on together. He would soon be on his way without me. It was never long before he saw the woods and turned in fright—cowards, all of them. I, however, was not concerned with my proximity to the woods and beasts that roamed just beyond the Fence. As a child in Aeda, I had heard many a talk of these Beasts and their dangers, and yet, somehow, being so close, they seemed almost to be my friends. None other was so consistently near me.

One day, as I sat pulling at the blades of grass which had found their way through the pried Fence and had begun to overtake my rock, I saw faint writing on it. I spent little time on its examination in the past, which lent small return in my knowledge of its cracks and crevasses. On my knees beside it, I plucked singularly and tediously away at the tares that had overgrown it. As the written words began to take form behind the greenery, I was distracted. I thought that in the woods (through a slat which I had pried way) I spied an unimaginable Beast. It was attractive beyond compare. It stared at me through my peeping-hole. Our gazes met. I forgot my rock and my work. Instead, I stared for as long as I dared at this majestic Beast; knowing that I shouldn't. It was well known that the Beasts which roam the edge of the forest are the destruction of many. It is the call of those woods which renders men to the teeth of the Beasts. I knew the Fence to be my protection, and yet, this Fence which I pressed close to—for curiosity of what was beyond—grew to be an uncomfortable barrier between me and the dark woods of Arqana.

The Beast which I saw was rugged and dark; its fur matted and shone olive in the shadows. I thought to myself how beautiful it was. Its rasping sounded to me like music. It gave me a melancholy urge to join it in destruction. In its eyes, which were captivating, I saw a city of stone, cascaded in orange light, so thrilling that I wanted to reach out and touch it. I caught a mysterious chill which found its rest in my spine. I realized that I wished to meet a creature which would quickly devour me; its job was to do so. I wept for myself, all the while I kept my eyes on the Beast. The power I thought it capable of attracted me and the city in its eyes fueled a new spirit inside of me. For this reason, it was given an ever-increasing amount of my attention.

For days after I seldom remembered my stone beneath me. I gave every thought to this Beast. I waited with my face pressed firmly between the boards of the Fence, hoping to catch a glimpse of the Beast as it led others lost through a hole in the thicket. They would not be seen again. From above the tree-tops I saw flames and smoke and heard the shouts and screams (that sounded strangely like cheers and hollers) of those who had disappeared into Arqana. It surprised me that this did not bother me at this point, and if not now, then I worried, it never would. My desire was to join this party of hollering woodsmen. But this thought was not so much as let to wake at that hour for it conflicted my very position seated upon Religion. I turned my face from the woods for a moment to give into the lake that grew in my eyes.

As I wept these, my black tears for myself, I heard new voices coming down the path. I cleaned the distress from my face and I stood to praise myself for being further along my way than them. As I came to find, these voices belonged to two sisters named Lyric and Ræla.

I welcomed them, "This is the path which I have come ahead of you and I know every turn and byway."

Ræla was not as welcoming as many had been before her.

"We have come to no turn and have seen not your reason for pride; you have torn to pieces that which was meant for your own protection along a journey, not as a home for the weary. Get up and finish your walk, lest some Beast come and seize you before you arrive at Saia."

Had I cared more for the content of her words than the way in which they had been spoken, perhaps I would have been frightened into turning from my ways; but alas, I took offence and ignored her wise, but poorly spoken words.

Lyric had her eyes fixed beyond me to the woods. Ræla saw this and pulled fast at Lyric who didn't so much as wince.

"What is that behind you, Sir? It attracts my attention and makes me think you must be its master."

I didn't want to share Arqana with Ræla for fear of a second chide so I beckoned Lyric to come join me in contemplation of all that is there beyond and here so close to the Fence.

"Do not be fooled, Lyric," said the other, "he does not know of his dangers. He looks only for the ferocity of power. This is not a man with whom you should associate for even as he speaks a Beast has its eyes fixed firmly upon him. He believes that this Beast will not attack him simply because he is loyal to it. The tooth of the Beast is indiscriminate in its prey."

"But, Ræla," said Lyric, "if this man is truly hunted, shall I not stand here and watch the back which he neglects? I see that this man finds himself quite wise, yet my heart has found for him a place which I cannot deny it fill. Allow me to stay here that I may help him on his way."

"This man does not want your help, nor mine. He is more set to his way than you are to yours. I fear that if you are left here in his presence it will not be you who aids him, but he who suffers you from your way to join him in his endangered-state. Those lost to destruction's power seek to share in their destruction, for death is a lonely place, although it is a companied journey. This Beast that hunts him may kill you with him if you stay. They want to feast on all who live within the borders of Aeda. We are fed with sweet milk and honey. Pray, do not join this man. His way is death, yet he thinks it to be life and this makes him the more dangerous for you." Not wanting to hurt Ræla, who loved her, she agreed to go on with her and leave me behind. But while Ræla had her eyes from Lyric, she slipped away to be with me. She was tempted by Arqana, so she chose to sleep by the Fence rather than journey to Saia where the men of Aeda were congregating en grande masse.

"You heard, surely, that we are all on our way to the mountain there yonder. We have been summoned in preparations for the coming war." Lyric said these many times, but my mind was too consumed with Arqana to pay her any attention.

"Good girl that you have a goal and follow it blindly, yet, I believe I can become a more weathered warrior here in the woods than to be always protected by this Fence. I've not yet seen the world; how can I know where my loyalty should be?"

"Nonsense. Truth is singular. When you know truth, you need nothing else to find your loyalty. Don't let your body fool your mind into thinking that there is something better where danger runs rampant."

"Good kingdoms, you are sour! I only think that it is wiser to go looking for what else is out there."

But she stayed despite her words. Her wisdom was only of the sort repeated by children.

"Then look, but do not attempt to convince me to follow. I don't need to see something for myself to trust when it is wrong. I don't have to throw myself from a cliff to know that it would kill me."

"Don't exaggerate. I'm no fool to throw myself into sure death."

Her stare was icy, and I chose not to argue any longer. We sat in silence. The silence seemed to be permanent. But she did not budge from her position near me.

I wished that we could share in discovering other lands together. Her conversation was good when it went easily with mine. I could see that her heart loved me greatly, it must have for her to argue with me so. None who despised me had the time. We sat for months, not moving. No talk was made of continuing our journeys.

After too long a silence, I hesitantly spoke to her.

"Do you hear the deep rasp of the Beast?" I said. "It has grown to comfort me, for it is always with me. Perhaps it is my protection from the wilderness beyond the trees. It keeps me satisfied to be where I am, looking upon it."

"Aye, I hear what you say but it is the sound of its heavy paws in the brush which brings me to tears, for it is a harsh sound. When I close my eyes, it lends memory of my feet upon the path from which I rest."

I was surprised that she answered me. She had been silent for so long. When she spoke of the Beast's paws, I lingered my eyes on Arqana, for one sat near to its edge with its gaze on the southern horizon which grew purple with the coming evening. I saw the crust of blood, both old and new on its paws. It was the blood of those whom I had seen go into Arqana.

After more time, all the while hiding my face from Lyric who still rested with her back against the Fence, I began to mimic the movements of the Beasts. Sometimes Lyric would hear my scuffs and pray tell her what I was doing. I imagine it would have frightened her. I did not know how to respond. It was a funny thing for someone of my age to mimic the movements of an animal, especially such an animal as this. I brushed her off.

"I am playing, simple Lyric, for I know how to make good fun. Do not fret for that of which you know nothing."

"You are becoming more like the creatures that roam the woods every day. I fear that, soon, I will no longer have your company here."

She was sad, sadder than I had seen her before. Perhaps she truly did love me with a pure heart. I sat and thought about her words. It was hard not to care for someone who cared for me.

"You don't have to stay here by me, but do not venture to the woods. Go to Saia so that I can be on my way too. Something about you keeps me here, yet I grow more fearful each passing day of the eminence of the King's arrival on Saia."

This was new to me. I had not known that he was coming here. Why would the King come to such an empty land as this when he has Paradise at his fingertips?

"Therefore, the people of Aeda are going to the mountain?" I asked.

Lyric looked at me with shock.

"You didn't know?"

"I must have missed that. I was preoccupied during my early years."

Lyric let me be in silence for a while. I thought about what the King's return might mean, but the Voices again began to rattle in my head. I shook them quiet.

II

HEART

A midnight-shadow, window to her soul—
Long umber locks off dainty shoulders roll…
Her lips so full—a sunset red and pink.
Infatuated, dare I but one blink?

Petit, blushed nose, white teeth that stir the blind,
And laugh of joy leave sadness far behind.
Her arms drape down to thighs of splendid grace,
Then dance, her hands, with fingers fine as lace.

And when she stands, her legs fall strait and strong,
No man who hopes to keep his heart looks long.
A beauty so unique to love stained eyes,
It's she who makes my heavy heart to fly.

The greatest of creation first and last—
No wish to share her heart, my mis'ry vast.

EDR

hen we had been together against the Fence for a long while, two more came to us. I heard their footsteps long before I saw their bodies. Lyric was asleep on the Aedic side of the Fence, softly humming as she exhaled peacefully. She caught my attention for a moment because she slept so serenely. I thought that I had never seen such tranquility in my short life.

I stepped onto my rock, which was only big enough to support one foot. I found this out in a rather painful way; I quickly mounted it with both feet to see the owners of the footsteps coming down the way and my right foot slipped, pulling my chin harshly on to the unforgiving Fence.

When I secured my footing, and finished my moment of watching Lyric sleep, I looked to the south to catch a glimpse of the coming as my vantage gave them visibility. Their laughs rang in my ear. I became excited thinking about what type of people might be joining us. I woke Lyric by dropping some pebbles on her face. She awoke slowly and gave me a look as if to tell me I had not amused her, but she followed my finger as I pointed in the direction of the noises.

The Voices were the first to present their thoughts of these two; beautiful and delicious. I shook the Voices away. I was frequently surprised by the strange suggestions that they would utter. Beautiful they were, of that I was sure, but they hardly looked like food.

Lyric stood, mouth wide open, staring in their direction.

"I think the King has sent one for each of us, as we are incompatible for anything but friendship."

The Voices laughed at her, but I put a hand on her shoulder and agreed. She seemed to think that it was our duty as people to procreate.

These two were passing us on the path before the male turned to see us at the Fence. The boy held his sister's arm as his feet ceased walking. Her talking slowly faded and she saw us, too. They spoke together in whispers for a few moments before seeming to come to an accord. They walked to the Fence where we were. I was struck dumb by their beauty. I squeezed Lyric's arm with excitement. They must have been as attracted to us as we were to them, I reckoned.

"Are you two alright?" asked the girl. I had to review what she said in my head before answering. I hadn't concentrated on her words very well.

"We are more than fine, now." said Lyric, obviously embarrassed that she was unable to retire her smile.

"You look starved and covered in filth. Can we get you help from the city?" asked the male.

I must have looked quite dumb. Again, I did not answer quickly. But the question had been directed specifically toward me this time. Even Lyric looked in my direction awaiting a response. She briefly changed her expression to that of urging, altering me to a prolonged silence. They didn't know how much conversation was taking place in my head.

After quite an awkward silence, allowing them to worry even more for my health, my voice cracked, and I whispered. "Just stay with us a while."

They shrugged and sat. The male sat a little closer than the other; too close to Lyric, I thought. I considered kicking her through the hole in the Fence, but I thought better of it. I looked at the sky and exhaled. I heard the girl speak again and I looked at her, perched delicately where the higher road slopes down to reach our ditch.

"What's your name?" she said.

"Delight." The Voices shrieked a new name as I had begun to say my own. I told her the name that my mother had given me.

She smiled and came closer to the same proximity as her brother.

"I'm RationHeart, and my brother is MuchHeart." She said as she extended her hand to me through the hole in the Fence. I shook it. Her hand was slightly warm. The only warmth I had felt in many months. I followed her hand back through the Fence and took up a seat next to Lyric who smiled at me for a moment before returning to her conversation with MuchHeart. I caught a second's glance of him as my eyes shifted from Lyric to RationHeart. There was something familiar about him.

"We did not expect to see anyone in this area; especially in such a dark place as the shadow of Saia."

"I came from that pathway to the west." I pointed across the path where, just a way south down the path there is an intersection.

"Why would you travel away from the mountain? Is there any other purpose in Aeda other than pilgrimage?"

I laughed quietly for a second before a Voice gave me words to respond.

"There's a new Voice in the wind here in Aeda. The land is some of the most fertile in the known territories. We should all take up residency where we are comfortable. Don't be so old fashioned; we haven't heard anything from the silent island for generations. Whatever king was once there is dead now. Why should we follow his laws?"

I felt eyes on me and turned to see that the other two had stopped to listen. Their eyes told me of their discomfort. Even I had been shocked by the words which fell out of my mouth. However, they left a sweet taste on my tongue.

"Perhaps you have spent too much time on the forest's side of the Fence to remember the power of the Law." Lyric said this in a condemning way that made me sit back and forget my stance. If they didn't want me to share my knowledge with them, I would keep it to myself for my own benefit.

I felt rather beside their conversation. The siblings brought news from the south of dangerous new territory being discovered in the mysterious East. I listened intently but decided to pretend that I was too busy rubbing the grass stains out of my feet to pay close attention. The grass on the other side didn't leave stains, it was too dry. I don't like stains.

Lyric shook my arm, "Listen to what they're saying!"

I brushed her off and continued acting. I listened secretly. What they said did not scare me, it excited me. I had never heard of the territory of which they spoke; a land beyond the woods—how invigorating.

They became more passionate in their warnings and Lyric ate up their cautions. Their brother, for whom they wander on the fringe of Aeda, had ventured toward the false promises of the East. Word was received of him that he had lost his way in a city made entirely of tents where no one stayed long enough to build a firm foundation for a house. They robbed him of his treasures and threw him from a cliff when there was naught left to take. I lost interest when I realized how tired I was, and I fell asleep. I dreamed of what the land beyond Arqana could hold; what mysteries, knowledge and people! Surely there must be people there!

My dreams were warm, and the Voices began to take on a body within my dream. I understood that they felt at home here. I allowed them access to my unconsciousness. They created a beautiful world.

When the haze cleared, and the forest fell behind me, the sun was too bright. I covered my eyes. My feet fell lightly on the golden ground—it was soft. There were more people here than I could focus on and each one loved me for me.

I knew I was dreaming. I didn't want to awake immediately. I continued in my trance while presently conscious.

A man stood forward from the crowd. His feet were shrouded in a hallucinogenic cloud and his body was distorted by the heat which rose from the sand. The sun was not overbearing on my skin—in fact, I could not feel its warmth, I could only see it. The man's hand was extended to me. I took it.

"I have waited for you; spoken to you along your journey, and finally, I have come through your fog. Come to me and I will show you a deeper reality. Come to the Desert. Come with me to my kingdom."

The dream ended too soon. The other three around me had fallen to sleep's warm embrace.

I sat up against the Fence and watched them jealously. I wanted to return to my dream. The firelight licked their pale skin. I watched MuchHeart's familiar face in the changing light. I buried my own face in my knees and growled at myself. I looked at RationHeart; she had the same face. I looked at Lyric. I feared her judgments. I fell to my left side and buried my face in the dirt. I argued with the Voices for the remainder of the early morning. I saw them now as the gatekeepers to the man who had come to me in my dream. We came upon a plan that went well with me.

By the light of the morning sun, I found my way to a patch of fauna and I picked the most luscious greens for breakfast. Only the plants that pleased me came with me to the Fence. I left the foliage in disarray, the best pieces torn from the ground and the least pleasing trampled underfoot. I returned to the Fence and decorated RationHeart with the herbs and waited for everyone to awake.

I became impatient as the morning sun grew warm. I tossed pebbles, made loud noises, nothing woke them. I stood and passed behind RationHeart, glancing at her, imagining her thanks for my gifts. I grew more excited. But out of the corner of my eye, I couldn't help but focus on MuchHeart. The hours stretching into midday, their slumber was undisturbed. The familiarity of MuchHeart grew on my curiosity. The Voices encouraged me to examine him to end my curiosity. Emboldened by my companions' stony slumber, I did just that.

I found nothing that told me why he was so familiar. I was more confused than I had been before.

I backed away and sat in my place on the Fence. I had not much more than reached the Fence before all three had awakened, as if by the same internal cue.

They sat up in silence. They all knew something which I did not.

"What?" I pried.

Lyric looked at me and then at the others. "When did we fall asleep?"

MuchHeart shook his head. "We were awake until we awoke. I saw the sun rise over Arqana."

Their problem confused me. What did it matter? They were awake and now I wanted to impress RationHeart with my gifts. I prodded her and nodded toward the garment of fine plants that covered her. She brushed them away and looked at me with fiery eyes.

"What did you do to us? You were awake well before us as is obvious by what you have done to me. What have you done to the rest? Is this a spell? Have you put us asleep to rob us of some hidden treasure?"

I couldn't think of what spell I might have caused; in fact, I felt as if some strange spell had come upon me, as well.

The Voices were silent.

Over the coming days, the other three grew closer as I grew more distant. I would wake from my sleep in a jealous rage over hearing their laughs dragging on into the nighttime air. I stormed across the Fence, looking for some way into the woods to which I could completely loose myself. At long last, dawn would arrive, and I would take my place by the Fence again. On the rarer occasions, the three would be asleep when I returned. I continued to search for why MuchHeart held my attention so. In the morning of the first fog of the season, I again become a part of the conversation; however, the two newcomers were still cautious of me. Lyric had given all her reservations to the healing of time.

I continued a pursuit of RationHeart, as I couldn't very well pursue the other, so that I could remain in the presence of both indefinitely while my curiosity pulsated.

I went to Lyric to beg for her help. Only she was trusted enough by both me and RationHeart to create a bridge between the two of us. We talked and devised a plan to make her mine. This was a dark and devious plan, for although Lyric was innocent in her thoughts, I knew a darker truth, for the Voices had again awakened and spoke of a different end. I compromised the two and Lyric accepted, but I kept from her a secret intent.

So, Lyric went to spend a day's adventure with RationHeart, a topic on her mind, while I stayed at the Fence to entertain MuchHeart. He and I had not yet spoken more than a few words together. I thought I might find the secret to my intrigue.

As we spoke, I forgot Lyric's quest and focused solely on my secret. I did not discover my answer that day. What I did discover was more damaging to me.

MuchHeart had the lightest heart that I had yet witnessed. Although it was obviously large, its weight was easily supported by his childish innocence and curiosity. As we enjoyed each other's company that day, no words were spoken of deep matters which seem to dull a good mood; only happiness was present. I grew an ever-increasing attachment to him.

When RationHeart and Lyric returned, RationHeart asked me to join her on a walk. To my surprise, she was rather mellow, and her presence was heavy. Quite the opposite of the feeling I had received from MuchHeart. She apologized for rejecting my gift in such a cruel way. I met her seriousness. Although I had not truly been hurt by her, I let her believe that I had. The Voices liked this. I did it without their urging.

RationHeart agreed to be my friend. In that moment, I had two contradicting thoughts. Firstly, friendship was not what I sought. I was dissatisfied with her hesitant approach to me. Secondly, after the lightness I had felt earlier, I was not in the slightest attracted to this somber mood. I faced her to reject her offer of friendship. I considered that I might be on my way again, finding that she was not as pleasing as I had thought. The Voices spoke as one: "If she leaves, so does her brother."

I accepted her friendship.

We pretended for far too long that we were happy as friends. I became a slave to the world which the Voices created in my head; this world included a different RationHeart. She was a slave's slave in my mind. I sought to control her in every way. Though her offer had been strictly of friendship, I perceived and took more than what I had been allowed. Our friendship shattered after only a few days. I am still surprised at the speed in which I effectuated the end of our friendship.

I introverted myself. My head became a hive of rage which was so intense that my face could not hold its ferocity and, instead, created a placid visage. A piece of me began to die; not because of the loss of someone who I knew full well was not the one I desired, but because of the control which I gave up to the Voices so that they might numb my senses and create a palace of my desires in my conscious mind rather than my subconscious thoughts.

The days were beginning to darken earlier, and the cold air rolled off the north shore and passed along the Fence. The fog was rising out of the selva and the Beasts called after it. The women shivered as the night rolled on, but I was warmed by the wind. My soul had become much colder.

Sleep was the best comfort. They had lost their hesitance toward me, so they slept often, while I remained awake. MuchHeart and I grew in our friendship during this time. We both loved cold.

When the women slept, I would whisper to MuchHeart alone. He would lean in close and giggle as I tickled his ear with jokes and crudeness to mimic joy. I spoke as though I had great knowledge of the world, when it was a grand display of falsehood. And he would listen. He was too polite to reject me for my constant interruptions of his solitude, but I could tell that he was hardly pleased by it. I moved more quickly than before for fear that he would soon be done with my company and take himself up and forward on the path with my dear friends, Lyric and RationHeart, in hand. For the first time, I shuddered at the thought that I would be alone with the Voices.

There had been rumor of a clan of Gypsy-Brethren near these parts and on this night, I heard their drums. Their rhythmic pounding aligned with the Voices and I found that their noise was musical. Their song called me to their bidding. Oh, what a place to find freedom as the brothers of the woods. I locked these drums and their sweet, soothing rhythm in my memory. When I awoke the next morning, my euphoria was not lost—the rhythm had become the beat of my heart and it pounded darkly in my chest, calling me to the source of its power; the freedom land of the Gypsies.

By this time, I had lost all control of my heart. It ran wild. It no longer desired RationHeart—MuchHeart had become my sole obsession.

I can mark with clarity a change in who I was. I thought at that time that I had discovered myself. I believe now, with certainty, that I lost myself that night in the chants of a strange song. I was no longer a struggling mind in a conflicting land. I was now a lost mind in a strange land, and I thought to myself that I could not survive here any longer.

But I could not bear to leave the object of my obsession. I went to MuchHeart and gave my best effort to entice him in a similar direction. I was neither so convincing nor suave as I had imagined. A clear expression of insecurity erupted on his face at my persuasions and I knew that he was about to deny me.

"It's only an adventure. Surely you are not so boring as to have lost your childish heart of exploration!"

"It's not that I do not wish to discover new territories, but the woods are not new to us. I know what lies there. The knowledge of this land tells us of its dangers. Let us go explore a land which will bring us closer to Mount Saia."

"I've not heard anything so dull in all the time we've spoken. Why do you change so? You are not quite the one I remember, although you have his face."

"I doubt that it is me that has changed, as I would have given you the same answer to venture out of the boundaries of the city had you asked me at any point in the past. I believe it is you who has lost your morals and destroyed the good conscience which I once perceived you to have."

I understood that I had lost. I would not make him budge. Dejected, I turned and found a place on the opposite side of the Fence to pout. The Voices went to work.

I didn't sleep that night. I sat by the Fence wondering how I would convince him to journey with me to the woods. While he slept—he slept just behind me—I decided upon a trick, for MuchHeart was unmovable in the day. I betook myself to plan an excursion in which I would carry him while he slumbered.

Upon his drowsiness, I snuck close to the Fence and reached over. I was careful not to touch the Fence nor even think of it. I feared the Fence would feel my deed and scream out *thief* for nothing else there could. No one else could see, nor hear my deed. We were two alone and my trespass was without restraint. The collar of his shirt was there and so I took hold of it and slowly hoisted him over and placed him beside my grass-covered stone which I toyed with leaving but I thought, at long last, that I might have use of it on my journey. So, I took it up and placed it on the sleeping boy while he slept. If he fell from my arms, so would it fall and quite possibly shatter. I then took MuchHeart in my arms and embraced the thicket; his body pressing the stone against my chest, making me quite uncomfortable.

Once at the first row of trees, I realized how many Beasts roamed in the bushes, but I believed myself safe. I saw in their faces that we were not enemies so long as I moved East. They stood aside and bowed as I carried my friend past them. They bowed to me. They worshiped me.

A Beast, humbler in manner than most, addressed me loudly from deep within the forest beyond the pack. It beckoned me deeper into Arqana, and made known, in a powerful and seducing way, that a land of desire was awaiting my allegiance.

MuchHeart was sometimes restless in my arms and at other times, he was pacific. I kept him asleep until we were near enough to hear the crackling of fires dying as the village before us slept.

I took MuchHeart's hand and pet it as I told him where I had brought him. He wavered for a bit, looking side to side as if he expected to see his sister and Lyric somewhere hiding and giggling, but then, he understood that we were alone, and he walked with me, eyes fixed on his feet. He quietly understood. He struggled to keep my pace as the woods broke before us.

III

GYPSIES

"Then cruel, by their sports of blood insured
Of fighting beasts, and men to beasts exposed ;
Luxurious by their wealth, and greedier still,
And from the daily scene effeminate.
What wise and valiant man would seek to free
These, thus degenerate, by themselves enslaved,
Or could of inward slaves make outward free?"

Milton, *Paradise Regained book iv*

e reached the outskirts of the camp by morning. The dew caught the glint of a morning sun as it passed through the stalks of the trees before reaching the canopy and disappearing again until sunset. The camp was illuminated for the smaller portion of a second. Men lay strewn about looking as corpses defeated in battle. I wiped my eyes, adjusting them to the light. When I returned my gaze, the color had returned to their bodies. I took MuchHeart by the hand and we stepped into their camp.

Their bodies were motionless, unclothed, but not untouched. Some were awake. What they were doing is not something I wish to recall in my present mind, but then, oh, how it intrigued me.

MuchHeart squeezed my hand and I turned to see a tear fall from his cheek and splash to the ground. I could hear it faintly; it resonated in my chest. He was frightened by his curious first steps into this savage clan, but he hadn't the strength of his own to return to where he had begun. He buried his face in my back, obstructing his view from that which was before us—Ç⍵d⍵mɜ.

From within the bodies crawled a woman, as a lion looking up from her meal. She was more beautiful than anyone I had ever seen within Aeda. Her stature was small, but her presence consuming. She, like a distant thundercloud brought forth by the early hours of evening—quiet and beautiful—emerged from the throng of tangled bodies. I was mesmerized by her beauty that would make a goddess jealous. Her hair fell to the ground in long amber locks, wet with dew, like everything and everyone within these woods. On her body were colorful

45

markings mocking the promises given to Aeda but here it was a new image altogether. I was captivated by it.

My knees trembled, for although she was nude, she was more elegant than that to which imagination can lend. She had the air of royalty. As my thoughts trailed on, less innocently than most would admit, she was announced by a man whose voice was sweet and charming, a eunuch of her courts, perhaps:

"Behold Queen MaraJipsa, Her Majesty. She awakes, and the tribe will cheer her as she walks. She conquers, and to her must be made a sacrifice all who wish to live within her dominion. Let her feet be kissed, as the sun rises in the East. Her face be kissed as the sun then sets in the West.

"Let no man go untouched by her effeminate power, and let all women be attracted. She is for all."

As her royal call resonated in my ears, she stepped down from the coil of bodies, which had been her nest throughout the night. She walked toward me, which made me bend at the knee and worship her body. She lifted my chin and placed a kiss on my lips. She was familiar.

"Welcome to Çɷdɷm3, the Gypsy Brethren of the Wood Arqana. Here you will have no need of your baggage." And with that, she and her comrades undressed me. I did not struggle, but rather, I aided them in their efforts.

MuchHeart, however, began to kick. His fear raged against all who would try to touch him. If I had not done something, they would have thrown him out of Arqana into the exposure of the sun. I wanted my companion to be here with me in all times, so I went to him and calmed him. The others took from him his garments, until he was left with only the shame to which he clung.

MuchHeart took, perhaps, more time than I had expected for his fright to fade. Nonetheless, when he slowly emerged from his hiding, he agreed to explore the camp with me and Queen MaraJipsa, so long as those who took from him not join.

"Delightful!" sang Mara; honey on her lips and berries in her breath. "We will make our way to the temple of Çⓐdⓐm3. Her buttresses are sturdier than that of mountains, for it was built with many more hands and through many more generations. Then built and rebuilt as a bone, fractured and mended. Surely, all can marvel at her splendor." Her hands were about us both and the choice was solely hers that we were to follow. She was much too strong for the both of us to overcome.

We passed many laying in the path, shaking the night from their bodies, rubbing the sleep from their eyes. It seemed to me that they all hungered after MuchHeart, which offended me, and yet, made me jealous in the same. This kept my concern from my own body. My worry would surely never encompass that of the well-being of MuchHeart, only fantasizing in his ability to fulfill my self-regarding desires.

"Queen Mother, how is it that your camp came to be found in the forest and not on a stage within the Desert?" I asked.

"Our home is where we choose it to be. None dare revoke our right to any land which we see fit, for, although many have tried, we are the victors at the finish. We preferred the northern shore of the Desert, so that we can mock and taunt the ocean waves, daring them to crash upon us. It's good fun and it is wonderful encouragement to see that the waves never overtake a single man."

"Then, have you never lost a man at all? That is quite an accomplishment."

"Oh, kingdoms, no! We have lost our fair share of men, but it is the war which we have never, and *will never* lose, for we are the makers of our morality."

"Is a moral something that can be different from land to land? Excuse my prodding, but much of what you say is beyond my understanding." I looked at her, her hair catching the wind and morning sun simultaneously in striking beauty. However, it was the silhouette of my dear MuchHeart, just to her left, that made her more beautiful in my eyes. She hesitated to answer; something she had yet to have done, but without waiting so long as would have been rude, she spoke.

"Oh, dear Delight, you have much to learn. But let us focus firstly on the task at hand and not be caught up by estranged and lacking subjects." I sighed; oh, how a lacking answer had become the bane of my existence.

As we rounded the path into a clearing, we saw the beautifully decorated temple of Ç∞d∞m3. Its spires topped the canopy of trees and its base, established and grand, carved out a niche for itself in this land which was fast filling.

"MaraJipsa," I said questioningly, "why have you built your temple in the confines of the Wood Arqana? It seems to me that this temple is worthy of a location within the Desert, which could be seen by all from miles around."

MaraJipsa laughed a roaring laugh which shook my stance and made MuchHeart cower below her.

"In the Desert? Are you mad? Do you not know what is within these walls? We are best to hide our treasures from the savage desertian creatures! Those foul goçips who feed in the Desert would ingest every soul that entered. Here, we are well hidden from all who want to prosper off us. No one can take from us if we are hidden. We gain our population by those who stumble upon our land. They were lost, and we gave them refuge. Without you, dear Delight, and those like you, we would die out and our beautiful culture along with us. You are our future. The strongest laws of this land make us unable to repopulate within our borders."

My curiosity was not, at this point, a good ally to me, for it stoked my interest and caused me to plead for a peek, so that I could know this mystery.

MaraJipsa had not answered my question before MuchHeart spoke up. He implored me to return to the camp rather than deeper into Arqana to the Temple. He would suit himself in a simple tent and hide from the ferocity which the Queen had in her eyes.

"You are not the more intelligent, I see. Information denied, is information against you. Come, let me do you a grand gesture of friendship and give you access to this temple for simply a night. When you are exited from its gates in the morning, you, as those before you, will find residency within our village perimeter, or suffer the wilds of the Desert. There is nothing in between."

MaraJipsa finished her warning and walked ahead of us, obviously still conscious of our footsteps, listening for them to fall in quick succession as she approached the Temple Gates.

I came to MuchHeart. I placed my hand on his shoulder to coax him toward the gate, so that I might enter. I stared at my hand upon his shoulder, thinking it something magical. We spoke quietly, and I saw my soul enter his body. The Voices sang with pleasure, as they fed upon the darkness therein.

At the time, I had thought Ç☉d☉mɜ something beautiful. I placed on his cheek a kiss and felt a spirit enter my body. It made me thirst for obscurity of the Temple. The spirit had not come from him but from within the darkness. The Voices fed upon this force and they flexed their strength within me.

My body was no longer mine.

MaraJipsa's hand was on my back as she pushed me through the gates. The doors were open wide before us, their black metal icy cold against the orange stone. MaraJipsa hummed a temptress song that I recognized from my infancy. The Voices harmonized with her. I became one with her song as my spine crawled toward where her hand was present on my back.

I looked at my friend. The envy that I had for his masculinity had turned into lust for *him*. My mind was consumed with some dark affair, the likes of which I had not previously known.

I was chained, each hand and foot as well as my neck, for this was my kiss of access into the lustful courts of Ç☉d☉mɜ.

The Voices were as silent as spectators at the climax of a terrifying play.

A darkness came over me as the grand doors shut behind us. Their creaking was the only noise present. At the clash of the doors shutting and locking from without, a wail of laughter erupted from the heart of the Temple. From the inner courts, there appeared a light which was artificial, yet magnetizing. I wandered in, dragging the chained MuchHeart at my waist.

We reached the center of the court. The eerie light cast visibility, but not clarity, on ten thousand faces looking up at us from the lower courts. They were souls ransomed to the Temple. They cackled and dripped spit, but they were not the goçips of legends. They were the beautiful people we had seen in the light, who had now become their true selves, illuminated in the reality of their own actions. Though they were apparently hideous, they had an air of their siren powers, and by that, they became attractive in a different way—I gave myself and MuchHeart up to them, to join in their party of the dead.

We were both bound up in the chains that hung from our limbs and our necks, and tied, one to the other, at the hip so that all in the Temple might have a way of their own with us. We were fresh meat. Once up-close, the populous became more disturbing than the pains which they donned upon us. Men, women, and children alike were unrecognizable now. Their bodies and souls had been destroyed. Their claws lashed torturously at the both of us. MuchHeart was well torn to pieces, and in tears, when he and I were finally come to converse:

"Why have you brought me here to such pain and death? Was I, to you, a friend whom you had a desire to kill? Have I somehow killed the good which I once saw, or thought I saw in you? Or were you so guarded by your lying soul that I saw your bad for good and hate for love, and anger for passion? You show me that you hate me, for you have brought me here to die!"

"Perhaps this is not of roses and incense; but we have a freedom here which is not found in Aeda, and we should enjoy it to the fullest before returning!"

"Are you so backward? We are in chains! We are not free! We have no freedom here; but in Aeda, we were even free to sell ourselves to this bondage and slavery to evil, though we had a King who owns us. We cannot return to Aeda. I fear we have disgraced our bodies too

51

completely. We will no longer be welcomed in Aeda's lush fields and golden hills. You have stolen me from my way, for I left myself vulnerable to a demon like you. Go back to the hole from which you first crawled!"

He then began to cry, and he vomited what was in him. He drank the spirits of this putrid city, but there was no reprieve inside these walls. All that was here was for his torment.

With his hands still bound and feet still locked with iron, he crawled to a damp corner and found himself in silence.

I followed—I had no choice—I was bound, and the irons yanked brutally at my waist.

"MuchHeart, if you give this city a chance, perhaps there is good beyond the smell and our first thoughts."

"I doubt this. The darkness is thick and permanent. Perhaps we are now here, where the light has been longest missed, and is closest to that time when war will start, and the sun shall return, and burn this place again with brimstone! Yet, we who should lead the battle are trapped here in iron chains, behind enemy lines. War may break this very eve!"

He raised his arms, clattering his chains violently. He was causing a commotion and I wished that he would be quiet. My chest rose with the anger which welled inside of me and I met his fevered pitch.

"Where is the promise of a King's return? Saia lay dormant and the world moves on in continual progress. What has the King done to promote goodness and kindness? I do believe MaraJipsa understands, for she whispered in my ear that their flag has done more good than the promises of a lost King. Do you wish for the death of all those inhabitants of this land? How unloving of you!

You ought to have more peace in your soul. We were told to love our neighbors and are these not our neighbors?"

"These surely are our neighbors and that is why I show them love by speaking the truth. None here will tell them of the death which they have chosen for themselves. It is not our King who chose their fate; only, long ago he arranged a punishment for such offenses which they now commit. He wishes, as you know, that none should be lost to the death of the Desert. It is not I who shows them a lack of love, for I wish to speak against their death. It is *you* who shows them hatred for you know the truth. Yet, you withhold it for your own selfish ways. It is not me who has decided this fate for them. They chose their own curse and they will bear it if they define themselves by it. You now know of this and not only do you known the laws, but you give approval to those who make sacrifice here against our King. You yourself give sacrifice against the King of Aeda! Your mind is debased, and you will die in this temple."

Having taken a long journey to get here, and having become obsessed with my companion, I did not want to part from this city. MuchHeart, having arrived with no time to decide if he wanted to enter (he would have decided against it), wanted nothing from this land, but his own right to leave. MuchHeart shriveled into a fetal position and began to weep. The anger in his cries and the utter desperation tugged at me, but, it wasn't his agony that pained me. I saw my own loneliness in his tears and it haunted me. I made for his chest to steal his heart while he was unaware, but even in his sorrow he did not forget himself. My selfishness left him furious.

"Can you think of only yourself? You are becoming a changed man even as I watch. I fear you will be lost forever. Do not touch me. I do not want to share in your destruction."

MuchHeart sat in silence for a while, with his hands around his bound ankles, and his face between his knees. Finally, he stood, with much difficulty, for his wrists and ankles were raw. I thought he would follow me now deeper into the temple courts, but rather, he pushed me from the comfortable perch of my stone. He ran without warning, back through the Wood and toward the Fence. He cried out for help all the while. I threw my stone at his head with both hands' power to render him immobile. To my surprise, upon impact, the stone crumbled and fell to the earth in pieces like fine pottery in the hands of a child.

The men of the temple heard his yelling and barricaded the path to hinder his escape.

"Boy! What will you give us? No one leaves this temple in possession of every piece with which he entered. You must pay your alms."

"I have none to spare for every part of me belongs to the King of Aeda. Remove my shackles, for I am not a slave to you any longer."

"Where then be your armor that protects you? Is not your home behind the Fence? Boy, you must think us fools. You have the look of a traitor, and for that, we will take two pieces of you and leave your bindings where they are."

They took poor MuchHeart's eyes. He was left to wander the forest blind, consumed by his pain and anger.

MuchHeart tore himself from the guards at the gated entrance and flew in a direction which seemed to be west, though, he could not tell. He was blind. He was not able to see the light of the sun—but neither could he feel it on his face. He ran toward the quiet, away from the shrieks of the Desert, deeper into Arqana.

I stayed in that city of Godoms for a while, but it was not a joyous place. I began to wonder if it was even a happy place when I had MuchHeart there with me. I had only the Voices to talk to, the rest were not interested in conversation. Although I was in a populated temple, I had never been quite so alone as I was then. I spoke to these Voices who had made this journey with me and given me support along the way.

"I hurt, and therefore you cannot have given me happiness, for I have none."

"Oh, but happiness is what you make of it! Perhaps if you sought more of what this fine city has to offer!"

"I pity the man who stumbles across this land without having seen first even the outskirts of Aeda. I have seen and felt her grass and for that reason, I see that all that is here is death."

"For what reason then do you stay in our city? Those here are full of happiness and merriment! They sing, they dance, they cry for joy!"

"I am here in the same place as you, and I see not what you say. They cry, writhe, and yell because they are being burned. They are dying as they sacrifice themselves. I want not to be one of them the longer!"

"Oh, but here you may keep your body and share in theirs, but if you leave, we will take that proportionate of what you have enjoyed here; just as we took from your MuchHeart."

"I have enjoyed naught and therefore shall you take the same? Even so, I would gladly cut off my right hand to be rid of this misery."

The Voices were silent. I yelled for them to respond—they hid. I was alone.

I was left on the cold stone to cry until I was dry of any tear which had been in me. I ate what scraps would fall to the ground and I grew slight in the borders of that evil place. My heart was weak and burned with the fires of the burnt sacrifices in that wretched place. I screamed. I cried. I grew sick. Yet, all the while, I was alone. No one paid me any attention.

I had been rejected here in a foreign land for I spoke against them in public. Yet, I groveled to drink the blood which dripped from the altars by night, for survival. For this, I was hated and cursed by all and shunned in my shameful state.

I was two men confined by one body; two separate personalities and neither in my control. My mind and body acted independently and in conflict to nature.

"Let the stone walls fall on me and kill me! Or let some fire consume me, that this misery might be done!" I was not heard; not even my plea for death. Death was nowhere to be found and yet it surrounded me. Its shadow was cast on the walls like writing. The flames from within projected this deadly shadow-warning for the lost souls of Çɷdɷm₃ were but an image of death, a precursory forewarning that few here heeded.

A day came when the temple doors were opened and MaraJipsa came to retrieve me from this oven of fornication where I was mindlessly confectioned to the ways of Arqana. She took me by the hand. "You look good enough to eat." she mumbled in my ear. "What a precious little Monster you are."

I followed her through the same clearing I had entered so long ago. The sun was different; its light did not give any visibility. I stumbled through the hedge, hand in hand with the woman who locked me in her temple. I didn't remember her violation of my freedom then.

We arrived in the center of the camp and she let go my hand. "You're free to go about your business here. You're now most like us."

I was dumbfounded. I was free—but from what—I did not know. I felt captive still in this land, though I knew not why. Some dark and sinister spirit held me within the confines of Arqana. I made it my home.

I was surprised by the lack of discrimination there. The young boys were picked over first by those long suffered from the paths, yet, there was no man, woman, or child left alone. No matter how (or how many times) one was coupled, there was only emptiness. I was alone.

I soon lost interest in watching others. I fell to the wayside and found my food at the base of the altars of Arqana. It did not sustain me, but it was food, and I was hungry. The more I ate, the hungrier I became. The cycle repeated itself until I lost count of the bodies I had ingested.

What felt like mere days went by, but soon I saw the same months come around again. I lay on the cold stones, exposed to the elements. My skin dried and cracked, until I, too, resembled a burnt corpse. A moan was little more than I could manage for I grew faint of drinking in sameness. I ate what I was and for that I was lost to the darkest trenches of my mind.

Late one day, when I had seen no light, though I knew the sun to be in the sky, I overheard men speaking of a cave in the dark of Arqana. The place of which they spoke was near to where I had once lived. MuchHeart must surely have tried to return to Lyric for help. I would try to find him and convince him to return here with me, so that Ϛωdωmᴈ could again be a beautiful place. With midnight on my shoulder, I crept into the wagon of bodies and I hid myself beneath the corpses. In a wagon, I was carried out and dumped in a cave in the woods with naught but a thought to my victim.

But I was not quite as clever as I had hoped, for before the bodies were denigrated, payment was taken from them; from each the highest price, for to lose your life in Ϛωdωmᴈ is costly in the least.

They took our hearts from us, many charred in their death, but none quite as dead and black as mine. They fascinated themselves with its state and I, myself, was shocked to find that it was nearly useless to them! I was equally shocked that it had not even a mark that would privilege them to know that it belonged to the King of Aeda.

Pace non trovo et non ò da far guerra
E temo et spero, et ardo et son un ghiaccio,
Et volo sopra 'l cielo et giaccio in terra,
Et nulla stringo et tutto 'l mondo abbraccio.
　　Tal m'à in pregion che non m'apre né serra,
Né per suo mi riten né scioglie il laccio,
Et non m'ancide Amore et non mi sferra,
Né mi vuol vivo né mi trae d'impaccio.
　　Veggio senza occhi, et non ò lingua et grido,
Et bramo di perir et cheggio aita…

Petrarch, *RVF 134.1-10*
I find no peace, and I am not at war,
I fear and hope, and burn and I am ice;
I fly above the heavens, and lie on earth,
And I grasp nothing, and embrace the world.
One keeps me jailed who neither locks nor opens,
Nor keeps me for her own nor frees the noose;
Love does not kill, nor does he loose my chains;
He wants me lifeless but wont loosen me.
I see with no eyes, shout with no tongue;
I yearn to perish, and I beg for help…

59

fter I was dumped at the cave, the men returned to Ϛѡdѡmꓱ. I stayed and ate bad meat. I grew fat on what I ought not to have eaten. I lost myself to some bit of insanity and did not depart from what I now considered *my* cave. I hid from the Beasts that hunted these parts. I was west of where they left me. I covetously hid the stench of the bodies which I kept for my own food. The Beasts continued to come closer. They must have known I was there—they are much more practiced hunters than me.

I was encouraged by discovering that MuchHeart crossed the path of my vantage point on a regular basis, always making the loudest ruckus trying to find his way home. I saw him in the shadows, but my gaze could not follow him. He hung amid the half-perceived and his voice was all that I could make out. It trailed off in a new direction each time he came into ear-shot. He was within my range of sight, yet I could not know where he stood. He was the blind one, yet it was I who could not see. We were locked between the menacing gray bars of the dense wood of Arqana.

My deranged mind had grown to accept the corpses as comrades in the flesh. I had no one else to listen to my poison. I believed them good listeners and the silent advice I divined from them was always solid and trust worthy to my melting ears.

I was lonely without the company of Ϛѡdѡmꓱ. I hoped for the true owner of the path to come and speak with me, and comfort me, while I sat in my cave. However, I would not have him take me from my cave. I was without trust. No voice came except for the quiet whispers which haunted my sleep and kept me awake. If I would sleep, they would wake me with a dream or some other fright. I stayed awake in fear; not in presence of mind, but in hiding.

Soon, I grew comfortable in my cave; I came to call it home. Not that it was a good cave—only that it had grown warm to my body. Alone, with no other company, my conversations turned inward, and the Voices began to become innumerable. One Voice was stronger (or simply more pleasing) than all the others. This Voice hated MuchHeart as vehemently as I. He called himself by a name which soothed me into trusting his words.

"If he is to stumble upon your cave," he would say, "be ready that you might woo him into trusting you, so that you might punish him for his wrongdoing."

This, to me, was a good voice. It pleased me to hear. Something stirred within me that this must be the voice of the King of Aeda—if Aeda truly had a king. I had heard that in some scenarios, his whisper can be heard in silence, repeating his laws for his countrymen.

"He deserves death for his curses. Nonetheless, I will be a merciful friend who he deserves not. I will spare his life and require only his tears of repentance."

"This is a wonderful thought," said the whisper. "I am proud of you. You are much like me." I sat back in my cave, warm, comforted, delighted that the king found me kingly. My grin stretched to my ears and I spoke pleasantly with the Voices. They were better conversationalists than the bodies, which now began to decay.

"I worry that I might be discovered for the stink that surrounds me." I relayed to the Voices. "If I leave, will you follow? For I dare not journey without company in such a solitary place as Arqana. I will need a sure companion."

"We will be with you forever and always, never leaving, never forsaking, never departing."

MuchHeart's body was sore and his ankles bled from the chains which bound him. He stumbled and fell many times, but he got up and continued his way until he felt himself safe again. He did not want any man on his way to Ϛѡdѡmꙅ to see him, weak and defenseless, and try to take him back whence he escaped.

Pointless! he thought. The chains were too thick to cut, too tight to pull off, but fastened far enough apart that he could still get half a stride before falling again to the earth. Each time he fell, he beat the dead sod with his chained fists.

MuchHeart felt as though he were a stuck pig, tied and ready to roast. Unable to push this thought from his head, he continued with all his might to cross the edge of Arqana to reach salvation on the other side of the Fence.

He reached the cold-packed dirt which let him know that he had arrived in a deeper part of the woods. There was no heat in the Desert. Its chill could be felt from the eastern side of Arqana in Ϛѡdѡmꙅ, and it quickly dispersed throughout the whole land. He clawed his way to the trunk of a tree, about his width around and straddled it upright like a boy clinging to his father's leg. It creaked in the breeze and he thought that it had given him welcome. Needles fell to his shoulder and in his hair. He left them there. They were not nearly as important as finding a good place to sleep. The woods now grew darker as day break came across the Desert for, just like in Ϛѡdѡmꙅ, the denser woods never saw daylight. Now that

63

the days grew shorter, he would not feel even the fleeting sensation of sunlight on his face.

He heard a whisper from the west. His heart leapt. Perhaps it was RationHeart calling for him from the Fence! He could not bear to stand. His knees were cut by the unforgiving rocky forest floor. They stung when he attempted to put his weight on them. MuchHeart lifted himself up on the pads of his feet and palms of his hands, and he crept like the Beasts that he had seen before— though, north, he assured himself.

His eyelids would have been heavy had he possessed them. He needed to sleep. He had not noticed before how much he relied on his eyelids. It wasn't until he awoke that he realized how tired he was. He had fallen asleep mid-stride and knew that he had to find a safer place to sleep. He paused to listen to the forest floor—he could do little else with any other sense—and he decided that the North was quieter and, therefore, safer for him. He turned and crawled a mere one hundred lengths before he came to a small patch of long, cool grass. He thought he might lay his head to sleep for a few hours.

His body was asleep before he could even make his nest. The ground was chilled and damp, not normally a place one would choose to sleep, but the tender grass made MuchHeart feel safe, and the dampness felt soothing against his wounds.

I walked back to the Fence where I had parted from it. My intent was to settle in to my place against the Fence, and rest there before returning to Çⓞdⓞm3. I knew my payment would be a piece of me each time I returned. In my present state of mind, it seemed a fair price. I thought I would do it often. All that while, I kept my eyes set out for

MuchHeart. I had no care for his safety. I meant to scold him for leaving me alone where I grew lonely.

I came to the Fence. I was pleased to find that Lyric was standing in search of her friends. They had both left her in the night, me included. She saw not where they had gone.

I went to her, speaking so that she hadn't the chance to speak. I saw her look. I knew she would not be one to welcome me lovingly. I stepped closer to her with caution.

She allowed me to speak until her ears bled. Then she shouted, much louder than I believed her capable.

"Be quiet, you foul fool! You have stolen my friend, MuchHeart, who was once beside me at the Fence and he now wanders amongst the Beasts! I have heard his cries. I listen to him as he wanders. I know your story is false. I have witnessed else. Cursed am I to have stopped here, where you beckoned him to rest upon this path. Doubly wicked are you for having pulled him away from this path! Your curse should be to have a millstone tied around your neck, cast into the deepest part of the sea. Part from me! I will stay here and call for MuchHeart in hopes that he return."

She chased me in her anger, taking RationHeart with her deep into Arqana. Although RationHeart had remained quiet, I knew that I had angered her more than any other for stealing her kin.

I did not see where they went. I knew the woods better and I knew how to hide in Arqana. They lost me, and I ran fervently from the Fence.

MuchHeart slumbered for many months. He had unknowingly stumbled upon a bog-of-separation, where his consciousness left him. These were common here in the lowlands of Arqana—he may have seen it had he possessed eyes. They normally glow quite vibrantly with spectacular colors. A shame he missed even that beauty. It was quite strange that he stumbled upon it without this lure.

Had he not been awakened by a horrid ruckus, he might never have come to. He awoke with a start. His eyes would have opened wide, but there were none there, save those of the bugs that had begun to burrow. The shock of the commotion was surely apparent on his face, nonetheless.

He heard a deep sob from one who had lost all hope. The sounds of the Beasts picking a sobbing woman to pieces faded into nonexistence as the woman's desperation grew more hopeless. MuchHeart tried to get up, hoping to save the woman whose voice he heard. But the grass he laid in to sleep had overgrown his body and begun to assimilate itself into his skin. It pained him to try to break free; but as he tried, he realized that there was little hope.

This was the first time he could remember not coming to the rescue of one in pain—and this was the worst pain that he had ever heard. Like a drop of red die in a pitcher, action of inaction tainted his whole being. The less he attempted to help the woman, the more the idea of leaving her to her own pain and death took hold of him. Now, he was not desiring her death—not by any means— only, he no longer carried with him the instinct to help. He let it die alongside his manhood. He was becoming the destruction he had warred against; now that he was in pain, he could think of no one's suffering more than his own.

The grass was stronger than what he had remembered. Perhaps the darkness of Arqana helped the grasses grow thick against the conditions. The water now covered most of him. The ground had been only damp when he had first laid there. But now the deeper waters made his skin porous and tender, so much so that he was not sure whether it was the grass's strength or his own body's water-logged weakness that held him there. Either way, he was hopelessly stuck.

Before MuchHeart could gash his own flesh to pieces, struggling against the sieve of grass, the Beasts left their prey and came to investigate his yells, which he had not realized that he made. "I was on the path!" MuchHeart shouted again, not knowing he yelled aloud. His ears were full of bog-water. "I stopped to talk to this demon that tricked me. He stole me away in my sleep! He is cursed above all others! He led away the faithful who were asleep! If I had not been against the Fence, but straight in my path to the beautiful foothills of Saia, this foul beast could not have grabbed hold of my collar to make me enter his sin. Is my temptation equivalent to his evil?"

His unconscious yells had not brought help to his side, but rather, they brought the threat of sure death. The Beasts slowly encircled him. He could not see them, but he felt and heard their breath. They were close enough that he might have taken a swing and hit one, if his arms had been free. He felt a paw on his leg and it tenderly cut away the weeds. He wondered if they preferred a chase. Or had they come to rescue him? Were these Beasts now, for one reason or another, his friends? MuchHeart became overjoyed that what would kill one person, became his friend, and so he lost all fear and gave in whole-heartedly to that which seemed to be to his safe-keeping.

Once the Beasts had freed him from his bondage, they began to lick his wounds and play with him. *Perhaps these Beasts that I once saw playing with my friend at the Fence are good after all*, he thought to himself. And they were won to his heart, knowing now why I, Delight, had followed them into Arqana. He made the Beasts his company. He followed with much hope in where they might take him. One of the largest of the four Beasts that had come to him let him ride on its back. MuchHeart held fast to the matted hair and buried his face in his protector who was now carrying him to the edge of Arqana, much faster than he himself could have walked.

The way seemed familiar, but, then again, all trees do sound vaguely the same, do they not? So MuchHeart fell asleep, as they carried him beyond where he had fled, without his knowing.

MuchHeart awoke again on the back of his rescuer. He did not have time to fully awaken before he realized that they had brought him to the Desert.

He let go of his grasp of the alpha and slid into the sand. He dug himself into a hole to hide himself from them. He waited, quietly and patiently. Perhaps the Beasts were not coming for him again. Maybe they had not realized that he had left. On the other hand, what if they were waiting for him to die so that he would not put up a fight? But now that he knew their game and true intent, he was sure to try to fight them off.

MuchHeart knew that his time was limited here in the Desert. His skin was still soaked and wrinkled. The sun was not drying him, but rather, the Desert temperatures began to freeze the water within his skin. He rushed to the humid cover of Arqana, being not far off. He had awoken at the first cool desertian breeze. The Beasts had brought him to some northern trail that was well-beaten, and he found that again. He could hear the Beasts yipping, but they were far off now and still traveling. He had not the faintest idea why they did not return for him. Instinct told him not to turn around to find his answer.

His hand grabbed a stick. He felt it quickly with his fingers, contracting a sliver or two, but with no mind toward that. He knew that where there was a stick, there must be a tree close by, and soon, the thick cover of Arqana.

MuchHeart pulled himself to his knees. He cradled the stick and cried over it. It was not the woods. Nevertheless, he spent quite some effort treating it as if it were.

He stayed to the edge of the trail, not wanting to be out in the open, but this made his journey more difficult. There is hardly a good place to stay for very long and the way was thick with pains. No path led to a safe place, only toward the raging desertian wilderness. There seemed no way to cross from this side of Arqana to that. But MuchHeart followed the northern path as best he could, without his eyes to see. Soon he came to a large clearing that he thought again to be the outer rim of Arqana. But when he found that it was only a rocky patch of Desert, he was so despondent that he made efforts then to rid himself of this torment by means of his own.

I do not remember my journey. It went without milestone or marker. I only remember what caused my first stop. The way was mostly downhill, so I felt at ease. For reasons unknown to me, I believed my way was parallel to the Fence, and perhaps it was. Interestingly, though, this path was as wide as it was long and had no edge nor end. It was the most spacious area in all my known world. It was spread with the sands of time. It was well tread.

Along the path I spied a quite peculiar sight. MuchHeart was on this same path. He wept and screamed for someone to rescue him as he sat in a puddle of his own blood. He had begun to kill himself. With much violence, he began again to do his head in with a rock.

"Kill me! Have the rocks fall on me! I fear that I am not a person who can be rescued. My way has been taken from me!" I hid behind a straggling tree and watched him to know what his fate would be.

"What shall I do for fear that You have not chosen me? My heart is wrought with sin-thought. I do not believe a good spirit lives in me. Shall I take this as a sign that a good path rests not within my grasp?"

Two travelers came and kissed MuchHeart on either cheek where his tears and blood had dried. He had been in their state for many hours. The blood matted his hair and crusted to his skin. They spoke with MuchHeart for some time and told him that their prince desired him. The men supported him on either side and walked with him in a direction contrary to me.

Immediately, I remembered my covetousness of him, even in my hate. I did my very best to release him of the grasp of these beings.

"Good Sir, I would have you unhand that man; he was first mine. I pray you not spoil him with fantastical ideas of a journey with the likes of you." They, in jest, responded.

"Deceit, for we shall call you by your name," which angered me greatly. "You are not welcome in the presence of this lamb, whose fall you aided. You have led him into peril, away from the land in which he lived. It was your voice that carried him to the border, and likewise your hand that plucked him up, and threw him to Godoms and the mercy of the Beasts. We come bearing news of your doom. You are not fit to lead. Leave the presence of this injured babe."

I, being quite wise in my own eyes, spoke to MuchHeart directly and said:

"These men are not surely the Beasts disguised in Aedic armor. Their business is in the woods and their lies are their master. Believe me, for when we met I was close to the Fence. These people met you on your travels in a place in which neither of us had found much happiness but for the company of each other. Let us betake ourselves to venture together as the friends we are, and care not for these deceitful beings of Light." At this point the Men of Light, having much desire for the child in their arms, let him speak for himself.

"Be gone, foul creature." said he "We are not friends. These men have told me of the error of my way and I have believed them. They have shown me selfless love and I wish them to take me to the place where I might worship the King and have my right spirit renewed. I once resided in Aeda. It was not me who decided to leave it behind, but it will be me who returns there to the call of the King. I have not rejected Him, for he is my Master and the reason I leave you in your death. I could not join you in what is contrary to my King. I have run in search of whence I came, yet I was asleep when you took me and know not how I came to where I am. These men have found me and wish to show me the way and I wish that they do."

"Dear lost one," I said, "do not let them take you now. You look tired and must rest with me here near the woods. There will be time for a journey, but not in your present bloodied state. Let me bandage you and kiss your wounds."

This was not worth their time in responding. They went on, having said all that they had reason to say. I, being unsatisfied and feeling quite dejected, bowed to let them pass. Then I took up the stone which he had used to bleed himself quite completely and threw it at his head in efforts to hinder him.

He was struck, and he bled, but he was caught in the arms of his companions and they pointed his feet toward the way in which he would go. The last words that I heard from them were these: that they went to a place where he could drink the blood of one who shed His own that all may be replenished and have life.

At this, I scoffed and left in my own direction.

PT 2

The Desert

Guarda 'l mio stato a le vaghezze nove
Che 'nterrompendo di mia vita il corso
M''an fatto abitador d'ombroso bosco;
Rendimi, s'esser po, libera et sciolta
L'errante mis consorte, et fia tuo 'l pregio
S'ancor teco la trovo in miglior parte,
Or ecco in parte le question mie nove:
s'alcun pregio in me vive o 'n tutto è corso,
o l'alma sciolta o ritenuta al bosco.

Petrarch, RVF 214.31-39

Look at my state from beauty that is new,
Which has, in interrupting my life's course,
Made me a dweller of a shadowy wood;
Give me, if it can be, unbound and free
My wandering consort; let yours be the prize
If I find my soul with you in a better place.
Now see in part my doubts all strangely new:
If some worth lives in me or ran its course,
If my soul's free or held back in the wood.

73

"He that wandereth out of the way of understanding, shall remain in the congregation of the dead."

John Bunyan, *Pilgrim's Progress*

"It is a beautiful place: the sound of dry, un-marrowed bones cracking beneath the foot; a dank mist of shrieks and laughter at head level, confuses the senses and lubricates desire. Our army can always feast at its gates; it overflows with the people of the Desert. There is but every way in, and not one out save by the mouths of Legion. Men here are long suffered from the valley where, it is said, they may still turn around and enter the narrow path which cuts away from Sodom and toward a Holy Land which boasts of Honey and Milk, Manna and Life. Disgusting, if fact."

EDR, *Pragma Letters*

For quite some time I wandered alone. I saw not where to go; the path became easier and more tread, yet wild as the desertian sun.

The wood beside me broke clear to the west. I saw, through its frailty, a thin path which looked difficult, as if it would purge my vocal companions from my body (provided I survive). That path was to Aeda. To the other side, I saw this expansive Desert which was wild and unknown to me. The setting sun cast mauve shadows before me. The further into the night I waited, the closer these shadows came to me as if they were large hands coming out of the sand to grab me, or a hunting tigress prowling across the veldt to where I sat, unaware of the dangers before me. The landscape was littered with paths that twisted in every direction like a snake. I shivered as the shadows retreated and were replaced by the much more ominous shadow of night which left no crevasse or crack with the light it may have held.

I ran in silence, arms wrapped around myself, partially for warmth, but mostly for comfort. I was afraid of the Desert, I had not expected such a vast expanse of nothingness. I ran for hours. At my first step into the sands of the Desert. I felt as though I could never return. The sand was cool and soft. It gave ease to my feet. It coaxed me to stay. My feet could not change course of my own will, only fall—one in front of the other. The darkness was so complete that I couldn't see my own body behind its obscure curtain of blackness. No more was the beautiful hunting purple dancing at my feet, enticing me with her slow and calming presence. Black was all that remained. The darkness made my eyes sting. It was less painful when I closed them. Somehow, I blamed my state on my country. It seemed to me that Aeda had abandoned me.

I heard whispers from the men who walked beside me in darkness. I couldn't see them, but I recognized their voices. They were familiar to me as those who encircled me, facelessly, namelessly, for months in the temple at Çɷdɷmȝ. I tripped and stumbled drunkenly, toward a city in front of me which covered the highest hill within a day's walk from Arqana. I was parched and in need of water—or whatever they could offer me for drink.

Visions danced in front of me. Men crawled in all directions on their hands and feet. It was as if all the ants of the world had been called to their queen, and on their way, they would gnash their teeth, tear themselves apart, and feast on the flesh of others. Yet I was alone.

When day broke, the Desert was covered in a frost. This frost was not beautiful as one might imagine frost on a desert might be. It is exactly as one might imagine it, only, to see and to imagine are two different matters all together. There is a certain disdain that comes from seeing frost in every direction when realization strikes that it is the cause of suffering through the night that ceases not in this forsaken tundra. That which makes you suffer can quickly lose all beauty in that moment where fantasy meets reality.

The closer I came to the city on the horizon, the more men I passed. They seemed mostly to be merchants or traders of sorts. They spoke loudly and with much confidence. Yet, I thought myself wiser than them, so I did not stop long to talk to anyone. I would not be seen wearing such crude clothing, draped in the carcasses of every animal and race known to the Desert. The first man I came to who could keep my pace was named SpeakGood. I could tell that he was an educated man; he covered himself in other men's catch and not his own. His language was the coarse tongue of the Desert. He spoke as though he knew many great things; therefore, I found favor in him.

Our minds were similar. We spoke of that which was attractive about this path. We had many different ideas, but most of our ideas were quite opposed to the other. However, we agreed upon the howl of the night and the breeze which chilled us both as something which attacked our minds and left us powerless against the wild call and the many kingdoms of the Desert. He loved that the sand was in all places. It made a soft footing for him, and he praised it in this way. I, on the other hand, found the sands to be a foreign nuisance to my body.

"How good it is not to change in direction, for our intent is ahead, to the desertian kingdoms—whichever one you would wish to enter. The sand beneath our feet guides the way so that we can turn neither here nor there, but to our destinations alone." SpeakGood said, visibly admiring his resolve and, presumably, his intellect.

When he said this, I turned to look behind me and saw that my steps had gone in many circles and were sometimes stopped and back-tracked. I did not understand why he said that the sand was aiding our way. We were trapped here and would make it to the East not because we were guided but because it was inevitable once one was in the Desert.

"Sir," I said, for we addressed each other with much respect, "I once had it said to me, by one with whom I spent much time, and trust with all my life, that this sand is a danger to us. I believed her not at that time, but I see now that it has captured my walk and raws the skin on my feet until they are well bled. How is it that you consider this to be in our benefit?"

"'Tis good to have pain if by good reason. If by necessity, the sand is our way to our respectful destinations, then be it painful or soft forever, it aids us in giving us path."

I did not like this answer. I thought my search was for there that I might find no pain; yet the conversation continued without my thought. When it came time to share our pasts, I remembered my stone. I wished to show it to my new friend. I reached into my pocket, to show him what I had named Religion. Quickly realizing I had discarded it in anger toward MuchHeart, I told him I possessed it, yet I couldn't produce it for his sight. Instead, I bragged largely of it.

"I have a beautiful white and gold stone from Mount Saia in Aeda which contains a spectacular array of gold ore from the streets of Paradise. With this stone, I have my laws and my promise."

"How great to see a man of background and of substance." SpeakGood said this as he patted my shoulder. "Surely you are the best of your land. You are proud and humble at once, accepting the Desert, while holding to the pride of your homeland. I boast of the earth and what it can do for me. I count myself not a religious man, but I have great knowledge of it, for I was presented with three stones as a child. I was told that they were all good." I, having had my interest stroked, listened intently.

"Please, Sir, tell me of these stones. Which did you choose and why did you choose it?"

"Aye, I had hoped you would ask. I was presented with three stones, as I have said. One of them I chose to carry in my pocket." He said this without breaking gaze and continued: "The first was a black stone with a center that was not visible. But it spooked me and told my heart that it could do me grave danger, while also giving me great power. I said *no* out of fear. I am proud of that decision for it would have destroyed me to have taken that stone. But I have remained curious of what could have been had I taken the stone. It was named BlackMagic. It is hewn from a hidden quarry guarded by a queen, who is more powerful than any other, though no one knows whence she ascended."

"How great to make that good choice. I have not heard of a queen in any kingdom this side of Aeda besides Queen Mara of the gypsies, and surely she is not of such darkness."

"Oh, surely it is not her; she is the most colorful in the land and cannot surely contain a black fleck within her."

"Then who is the queen of whom you speak?"

"Surely she is simply a legend. Nonetheless, I assure you that the black stone was of the purest black. It was all sorts of real. But enough about such dark matters. The next stone was a stone of whose name I shall tell you first, before I describe it, so as not to confuse you. Its name was Religion. This was most likely from the same quarry as yours. It has the same name here in the Desert. I tell you this, not in offense, but simply to describe the truth of which stone I have chosen."

"I take no offense, good sir, for I am but a humble man of religion and I wish to hear all stories if they please my ear to hear."

"Yes, well. I shall tell you why that stone did not suit me. It was gray, and it crumbled in my hand. I had only a small piece. I thought that perhaps a larger piece would be of better substance. However, having not the luxury, I quickly moved on to my next stone which was brown.

"Before I continue, I would like to request sight of your stone, Religion. Perhaps it is larger and of better composition so that I might learn better of Religion."

Feeling quite shy of my loss, I held out to him the dust which it had left in my pocket.

"Sir, this is the dust from the stone which rests in my pocket. The stone shall stay there for protection, for it is of precious material. Study this dust. See that this stone is not gray but white and gold as those mined only in Aeda and Paradise beyond."

Holding my handful of dust up to his eye. I noticed his expression only changed slightly from that of confusion to pity.

"Deceit, for this must be your name, you hold gray dust that fell from your stone, which must also be gray. Why do you tell me that it is white and gold? It is clearly not. Please, take it out of your pocket so that we can study its color and quality together."

"What attack is this? I deceive you not for I know my stone is from Aeda! It is of white granite and gold ore. It is both sturdy and precious."

At this, I turned to face him. "SpeakGood, you have not finished your story. It is important to me that you do so with much haste! If we are to travel together, we must know each other well and not be caught in the rhetoric of argument."

"Yes, I will continue. I meant no offense. My stone, which I took up, is brown and its name is earth, for it is the stone which has made the sands of this Desert. It is made of many minerals. I chose this stone because most men I met along my journey carried the same. I, being a wise man of the world, choose nothing better than the next. I am humble and kind, and not overcome easily by pride."

We were interrupted as a man came upon us out of the desertian haze. He lumbered through the icy air, his gate rigid and strained; he was in obvious pain. A gust of wind caught him off guard and knocked him to the unforgiving frozen sand. SpeakGood and I ran to him, forgetting our conversation.

The man was not dead, though he looked as any dead man might—gaunt and green. His chest heaved, and he rasped words which were unintelligible to us.

"What hideous words does he utter in such a lack-luster fashion?" SpeakGood asked me, looking up from the man on whose chest he rested his hands, but did not help to resuscitate.

I leaned in closer to hear his words. They slithered like serpents. My choir came to life in my head; the Voices spoke back as any native speaker lucky enough to find its kin in a foreign country might.

"These are not words of my home." I said, to which SpeakGood informed me of the same regarding his own native tongue, which was more closely related to the language which I had spoken in my birthplace. This language was dry and harsh but flowed off the speaker's tongue like warm spit. He spoke again, and my Voices responded. They were spoke so fluidly through me that a familiarity grew within me, and soon I found that the Voices no longer had to give me the words to say, merely the ideas to convey. But this man soon caused the Voices to hate him.

"Do not go to the East!" The man choked. "There is naught but death and rot and foul beasts of all shapes, sizes and degrees of evil. They rage, one against the other, but they hate man most of all. Flee west while you can! Be free of the Desert and her mutilated whores!"

I translated his warning to SpeakGood who was not so lucky as I to have an internal Voice to teach him the strange desertian tongue.

"The man's delusional, surely. Look at him; he can scarce sound a word. Are you quite sure of your ability to translate? I'm not sure the man enunciated well each syllable. That ought make a clever difference, child-language-learner."

I looked at him harshly, my eyes telling him more than my lips, and responded snidely:

"He's more understandable than your mottled dialect and poor grammar, I dare say. Besides, this is not a language of sounds, it would appear. They merely seem to decorate the meanings of such sinisterly formed ideas.

The man spoke again.

"Beware the snake that eats the new moon. He knows who walks in his Desert. He will find you."

We decided we didn't like his warnings. We killed him and left.

TENTED CITY

VI

"Hasta que al fin caemos en el tiempo, tendidos,
Y nos lleva, y ya nos fuimos, muertos,
Arrastrados sin ser, hasta no ser ni sombra,
Ni polvo, ni palabra, y allí se queda todo
Y en la ciudad en donde no viviremos más
Se quedaron vacíos los trajes y el orgullo."

Pablo Neruda, *Ya se fue la ciudad*

Until, in the end, we fall in time, exhausted,
And it takes us, and that's it. Then we are dead,
Dragged off with no beings left, no life, no darkness,
No dust, no words. That is what it comes to;
And in the city where we'll live no more,
All is left empty, our clothing and our pride.

*W*inter was coming and the Desert was a brutal tundra. Water could be found only in the ice that grew in the cracks in the rocky terrain. There was no food to be found. Ice was all there was to eat for miles. Aeda had never grown cold this early in the harvest season—if in fact there was a harvest to be made here—but the Desert made no attempt to be like my former home. My companion and I feared what might come of us in the cold wilderness without company. Before the sun sank into the colorful east, we saw afar off a tent-city of rag-tag men and loose women. We decided to stay, though neither of us were certain of our safety in this universe of intolerant tolerants. In the end, we chose the fear which threatened least our bodies and most our souls.

These tents were by no means mediocre. The people may have been second-rate, but the tents were as I had never seen before—colorful beyond imagination and stacked, one atop another, as far as the eye could see. The people here were as varied as, or more than, the tents themselves.

SpeakGood and I were yet some way out, but the city seemed already to encompass us. The populous was outside of the border. No law could contain them. The law had become to have no law. In this way, every decision was accepted as good. All cheered and drank. The coy smiles that danced on the lips of those to whom we came to know first transferred seamlessly onto our own lips.

The first man to greet us was called FreeThinker. He was the now-decrepit leader of this nameless faction of men who robbed the citadel of Aeda its nearest out-post, the mount upon which these tents spread and festered as the disease they were. FreeThinker was funny company.

His jokes were simple and at times made me cringe; but his mastery of the vernacular was more proficient than I had yet heard. It was not difficult to see why the erudite were those to join in his rebellion. In his company were three: his daughters Crude and Lewd, and their strange cousin from the East, Mystic. SpeakGood found great kinship with them and was frequently invited to their home. I could tag along. I was not easily recognized at this time as an Aedaite; my complexion had been worn thin and my skin was covered with the dirt of Arqana. I appeared as everyone else who pollute the Desert as the wandering stars pollute the mariner's sky.

The house of FreeThinker was ill constructed. The entryway seemed to be the heart of the house. The back rooms were dark and secretive. I bid my time listening to his thoughts in the foyer. Chairs were brought to us by his daughters. I was slightly uncomfortable by the way Lewd looked at me as she placed the chair behind me and pulled my arm so that I would sit. It was as if I was her next meal. I felt as though she were planning how best to prepare me.

I sat with an awkward lurch. I awkwardly held her gaze until she smiled from the corner of her mouth and slithered out of the room. Crude soon followed her, having had a similar interaction with SpeakGood.

My smile was uncomfortable, and I tried to hide it. SpeakGood, however, was beaming from ear to ear, not the least bit shy of his joy. I watched the floor out of embarrassment. I was unexpectedly attracted to Lewd. I did not want FreeThinker to see my face while I imagined myself with his daughter. The floor, I humored myself to believe, would be more understanding.

FreeThinker let out a squealing laugh and I looked up, shocked to see that he was staring right at me!

"Boy, don't be shy. You're hardly the first to have eyes for my daughter. I raised her to be sought after by every man, good or bad, that passed her way. This is my way of opening the world to her and showing her my fatherly affection."

Something about this didn't sit well with me, but I said nothing so as not to seek conviction where I might liberate myself from it. I felt in a fog. I couldn't quite wrap my mind around his words.

"I can continue to think as I think, then?" I asked. I was surprised that I was bold enough to speak. Boldness seemed a pitiful name for my question, though. It would be more accurate to say that a desire had taken hold of me and I hadn't the boldness to deny myself. I spoke out of fear and desperation of losing something that caught my eye.

"Surely you can think about her, but if you touch, I'll have you strung up by your ears and skinned by the women of the town."

"I understand, sir. I will be cautious."

"Don't let your caution get in the way of your fun, boy! Just do as I say and do as you will."

This conversation confused me more so than I had been at my arrival. I was relieved when the subject was changed.

As FreeThinker began to speak on the harvest festivals that would take place in this city, he became passionate and lost his collected composure for a frightening moment.

I heard a scuttle in the hall that runs along the foyer. I saw Crude and Lewd had been listening but scurried off at their father's anger. I watched as they ran the returned my gaze to the now calm-and-collected

FreeThinker. He watched me watch his daughters with a disgusting pleasure in his eyes.

"Now, where was I? Ah, yes, the events of this season in the Tented City. Let me first say that our city is well accredited by the kingdom rising in the East. We will hold a celebration of our new standing, the first western outpost, in the coming weeks. You would be fools to miss it!"

I made a mental note that I would not, for the life of me, miss the event. FreeThinker continued.

"If you are at all interested in these other events, please feel free to attend. Our first event of the season will be held in just two days' time in the center of the city to welcome the shortening days and praise its unfaltering cycle. You are best to pay your respects to the Queen in all that she gives, otherwise, you know, you may not be found well in her favor."

"I believe I have already met Queen MaraJipsa. Does she hail from these parts?"

"Silly boy," chuckled FreeThinker. "MaraJipsa is not a queen any more than I am a horse. She does, however, share an unabashed reverence among our citizens. She really has learned true freedom and taught it to her captives. They have much to thank her for."

I smiled; I did miss her haunting whisper in my ear and the fiery touch of her talons on my skin. I nearly forgot myself in choice memories of a fictional sort. FreeThinker brought me back to reality—or so it could be called—with a sharp jab-to-the-knee with the tip of his luxurious leather shoes.

"Do not interrupt me again. I have a right to have my thoughts heard."

I had never heard of such a right in all my days; but this was not the world as I had known it, this was a world created of those within. It was his bluntness that silenced me, not his logic. But I sat quietly waiting for him to finish.

"The celebrations are once per month according to our stellar calendar which is interpreted by my niece. The Celebration of Mwna will be held three days from now and extend eight days and nine hours. The Celebration of Mæsma begins immediately at the setting of the sun in the ninth hour of the ninth day of Mwna. The Celebration of Rælw begins then, naturally, on the ninth hour of the nineteenth day of Mæsma and extends through the fourteenth hour of the thirty-fourth day of Rælw. This is the day the sun is reborn.

Each celebration is well attended, but they gain popularity as the days grow darker. All, however, are pivotal for understanding the culture here, which I can only assume will be yours as well, before the season is over. Oh, that reminds me. The Festival of Babel will take place on the first day of the next season, but you are best to begin preparations for that which you can contribute. My daughters have begun practicing their performance and I must say, I am loving where it is going!"

There was murder in his eyes when he said this—an odd hatred that fueled his ferocity. There was no way of separating the emotions he was displaying, both of hate and of love as if he either hated love or loved hate.

"Sir, will we be expected to contribute?" asked SpeakGood.

"Why, of course! You would like to be a contributing part of society, would you not?"

"Well, yes, I would. What kind of presentation might be appropriate for this festival?"

"Whatever you might wish, so long as it pay homage to the Desert and its kingdoms."

The meeting ended with room assignments. We were both roomed in FreeThinker's house but separated to rest on opposite sides of the habitation. I was placed in a dark room, farther from the foyer, whereas, SpeakGood took the room just beyond the great hall in the center of the grand estate.

My room smelled familiar as if some well-known spirit had inhabited it just before me, so recently that I could still see its presence in the shadows.

The first night was uncomfortable to say the least. The Voices held a festival of their own which woke me in the night in cold sweat. They were slaughtering my countrymen and it was a game to them! I thought it impossible that I held no control over what entered or existed my mind anymore.

I sat up, rubbing the stress out of my shoulders, while holding my knees to my chin. Suddenly, I heard something unusual and intriguing. A voice hummed quietly in the wall beside me. I thrust myself, without hesitation, from my bed and sat against the wall to listen. The wall bordered the last room in the back hall of the house, or so I thought. But there must have been one room beyond mine, to which I had not seen a door. The strange cousin of the household, Mystic, must lodge there. I felt her.

Her voice was low and raspy and her words foreign to the world, but not to my ears. I heard this language years prior, in my first house, the night my father died.

I listened to her. She formed her words so beautifully. A chill ran down my back which culminated both in the top of my spine and in the pads of my feet. The audible words that I felt in my head for all these years had a new power that awakened something physical in my body. What words were inaudible I now felt in the entirety of my being.

The Voices began to whisper along with her. Startlingly, they stopped at the same moment she did. I sat there listening for another few seconds, for any words. There were none.

I pulled my ear from the wall and sat looking at the wall across from me. There was a strange shadow there. The shadow had the same presence as the one I felt when I had first entered this room. However, this time, the spirit was almost distinguishable in physical form. I saw the image in the corner, just in front of me, no more than a length away. It rocked back and forth as the Voices began a low hum.

Suddenly, and without warning, the hum reached climax and the creature in the corner became perfectly visible. I heard a loud thud on the wall of what I assumed to be Mystic's room. It was as if she had thrown her whole body against the wall with all her might. The Voices shrieked and disappeared. The ghostly spirit in the corner of my room disappeared with unprecedented speed. I was left in dead silence. I fell into a deep sleep where I sat. I did not move until I woke the following morning.

The events of the night before felt more like a dream. In the morning, I dismissed them as such. However, Mystic looked at me differently from then on, as if I knew a secret of hers—or she knew a secret of mine. Her icy blue eyes intrigued me as much as her mysteriousness. I found Lewd's advances infantile after that night's experience. I grew attracted to the oddity which sat before me known as Mystic.

This only made Lewd frustrated. Her advances became more juvenile, yet beyond the ability of a child. The more I sought after Mystic, the more she seemed to disappear, and the more Lewd seemed to be ever present.

Soon it became quite difficult to live in the house any longer. So, I built my own tent for privacy. I left without saying a word. Not one member of the house seemed to notice, not even Lewd.

The Celebration of Mwna came and went without much excitement. It is hard to say much about any event that was void of controversy. The festival praised the antiquity of the Desert and its mysterious beginnings. I learned a much different science having grown up in Aeda for most my life. However, I compromised my knowledge to that of the knowledge of the Desert. I felt quite knowledgeable. I ignored all fallacies because no one seemed to care. Why I should care, either, was beyond me.

The Celebration of the Mæsma was what I had expected. There was little difference between this desertian community and MaraJipsa's Queendom.

I wondered if anyone here had experienced Arqana as I had. Either way, I preferred the woods to the seeing eyes of the Desert. I returned home but did not neglect the festivities of the season.

The Celebration of Rælw was the culmination of these festivals and the climax of the season. The people of the city exchanged gifts of cosmic origin and no earthly good—mirrors, mazes, cards and crystals—throughout the whole of the week preceding the festivities. It became apparent that it would take the entire week to prepare for the celebration.

Men and women swarmed the city to partake in the festival. There were easily ten times more people than had been there for the previous events combined.

The festival was to be held on the highest peak of the city, a hill that the city had surrounded and smothered out until it was completely uninhabited. It loomed in the foreground of their lives like death; the people generally despised that this hill blocked their view to the East, but on this day of the year, the last day of the harvest season, the people climbed this hill and praised the Soul as they sought its power. Ironically, they only believed the mount held any power because it resembled that of the face of Saia. They could have known, had they wished, that it was a mere golem of the glorious and singular mountain that united Aeda with the heavens above.

It was the day before the festival when I discovered that this festival was led by Mystic herself. She came to this city and lodged with her uncle, not to enjoy the festivities, but to complete them. I watched from my tent as she was led up the mountain on a path. The hill was too high to see its peak. As Mystic and two assistants scaled the part above my vision, I turned back to my room and conversed with the Voices, inquiring more of her. They were silent since my first night at FreeThinker's home. I was growing lonely and frustrated.

As Mystic ascended into the clouds, the sky darkened, and night came hours early. Some shrieked and ducked into their tents. Some stared in fascination. Others were glad to start their nighttime activities early. The people danced and sang their thanks to the sky for darkening the sun so that their wilds and parties could have the time and obscurity which basks their actions in secret.

I was not nearly frightened by the sudden darkness. Rather, I fascinated at Mystic's power. I assumed that not many others had seen the source of darkness. I felt much above the rest for this secret knowledge that I held. I walked through the streets trying to tell people who it was that conquered the sun's rule over the Desert, but few were interested in its cause. I was surprised to find that I was the only one more fascinated by the creator than the creation of this divine darkness.

The parties were wilder than any I had ever attended. The night grew old, and the reveries became more and more free-of-thought. The noise of the city reached a feverish pitch when the sun had been longest gone from the face of the earth. Each person that I encountered had only one thought: to liberate themselves permanently from the light so that the festivals might continue indefinitely. This was the night before the winter season, the eve before the final night of the harvest season. A soul-harvest began in the Desert the likes of which had not been seen before. Yet, its affect was to be hidden for some time. Evil breeds better in secret.

The morning glowed with the light of the transitioning sun. An ice-blue dew fell over the city as each person fell, one by one, to exhaustion's sleep. The cold bodies hit the ground like corpses. My own body landed on top. I watched the mountain diligently for Mystic, but sleep took my sight.

The slumbering people of the city roused early in the evening, to a sound which rang from the heights of the hill. Neither instrument nor man could make such a noise. The musical tones were divinely orchestrated by a skyward choir, calling for our immediate attention. My experiences told me this must be a good power. Because it felt good, I believed it good.

I got up and looked toward the evening sun, setting over Arqana, too far away to see, though there were no hills—not even one—between this city and my origins. I slowly shifted my gaze toward the sound which had awoken me. The sun distracted me for only a moment, long enough for me to remember it and feel resentment over its parting. It wasn't my position at the time to remember that it was I who stayed to watch the darkness while the sun had come and gone.

I fell to the call of darkness and, in my resentment, forgot the sun behind me. The crowd travelled in the same direction as me, though they had not been directed—quite an oddity, I thought, for this land. Their travels were as my first steps into the desert—winding and lost, though, in a compulsory direction.

Strange clouds covered the night sky as we, thousands in number, followed Mystic's small path up the hill. It swallowed us with the flexibility of a serpent's belly; widening to give ease to our feet. It consumed us as we found altitude above the clouds, claiming co-creation of that which we did not create and thus losing, though unknowingly, our right to both land and sky.

The clouds were cast with light from below, but rather than the usual reds, they reflected blue and green as though we had found our way to the Island Paradise. Its spoils lay in our midst though the peak of the island in the clouds had been long abandoned. I felt the presence of a power I had long forgotten; power itself. The Voices awoke. My eyes closed slightly as they sent their waking scream through my body. And I knew this was an unholy land.

Mystic stood above the crowd and welcomed her co-creators with a motherly coo. She seemed like an adolescent until given authority, which she ate up with all the throws of pageantry that I could imagine.

"Children," she began, "welcome to the last night of the Harvest Festivals. Let us thank the earth for bearing her fruit to us; the Queen looks upon you all with grace and mercy, though you have been poor stewards of her body.

"I have come from the distant reaches of the eastern region to join you in this special festival so that you might be enlightened by the inherent wisdom which is found within me.

"Let me start by saying, there is a land growing out of the East which is perfected under the Queen's authority. I speak here today on her behalf as well as to bring report of your progress as an educational establishment to her. This city has surpassed my wildest imagination! On behalf of the Queen, I would like to offer you entrance into the coming new order. You will be among the first in the West to join this side of the ancient cities. But we would have you placed on a pedestal above all others. The religion of intelligence, as should be obvious, is the only religion which can never be a danger to this earth.

"This hill, as you all know, is the highest peak in the land. Though not the tallest in stature, its location makes it ideal for considering all aspects of the physical land and even beyond. My promise to you is this: you will be taught knowledge above your wildest dreams. If you donate this land to the queendom. You will be rewarded with wise teachers who will give you divine insight into the new religion of the East. We will instruct you on how to worship the only true god-force."

The crowd sat in silence as Mystic held her arms out wide, as if trying to unite the dark sky in her grasp. I looked around to see if any stirred. Some had a look of impatience, others of humor, most of poor expectations and speculations.

"We are gods." She whispered through the silence. The crowd erupted with unexpected applause which must have carried to every land. Rather than cheering, the Voices hummed a mantra. I understood them. I cannot write it for the power which it contains in its mysterious speech terrifies me; however, their whispers were of their godhood and mine, a mockery of the future, yet revealing in the same.

Mystic silenced the crowd with a villainous smile that reminded me of my strange attraction to what only the crude in heart could call beauty.

"Let us consecrate this night, this land and our souls to the queendom."

The clouds consumed us as an ethereal trance came over the body of those gathered there. Mystic led a mantra—the same mantra known by the Voices. My mind and body worked against each other as I sat there in the dead altitude of a forgotten hill.

Wild yelps began to sound in the paramo. I saw others writhing as I was, from some attack that had begun on our bodies. Mystic's prayer continued through the wailing. Silence struck as calmness took over my body... and then I heard it: a slither, like slate on slate I could hear it ransacking my body, and I convulsed horrendously.

"Tonic exercise; it's good for the body's health." That is what Mystic said, repeatedly. Each time she revealed to me a new way to control yet more of my body's reactions. I admit freely now that this control was satisfying, yet not altogether mine.

"I've never felt such hectic peace. Is there nothing purer within me?" I asked, now hardly tired at all.

"Sit here and align your body to the heavens." She had only shown me things which made me feel good thus far, so I gave my trust to her again.

She then addressed the crowd, once more. "The mountain here is but the beginning of your journey. Yet, you must sit at the foot of the hill so as not to be disturbed by the sun rising in the East. Now is when the sun has been longest missed, and now is when the hill has its fullest power. Give your body to it and awaken inside of you a spirit so long suppressed." This sounded strange to me, but she did say that spirituality had been her longing.

This was exactly what Mystic was presenting to me, and so I did it. "Descend into the city." she whispered cooingly, and my feet rose beneath me. My body was not my own, it twitched and writhed uncontrollably. I could feel the snake in my head, as if it sought to rupture my skull and find its way without. I hurt. I cried, and I was left atop the face of the hill in the morning sun. The snake fled the light, and I felt him no longer. My consciousness was lost.

VII

WAYS OF THE WORLD

Or incomincian le dolenti note
A famisi sentire; or son venuto
Là dove molto pianto mi percuote.
Io venni in loco d'ogne luce muto,
Che mugghia come fa mar per tempesta,
se da contrari venti è combattuto.
La bufera infernal, che mai non resta,
mena li spiriti con la sua rapina;
voltando e percotendo li molesta.

-Dante, *Inferno Canto V*
"Now notes of desperation have begun
To overtake my hearing; now I come
Where mighty lamentation beats against me.
I reached a place where every light is muted,
Which bellows like the sea beneath a tempest,
When it is battered by opposing winds.
The hellish hurricane, which never rests,
Drives on the spirits with its violence:
Wheeling and pounding, it harasses them."

*H*o! Little boy, by the hill of Transcendence. Why do you sleep in a dangerous way? This is a happy place where men and women do their travels by night! Go home and sleep! The sun is up." A female voice woke me. Her words were comforting. Her voice was sweet. Her eyes smiled brightly, and I trusted her, although I had never met her before. She was loud and boasted greatly of herself. So, she made great company to me. I became so close to her that I nearly forgot about Mystic and SpeakGood at the house of FreeThinker.

Her name was Moveable. She emanated an air of strength. She did not exude much intelligence upon our meeting. Rather, she would talk about her intelligence, yet, lend no example. Therefore, I thought her dumb. Nonetheless, I was grateful that she had come to me, so that I might have company in this lonely land of learning that the Desert had made a gate of access to its strangest of lands. I thought surely that Moveable must be an angel. I saw that the sun shone behind her. She took me up as a child and comforted me, all of which qualify as angelic qualities on my account.

"How have you come to such a fine land as ours, this City of Tents?" questioned Moveable, for she had seldom seen one of my heritage in this city.

"I am but a sojourner in need of keep. I travel to East for respite from my homeland. This journey has grown more difficult than I had expected at my first goings. I have begun to think that perhaps I should have turned onto the short path to Aeda, when I had the good chance to do so. But once beyond the Fence, it was difficult to escape the labyrinth of Arqana."

"Why such a thought? There could be nothing here to cause you to miss that from which you come. This city was built for the enjoyment of every individual, that he might make for himself whatever it is that he desire. There is much more to be explored here than in whichever homeland was yours. The Desert has hills and mountains and beautiful geysers; castles and temples, and things which would give the saddest of men true happiness."

"But Moveable, what is this hill? What is its power? I feel I was nearly destroyed by its ferocity in the night."

Moveable looked puzzled. "The hill has no power. Only people have power.

"This hill was once quite full of men. This was the old hill of the city. Yet, it has been long abandoned. Its borders were sure. The men and women of the city desired expansion. So, the hill became desolate while the base became well inhabited.

Without much hesitation, it was surrounded in efforts to choke it out so that it might be smothered and die under siege. This hill, had in fact, belonged to Aeda, as an outpost from the city. The Deserts, at that time, were full of life and vegetation, and belonged to the people of Aeda. But the Desert had a new royal and she kept what was good and beautiful in her palace yonder over the dunes, rocks, and ravines."

"Have you seen the Kingdom of the East?" I pleaded excitedly.

"No, but we were all present for the ritual which took place last night. Were we not? Surely you understand the beauty of the Eastern Kingdom." said Moveable. "My brother built a house of stone, just outside the Kingdom. I am going there for ease and familiarity, and to hail the coming queen. Come with me, and make it your home, too. Those within, are no different in race than those which consist Aeda. They are an ancient outpost of your people.

These Aedaites were among those who were first to elect the king, who is now your King, as well. He is still our king, only, we have expanded his government to include many sub-kings, viceroys, queens, and any that might help the kingdom come. We do not discern who gets our praise and worship. We give to all equally. But, we are still the same blood as you. Is it then false to say, that you and I are anything less than brother and sister? Let us venture on together to this beautiful city. It has been many a long year since I have seen my home in this painted Desert, just beyond the Badlands. You have come this far already on your lonely journey?"

So, I went with her to hail the coming queen.

Moveable was the first to take an interest in my wanderings. My experiences reached beyond hers. I promised to make this journey with her immediately following the festivities. which would be held tonight in the house of FreeThinker.

Moveable and I conversed intimately without regard to our settings or anyone around us, certainly not paying any attention to the setting sun on the horizon. Light of the new winter sun's setting fell upon us. We raced down the face of the hill. We were late for the final festival. I had been warned by FreeThinker of committing such an offence while in the Tented City.

We arrived after the acts had begun. Crude and Lewd were performing the dances of each land. They had begun with the Eastern Kingdoms of Babel and the City of the Ancients, much to my disappointment. I contented myself with watching the festivities from a distant lounge with Moveable. We discussed these dances.

The seventh province, Babel, was, for the rest of the party, quite the topic to be recalled, yet, I had missed it.

Crude and Lewd continued. Their interpretive dances covered all the provinces. Their third dance, for which we had arrived just in time, was spectacularly beautiful. It portrayed the Outer Land of Babel, an oneiric land of vegetation, scarcely seen in this scorched land. The depiction was performed under candlelight. Their solemn movements gave me chills. Their garments were colored as the stones from my homeland. A mockery, most would say, but the familiarity eased my soul.

Their scandalous costumes were more applauded, perhaps, than their dances themselves. I was not captured so much by their vulgarity, but more so in the rhythm of their music that secretly captured my heart for the familiar comfort in my head. It seemed the Voices had a divine taste in entertainment as well. There was only peace in my mind when they were satisfied.

The dance of the Badlands was rhythmic and dark. The candles had been combined to create one large bonfire in the center of the stage. Only the shadows of Crude and Lewd could be seen on the wall, pantomimed by the glow of the fire burning in the Great Hall. At times, I thought that I could make out writing on the wall, over their figures. Spell-bound, I focused on their beautiful darkness.

All of Crude and Lewd's performances were applauded grandly. I could hardly contain my excitement, waiting in anticipation of what they had in store for their final performance: Aeda.

Midway through the ominous dance of Arqana, Crude and Lewd gave their representation of Ϛωdωmз.

Crude dressed herself as the gypsy, MaraJipsa, and Lewd danced around her as a rainstorm comes upon a valley, darkening her fertility and filling her with noise. It was delightful, beautiful, and not at all representative of my experience in ÇꙬdꙬmƹ. However, Crude mimicked MaraJipsa's beauty with stunning accuracy. At the end of their performance, there erupted from between them, a beautiful display of every color and light; a fantastic conclusion of the border of the Desert.

Aeda was finally next. Crude and Lewd took more time than usual in returning to the stage. This pause was quite unlike them. Although each performance seemed better than the last, Babel was still praised as none other. It remained shrouded in mystery to me.

Crude and Lewd finally arrived on stage. But they were not alone this time. A hush came about the crowd. Two girls were shepherded onto the stage. They were dressed in rags, head to toe, much differently than all others present. That waif looked so strange to me. It was a while before I discovered who these women were. These two women were my friends! I recognized Lyric and RationHeart. They must have been caught by the Beasts beyond the Fence, where I had left them without a guardian. The Beasts had led them too close to the Tents

Lyric and RationHeart's eyes danced wildly across the ferocious crowd. For one reason or another, even though they were in shambles, the crowd despised them.

"Get them off the stage!" yelled one man near the front left, much louder than his stature made seem likely to allow. Others followed suit. But Crude and Lewd continued with a smile that told the carefully-watching crowd that they had in mind something sinister.

The dance slowly reached fever-pitch, and the display was obvious. Lyric had been selected as the preferred citizen, and RationHeart was slain on the stage, there ending the performance with a roar of applauds and wild whistles.

I was heartbroken and disgusted.

I took my leave from the party in haste, taking Moveable with me, arm-in-arm. I feared the danger I may be in if my heritage were to be discovered.

We searched for a way to reach Lyric before she is slain. We were separated in the mass of bloodthirsty citizens.

I did not see where Lyric was taken. Moveable gathered my arm and pulled me into an old room that smelled of death. There was no ventilation but for a small window which was shielded by three iron bars, blue with the moonlight on their metallic skin. The window looked toward the face of the mountain, its height gave it great vantage.

I looked out the window to see the town square filled with a murderous riot. They chanted "kill them, for they kill each other and call it justice!"

There words seemed to lack consistency and truth, but truth was not well embraced in a city such as this.

"I need to find my friend. She is helpless in this city with these wild men who would like to kill her!" I said, realizing the peril that even Moveable may be in for her simple act of association with my kind.

"Quick, let us escape to my brother's protection. Your friend is safer than you. She was spared. You are yet to be discovered. Let's ru—"

Moveable was cut off by a loud noise in the foyer. It was a terrifying shriek that landed my hands over my ears, then my knees hit the ground.

"Aedic filth! You dare taint the house of my family! I smell the nastiness of your ancestors!

The sound of talons in the wall filled my ears. We could hear Mystic tearing through the wall. I had been discovered as that which I had so accidentally concealed— a citizen of Aeda. There was no way of escaping this single-entry room. Moveable was simply too large to fit through the bars on the window. Even if she were to fit, the multi-story fall would flatten her.

There was one way for both of us to escape: through the door which was being eaten away by Mystic's acid-like claws, scraping away the wood of the door which encased us in this forsaken hole in the wall.

We ran headstrong through the door, just as Mystic had weakened its structure enough for our escape. Moveable planted her forehead in Mystic's breast and collapsed her to the floor. This gave us the time we needed to get ahead of her swift pursuit.

As we ran, we encountered SpeakGood who greeted us jollily and with a great embrace.

"SpeakGood! Friend! I must run from this city! Come with Moveable and I to the East, so that I might escape sure death in this ferocious land!"

"My place is here, for these have become my brothers and I am comfortable. I should not travel with bandits of my men or outcasts and the likes. I will stay here in a more comfortable company. Just be Thankful I have not found pleasure in a similar bloodlust like that of my compatriots.

"I have wandered quite far enough and quite long enough that I see no point in continuing until I have eaten my fill and danced my welcome. I shall content myself with my place among the tents."

We left him to his wishes.

Mystic recovered herself, red-faced from what was either rage or embarrassment; either would have had the same result, and so it did. Her anger halted the cacophony. Her actions were insidiously untamed.

She brought herself up to the heights of this structure where there was a balcony which was left rather unused in the recent decades since the town had, regrettably, become more of a shanty-town than the mecca of education for which it was well known.

She took to the platform to address and organize the masses.

"Halt." she hollered. The crowds ceased their rioting and turned, as an army, still before their master.

"Find the wretches that infect this land with their unclean aedic bloodline. Wipe them from the land. We must rid ourselves of their violence if we are to have peace."

The men and women watched her in admiration while she gave her orders.

As she spoke, the floodgates of Arqana broke open, and so began a hunt that none would survive. The beasts that had once been held in the woods by the power of Aeda were loosed and the land awoke with the pillage of the Beasts.

These vile creatures were not often seen in the daylight; the mere image of these foul creatures was enough to strike fear in the hearts of men.

Mystic watched as a stronger power overtook the weakness of mankind. She was pleased, for humankind seemed nothing but a tool to her. Death and destruction made her feel alive. She watched with such contented pleasure that she had not noticed the man who followed her to her balcony, secretly disenchanted with her. He saw her for what she truly was: a whore of the East on all accounts. While she laughed a wicked laugh, he was overcome with rage and he pushed her from the tower and that flightless bird.

We fled through the path which crossed the hill of Transcendence. The city was overcome in chaos. There was a small forest in our trajectory. The forest was white and welcoming. We made that our direction.

I looked at the terrified eyes of my companion. For her type, she was very quick. She was well-built beneath her deposits and she had the stamina to outrun me.

I paused, panting. She came to me.

"Will you be able to continue? We are not nearly safe yet."

I looked at her. I was exhausted. Her forehead was bright red; I wondered if she was red from effort as I was. I wiped my eyes to be sure. She was not exhausted, rather, wounded.

"Moveable, what happened to your brow?"

She looked at me curiously and wiped above her eyes. Blood. She put the hemline of her shirt to her forehead and lightly dabbed away the blood. She was punctured in the center of her brow.

"There is a hole in your head!" I muttered quite unintelligibly. She felt the spot where blood oozed from her cranium. The tip of her index finger disappeared within the spot. She pulled out a gob of coagulated blood and sand.

"How were you wounded?" I reached to touch her wound myself; she batted away my outstretched hand.

"I felt a large stone on the breast of Mystic when I ran into her. I saw it as she fell beneath me. The shape of a tear, a black tear, as one cries for one's self." She was silent for a moment before she continued with a new attitude.

"No matter." she said. "We must move if we're to make it to the white forest." she looked off into the East as she said this.

It was the evening of the first day in the New Year. We had neither baggage nor time to prepare. We had only what we could collect along the way in the trash of the riots. Our plan was for a journey of a few hours through the night. However, upon day break, we were little farther than where we had begun.

"Do you see the forest growing farther from us, Moveable?" I asked, a few hours into the late morning.

"That, perhaps, should not be our worry. It is what draws near that I fear."

I followed her gaze; there was a group of Beasts between us and the white forest. They dragged behind them the remainder of corpses which had fallen to them in the Tented City.

"We will make our way toward the dunes of the Desert where they cannot follow." She was right. I followed on this altered course.

It was not long before we found our next obstacle. It is a strange thing how speed is always in favor of danger to come, yet safety always seems to be out of reach.

"There is a cliff just ahead. We must go down to the depths before we will be able to scale the dunes." said

Moveable. I was not listening. I had stepped in something that smelled putrid. I was scraping it from my feet as she spoke.

"What?" I said impatiently.

"The cliff before us is at least thirty body-lengths. We must scale it before we will be able to pursue safety." She said, leaning over to judge the difficulty of the ledge. I sighed as I looked to where she pointed toward the edge of a rocky cliff. My right foot still hung suspended beside my left knee, sand clinging to it, the stink wafting its way to my nose. I was disappointed but saw that there was nothing else to be done.

"Then down the cliff we must go."

We both sat at the edge, much like we had on the hill in the Tented City. Had I seen that this path was at the bottom of a similar hill, I would have gone my own way to the East and left her to fend for herself. However, I needed her help and she was in search of her family, so I stayed.

"What have you stepped in? It is rank!" she cried, covering her nose.

I lifted my yet uncleaned left foot. Dung filled the arch of my foot. The stink would drive any man away from it, but not Moveable. Something caught her eye. She reached for my foot, and with her bare hands, dug into the feces. She removed a shard of shattered stone, blacker than midnight.

"The Beasts have been here." I said. I had smelled this before in Arqana.

"And part of Mystic's remains." She said as she held the black shard to my eyes. Its edge was smooth and formed a partial teardrop. She had been devoured by the very Beasts she called into the Tents.

VIII

GREED

Quando giungon davanti a la ruina,
quivi le strida, il compianto, il lamento;
bestemmian quivi la virtù divina.

Interesi ch'a così fatto tormento
Enno dannati i peccator carnali,
che la ragion sommettono al talento.

E come li stornei ne portan l'ali
Nel freddo tempo, a schiera larga e piena,
cosii quel fiato li spiriti mali

-Dante, *Inferno Canto V cont'd.*
"When they come up against the ruined slope,
Then there are cries and wailing and lament,
And there they curse the force of the divine.
I learned that those who undergo this torment
Are damned because they sinned within the flesh,
Subjecting reason to the rule of lust.
And as, in the cold season, starlings' wings
Bear them along in broad and crowded ranks,
So does that blast bear on the guilty spirits:"

115

I shoved myself off the cliff, and onto the first ledge, only moments after Moveable had taken her first leap. I was a step behind her for the first ten or so lengths. I watched her careful footing. After seeing that her footholds were sure, I gained more trust in my own way. I repelled myself much faster than her. Unexpectedly, my foot slipped on something that was neither rock nor earth.

I heard a choking-snarl from below me and I quickly moved aside. A body came out from the face of the cliff.

From out of this sand crawled half a man; his arms were shredded, and rib bone showed through to his torn chest. Chunks of flesh had been removed from him in horrid succession, and his every inner part could be seen. Nothing was hidden.

"Halt!" cried this decrepit man, though his words were hard to understand. Even his tongue was mangled.

"Oh, poor man, what can we do to help you?" pleaded Moveable, a tear running down her cheek. She was much kinder than I.

"Give me pieces of your flesh that I might patch myself together and escape the dangers below!"

"What is it that you will have? I can spare some. I do truly have more in all places than is necessary." At Moveable's words, I pleaded with her not to give into his demand. To give of herself that which can never be returned seemed to me to be a larger favor than anyone should ever ask.

"What dangers lay below?" I prodded, nudging Moveable so she would be out of this creature's eyesight. The Beast, for that is what he was becoming, dripped spit through his lips as he lusted after the pieces of us which he had not. He looked up at me. Lust oozed from his eyes as fluidly as the spittle on his lips.

"Darkness looms below and they are hungry," he said, more dramatically than I was pleased to hear. Oh, he annoyed me so.

"Sir, what is your name?"

"My name is GreedHeart. I was once an Aedaite."

"If you are a Heart, have you relations remaining in Aeda?"

"Oh, I do hope so, for it is a cruel world beyond the Fence, as you well know."

"GreedHeart, I have met your sister, RationHeart, in the land of Aeda. That was also my home. How have you come to such a terrible state? You are from a beautiful blood and a strong people."

"I am from RationHeart's estranged relations. Our family taught her to ignore her own flesh. I, on the other hand, was true to myself. I saw what I wanted, felt that it would be good for my body, and so I took. The bodies of thousands have come to fill me. My flesh is now less my own than when I paid it no attention at all. Soon, my heart, too, was less and less available because I gave of it so often. Its pieces are strewn across the land. So, then, my body became my trade. I now have no other option for survival. I offer a piece of me for a piece of any other. Still, I have not found any creature to be compatible. All rot away. I seek more fervently now. For by chance, I know that one will come along who will fill me and whose flesh will cure my infection rather than become infected. Then I will steal myself back to the West." But it was obvious he would not live through the coming night.

He paused for a moment in troubled thought. And then he continued, rather hesitantly.

"And my brother, MuchHeart. Have you heard of him? He was such a troubled child. His joy penetrated even the hardest of Hearts in his youth, but a day came in his jeunesse that his laughter quieted, and his eyes grew heavy with the world and her burdens. Do you know if he has regained his light?"

I was silent. I was not sure if for anger or guilt, but no words came in response. He hung his head in defeat. Perhaps a look on my face had told him what he had most feared. I changed the subject so as not to hurt him the more. I could not bear if the question of his sister's current welfare were invoked.

"Oh, friend, GreedHeart, I wish to help you, but I cannot. For I am like you, and I fear to become you. Trust me, there is nothing in the west. I came from there and they are themselves. I learned of their treacheries in the City of the Tents."

"Do you think that the East will be any different? Our people die everywhere. Best to become like the world and lose a figurative blood rather than our lifeblood.

I had no rebuttal. Moveable was terrified! Being fast to disregard her own skin, she cut a piece from her stomach, and thrust it toward this pitiful man.

"Here then are my alms to the poor that I might gain access to the East. I believe this to be a test of my worthiness."

"Not this stink!" he shouted. He was not content now that he had smelt familiarity. Perhaps the stench of Çɷdɷmɜ still clung to my body; such a stench that can never be hidden, more infectious than cancer in a body that destroys first the mind before killing the man, for in it there is naught but death. He longed for that similarity. He wanted to feed on my flesh rather than that of strange skin.

119

"Moveable has cut out a piece to fit you! Her charity is larger than I can even spare. Take what has been given you and let us on our way. She has done a foolish thing to feed you."

"I am surer than I have been of anything else, that if we can share your body, we may both be more than the one you are and the piece I am!"

"What foolishness! I might give you money or real food, though we have little of either, but I know that my skin is my own and that I have already lost too much of myself. I know that my body would not feel like mine if I were to share it with one who wished to consume it for himself!" He saw that my abstinence would not be hindered. He sprang upon me and bit at my face like a Beast that lurks in Arqana. I saw in his eyes a familiar orange hue and I discovered a horrible truth of the Desert.

There was no time to ponder. Who bothers think while under attack?

Moveable did little more than scream. By my good chance, this man was only half of what I was, and he was easily overcome. His mouth was ferocious, but his skin frail. His movements were ungoverned. I put him to the ground with minimal effort. He shattered in pain and tears at the base of the cliff. I was terrified by my own pleasure in destroying another. In my newborn fear of my own pleasures, I took my hands from the face of the cliff to cover my shame. Without hold, I fell in the same way as my victim. I had not been the death of a man before—not even half of one. His body would lay to rot in my wake. All who came to this would see and know that I had been his end.

Yet, what was worse to me was that this man, GreedHeart, was but a shadow of myself. I had sought to do the same to RationHeart—to take a piece of her heart and sew it to mine. She would have surely died soon after.

My eyes flickered like a candle and went out. My suppressed thoughts awoke to the freedom of a dream that tricked me into thinking it was real.

I cried out to the sky with shrieks of horror. I was angry. I was lonely. I was tired. I sat there in the sand with fists buried to my forearm. My face lay flat on the ground. I could not help but eat the sand. My tears mixed with it, and my hunger made me think it was delicious. For the time being, it satisfied my spinning and cold belly. As I feasted, the Voices, which had been silent since I fled the Tented City, stood beside me with hands on my shoulder. I had entered their world—a world between sleep and death, where they were real, and I was but a figment, a toy, a manipulated consciousness. The Voices were familiar. They spoke from my heart but fell from lips that were not my own.

"Oh heart, you are fit to your master, and he knows it not. In all irony, he follows. Come near. I will tell you what you want to hear."

Thus came the Voices of the Crooner who rested his many hands on my back. He rubbed me to comfort me. He continued, taking my silence for permission to do so.

"How is it that you come to eat this sand? You are of much richer breeds than to eat hereof. You should eat the sweetest bread which the desert can offer."

His soothing voice pleased me. So, I took my hands from the sand, and put them in his. I kept my face buried so as not to examine this gift of an embodied comfort, who had been given to me from the well-known inner Voices.

121

"What will you tell me? What will you give me? Can you then feed me?" I asked with much desire in my heart.

"I'll give you food which alone can sustain your life. I will give you angels to carry you on your way. I will give you the land to which you travel on angel's wings, if you will but kiss my feet."

These words sounded familiar to me and so I took no warning by them but gave into them with all my heart.

"Sir, will I truly go to any land I seek? Can you take me first to Ͼꙍdꙍmӡ and then to Aeda, where I can return to my home?"

"Why, yes, I can give you anything! But first, I will take you to Babel. I will feed you and have you carried through the streets. After that, you may decide in which country you would like to venture."

I awoke as if I had never fallen asleep. By that, I simply mean that no rest had found me. My exhaustion threatened to steal away my conscience. How I wished it would.

I felt a presence lingering with me. It came close, then fell behind, but never left my shadow. It appeared this auric spirit thought it hid, and yet, it was more real to me than what I saw before me, a sand dune which crawled like a wave into the red, evening sky. My follower did not bother me; it seemed the least of my worries in a Desert much wider than any eye could behold, and kingdoms of my choice rested in its loins.

Moveable was, presumably, frightened into retreat. She must have climbed down another way or returned to the top of the cliff. I looked up in the direction where I expected her to be; not even the dust of footsteps hung in the air. It was perfectly placid. Perhaps she was attempting to find me.

I called out to her. I became suddenly aware of the silence that had filled the ravine between the dunes and the cliff where I sat. My cry, which was weak from the dryness of my parched throat, erupted into the silence like shattering glass. I stepped back at its sound, closer to the dunes.

A breeze glided through the ravine. I smelled honey and spices in the air; the breeze was thick, unlike the air I knew in Aeda. It was also quite different from the wind in the Tented City that stole away any moisture, greedily hoarding its life-giving comfort. No, this was a much different breeze, it came in waves like pre-sleep consciousness, it was moist, but not wet.

I closed my eyes to enjoy this refreshing breeze.

Crack.

Something collided with the back of my skull.

Movement woke me. I was still alive—if it could be called life. My neck ached, my back was sore, my arms and legs shattered like twigs under foot. My state bemoaned, I dared a cry which was met by an ardent slap to the face which shook me from my stupor.

"Wake up, rodent!"

A howl of laughter met my consciousness and made the hair on the back of my neck stand. My eyes adjusted to the dimly lit cavern. The light that might have been, was swallowed by its mere depth. The air was stale. It ate away at my bones; I felt their fractures. I couldn't move; I couldn't tell whether because of my weakness, or by effect of some paralytic, but I was hopelessly immobile.

Eyes flickered against the wall of the cave. The light came from within; there was no source of light to be reflected from without. They moved in pairs in erratic twists and turns, some flickering and disappearing and others appearing, always spinning, hypnotizing me like prey. A few eyes moved without partners. How lonely. All the eyes watched me, and only me. Each eye was a most entrancing yellow with a deep-black, rectangular pupils.

The noises which emitted from the wall were horrific—cackles and moans, screams and heaving. My mind struggled to make my body move. My muscles were not ready to obey.

In the cold air, just before me, I saw frozen breath, but it was not my own. I couldn't see the creature from which it came. But it must have been just in front of me and invisible. I felt a blow to my left cheek. I coughed and spit out a tooth. Apparently unsatisfied, whatever had hit me struck again from the top of my head, sending my jaw into the bitter dirt. It tasted as though hundreds of others' blood stained the rock-floor.

"You killed my favorite pet, you foul waste!" My eyes were adjusting at last. I began to see what was before me. The creature moved like nothing I had ever seen before. It flickered in one place, like the light of a campfire about to die. Then without warning, reappeared in another place. Its speech was a piercing scream. My ears hurt to hear even a single word.

"You FOOL! I will shred you! I will eat you! I will tear your living body to pieces and feed you to the Beasts. Why you small insect; what right was it of yours to touch my property?" Her rantings continued, most of what she said was little more than unintelligible shrieks, however, she made her issue plentifully clear.

GreedHeart had, in some way, been a pet to her. She flickered in and out, here and there. She always

124

returned to one spot near the rear wall of her cave. Her favored spot seemed to be together with the glowing eyes. She would retreat among her coven, they would speak to her in slow, sultry hisses. When the apparitions again became furious, she would fly into a rage, provoked by her sisters.

While against the wall, she petted something that hung there, above eye-level. As my eyes were now adjusted to the darkness, I noticed her shed a quivering tear.

To my horror, it soon became apparent that she had collected GreedHeart's body from the floor of the ravine. Oddly enough, she had hung his body, as if it were art, on her wall. She petted it, and crooned loves and flatteries to the masochated corpse. Again, without warning, she flickered and disappeared, and returned to my side, for a fresh beating of frantic insults.

Before I lost my grasp on my waking mind, I saw a flash emitted from the mouth of this hag, as she opened her mouth wide to fill herself with GreedHeart's flesh. The rot was too pungent for her to resist; she had to consume it. However, the light that came from her shed light on a terror that was worse than I could have imagined: they were goçips. Gaggles of them, crawling up the walls, over one another. They crawled on all-fours, joints bent out of place like spiders, their hair tattered and dreaded; all different colors of earthen dirt and stone.

When the light was nearly dispersed, the one nearest me, an older, scarred, and horrifying goçip, arched her back, put her face near mine, and let out a foul hiss, spraying my face with slime. I fainted of fear.

This cycle seemed endless. Their torture was always soon recycled, time and time again. What must have been days passed the same way with no rest. Inside this cave, I couldn't see the sun to tell me when the night had come. I slept when I could, but never more than a few moments before she beat me to consciousness and again to unconsciousness. I began to think that this might be my death—sleepless and tortured. For some time, I gave up, and once, I tried to fight back, but to no avail. I was a broken man and a slave. Within a week (I can only assume) a loud ruckus was heard outside and she flickered and disappeared without return.

I took my opportunity. I was not bound by chains or ropes, but my body was weak and my vestiges inutile. I moved across the floor like a worm on my side, inching with all the speed I could, toward one of the many holes from which the goçips would come and go. They truly were more like insects than humanoids. This point cannot be stressed enough.

The largest hole was little bigger than my shoulders. I could not, after all, contort my form as the goçips. I went in first with my feet, as they were closest to this small cavern. The floor curved downward; I began to slide. Slime lined the walls. I caught one last glance at the cave from which I escaped; he lifeless, mangled corpse of GreedHeart dripped bile to a puddle below. But this sight was nothing compared to the abominations which filled the place where I landed. The goçips that had begun to follow scurried away with much haste into their holes when the sound of an epic battle of swords filled the hollow air.

At first, all was dark; but I knew well enough into what I had fallen. Bodies. I did not know how deep the pile was; but I could feel them all around. I was not the only one moving. Arms pulled at mine and I was sinking quickly to the depths of the masses.

I heard a beating like the rush of wings—large wings. My eyes were adjusting to a blue light that moved towards me. It was hard to see because of the movement below. As the light came closer, I made franticly to hide myself from the creature that emanated it. I feared I had entered a den worse than that of the goçips, beneath the mammoth dunes of the Desert.

Each wing of the beast spanned more than two lengths of my body (and I was a tall man), with deep florescent black feathers, each shaped like a sword that could shred me in a single wingbeat. The body was that of a wild animal. The beast was serpentine with an appearance of seductive beauty, perhaps lent by the face of an androgynous human which graced the head of a goat atop the slender, strangled neck. This was not an awkward creature by any means. Its elegance was fascinating, but elegance in this sense was far from amiable. I had thought of the specter-like goçips as frightful, but I could not have imagined this was in the pit of the goçips. The winged snakes were unmistakably angels, but such corruption of their mere state of existence was more terrible than I had thought possible. They were the Fallen; those born on a single day and fallen on another. They masqueraded as beings of light, but their light came only by subtraction so that all light was drained from their surroundings.

It grabbed a body in its mouth and used her talons to climb the wall of the cave. It moved quickly, like a spider running from a boot. It leapt into the air with its catch and flew, quite raucously, toward the cavernous center of the cave. As it flew, the blue light which came from her darkness was met with that of others like her. In unison, they lit the cave to a darker hue which made the place at which they congregated barely visible, for their light was truly darkness.

A tree of mammoth proportion stood ominously and strong in the center of the pit. Its branches stretched hauntingly to each end of the abyss and vines hung down like one million nooses, clinging lifelessly to the hanging tree. In fact, that was precisely what it was. As the creatures met, their light was emitted strongly enough that I could see with some detail that of which consisted this tree. My heart sank. The tree became a silhouette in the darkness of the angel's light.

A body hanged on each vine. Some writhed with death-pains, but none seemed to be relieved by the arrival thereof. The winged beasts were hanging their prey from a tree, awaiting the ripeness of decay.

Another angel was nearly upon me before I finished gazing at the tree. I wrestled it aside in time, and it grabbed my neighbor instead. It hesitated as if it considered tossing back its prey in exchange for me. Apparently, I had been its intent, but it had found its claws in another. It brought its face near to mine and I smelled honey dripping from its mouth. It growled at me with a fearsome rasp that sprayed me with sick. It leapt into the air and was again gone to repeat the deadly pattern.

SpeakGood grew restless in his tent. He was no fool to think that he would not be found out among the people of the Tented City. SpeakGood sat up, spilling a bowl of uneaten grapes to the floor. They rolled in every direction and found a stopping point at the bodies of those laid drunk on his floor.

He stood, took up his things, and with that, was gone. There was no need to stop and say goodbye. The parties would continue each night as they had before he arrived. He only found solace now in the road ahead for he found himself done with all matters of foolishness of this sort.

SpeakGood moved forward in a manner that few men had walked. He chose a way that was not well tread, not because he was a solitary man, intrigued by a challenge. Rather, he was fearful of the Beasts which hunted the highways.

A glance over his shoulder was little more than he had to offer this city from which he departed; and that, he thought, was little more than it deserved. All that the Tented City had given him was temporal and lost. SpeakGood now knew that his thoughts defined a lifetime, and it was Saia he sought, only he had been misguided. So, he continued, in every hour finding some little place to sit and regroup. The Desert was gruelingly xeric. The cold bit at his skin.

The quiet was painful, too, not peaceful. The sand seemed to mute all noise. The common pathways were dreadful sights, but a man who wished to take himself away from the insanity of the Desert had only to find his own private pathway in which to walk. There was much enjoyment in that, for he had a lot of time and solitude to ponder that which was before him. Silence is a welcome friend to one who has nothing to keep from himself; it is a terrible foe of the man plagued by a double mind.

The sand was red in color but collected no heat from the useless sun. The cold gave off an iridescent glow that wicked the green-blue from the sky and descended to meet the dry dust. The clash of hues was offset only by the blur of the horizon, and the dark lights that cut the sky from the land.

SpeakGood stopped then and stared. He had not noticed these lights before. Their power was captivating and moreover, their light gave off sound. Oh, how beautiful these lights of the world were to tug at his heart and now finally, in turn they were that which caused his feet to stray from his self-made path. Few can deny themselves the Lights of the World.

And so, this became his love, and the lights served his interest brightly. The sunless winter days consumed him. He did not miss much which could be mimicked for less a price and a more mysterious attraction. His eyes darted left and right, along the ridge which cut the desert north to south, east from west, to find a way that he might scale. He saw where Moveable's and my path led, and to the cliff we had the most reason to have attempted. He stood still to be sure that he clearly saw its steepness and grandeur. It was perhaps the largest cliff which directed itself toward the mountain in the East.

His heart ached for me and our friend, of whose fates he was unsure. His gut sank, for he felt that he knew well what our dual end might have been. With the corners of his lips tightened and the center curled inward, he brought his eyes to his feet in pity. But a silent moment was a sacrifice to give. SpeakGood could feel, hear, and see the lights whether he watched them directly.

He spent the largest portion of time looking at these lights that he could but bare giving them the next piece of himself; his travel. He set out by the nightlight of the winter moon, which yellowed the sand to a pleasant glow and illuminated his way fancifully. He felt as a king would upon entering his own royal courtyard. The world was at his fingertips. There was nothing between him and his stayed desire for the lights on the horizon.

He rose. His feet were ready for the journey, though his body resisted. He had not slept in all the days he stood watching the horizon. He thought perhaps he could find a place to rest, where he could hear the song of these lights which called to him—a place where he might see them more purely. He made his way to the slightest ravine which could be walked in minutes.

The rock was gray and loose and hung weakly to the face of the ravine. The way looked easy, but his feet slid, and he fell on his side many times. To his luck, there were dead roots protruding from the slope. He used this death to cling to find safe footing at the base of the white ravine. This was not as pure white as it had appeared in the dim moonlight, but it was deceptively close.

The ravine gave him a spook. Moss hung from the scrap of trees which had seen little life, other than lichen, in their branches for many years. He had seen few trees in any greater congregation than the scattered single, couple, or the occasional triplet, since he left the Tented City. Though dead, it was refreshing to see something that had once lived.

Through the bearded lichen, SpeakGood saw a wisp of smoke. *Uncharacteristic*, he thought to himself. *A forest giving off smoke with no fire?* He redirected his course for a brief investigation, whilst designing in his head a bed of moss collected from under the shade of the trees. He had not heard kind stories of any woods. One had been my own tale, but hardly was that his sole woods-experience. He was not so foolish as to let himself be led by a woodland creature that lurked in the shadows. Why, to his surprise, there was not a wild creature to be seen

131

anywhere, not even a bunny, a squirrel, a spider, or a rat. The wood was barren and lifeless, except for the smoke in the distance. The smoldering must have been a very old smoke, for all things here were covered in its ash. He picked up speed. SpeakGood was now irritated by his curiosity. He barreled his way through the throng of dead forest.

SpeakGood burst through the first clearing, at the highest point in the wood. He came upon a cabin of grayed brick and a dusty type of wormwood, lofted there on an incline. Caught much off-guard by the out-of-place shack, he ceased his rampage and walked softly to the front door where he read the door-sign: *Hostel for the Weary. Full-board only: Vacancy.*

LIGHTS OF THE WORLD

Di qua, di là, di giù, di sù li mena;
nulla speranza li conforta mai,
non che di posa, ma di minor pena.
    E come i gru van cantando lor lai,
faccendo in aere di sé lunga riga,
così vid'io venir, traendo guai,
    Ombre portate da la detta briga;
per ch'i' dissi: "Maestro, chi son quelle
genti che l'aura nera sii gastiga?"

                  -Dante, *Inferno Canto V cont'd.*

"Now here, now there, now down, now up, it drives them.
There is no hope that ever comforts them—
No hope for rest and none for lesser pain.
And just as cranes in flight will chant their lays,
Arraying their long file across the air,
So did the shades I saw approaching, borne
By that assailing wind, lament and moan;
So that I asked him "Master, who are those
Who suffer punishment in this dark air?"

133

My time was short if I was to escape. The Angels of Light were returning to the tree. They would be upon the pile of bodies again before even one man could escape the grotesque pile. My pursuer had its eye on me again. I had to hide. This was a more difficult task than at first, I thought, for the bodies beneath me were of the living. I knocked one woman in the teeth. She fell back onto a man, who pulled her into the pile and crawled atop her to reach the heights of the pile. His grin was savage, and his teeth stained with blood. Perhaps it was his own. But what better defense for one trying to dig his way out of a pile of death, than a sharper tooth than those who held him back. He spit flesh from his mouth. Each body concerned itself with the destruction of the others so that they could use the bodies of the wounded to elevate themselves to escape. Or their hopes laid in the tree at which they would glance longer than one glances at that which they fear. Indeed, some were attracted to the tree, all the while knowing that the tree would be their death. They hoped for more bodies to fall from the caves of the siren goçips, so that they could climb upon them and reach the tree as the angels did.

Realizing that my escape could be found only in destroying others, I became furious. I saw no simpler way to be free; I joined the others in tearing apart the mass of defilers. We acted in war against ourselves as our own enemies. We quickly becoming one mass of carnage.

Before the thought reached my head, my body realized that it had left the ground and began to flail in the sour air of the Under World. The foul angel had captured me while I was preoccupied with slaying my company. I watched the mass of tortured souls grow small as I was

taken further from their death to a tree which was dark.
Evil had more an air of death than that from which I had
just left.

O

What Luck! Thought SpeakGood. The glow of a fire
illuminated the cracks in the door. SpeakGood felt warmth
before he so much as laid eyes upon the flame. He knocked
on the door. It rattled. It was not a heavy door. There was
silence inside that seemed ominous to him. The glow
disappeared. He took a deep breath and lost it in the same.
Two eyes, lit with the moon that shone through the
slender, dead tree branches were the first to catch his sight.
They came from much lower than his; as if from a child.
SpeakGood knelt lower to see this small creature. It shied
away slightly. Yet, when SpeakGood had been motionless
for more time, the creature lowered its head as a dog
inspecting a movement where there should be stillness.

"Who?" came a feint whisper, desperate with either
fear or shyness; SpeakGood knew not which. He was
taken-a-back. The creature seemed nearly frightened to its
death.
"Who am I?" questioned SpeakGood, softly. "Why, I am
SpeakGood of the Southern territories of the Desert." The
thing moved closer and wrapped its arms about
SpeakGood. It sobbed quietly before it took his hand and
whispered in his ear.

"I am Lonely, from the East; a land called Shadow.
We are without light in the shade of the great Mountain."
The creature smothered SpeakGood's feet in kisses and
begged him enter.

"Come, come. The food is made, and you will find
that you never wish to leave. Please don't leave."

SpeakGood crossed the threshold, hand in hand with the creature, Lonely. The dim, smoky interior within consumed first his hand and then his arm, before it overtook his whole body darkly.

"Why is the fire not lit anymore?" SpeakGood prodded patiently. But Lonely was gone. He felt his grasp in which Lonely had bestowed his frail hand but there was no longer keep of it. Its slenderness had fooled SpeakGood and he was alone.

"Hello!" He shouted.

"Shut up!" shouted a gruffer voice from the length of the far wall. "Shut up you rat! Tired has just fallen to sleep and he should not be woken before we sup!" SpeakGood, embarrassed and annoyed, said this.

"Lonely said that dinner was made. Is not now a good time to feast and meet? I'm a traveler in need of your hospitality."

"Why do either? Hungry is not home yet, and you best fear his wrath if you eat his portion of the food. And neither would we like to meet you. Be gone!"

"Angry, stop your barking. You will scare off the guest." said yet a third voice. It spoke from the sacks of food (or so he assumed that it was food). He never actually saw the contents of those bags. But he well assumed that they were edible with all this talk of food.

"I don't want another guest! Lonely tricked us to put up the vacancy notice when he said that—"

"Stop!" shouted that same third voice. "We have a guest and we dine him before he parts."

"As I am a sojourner, could I trouble you for a sleep as well?" SpeakGood could not see, but he could sense by the silence in the air that both creatures in the room stared at him with a devilish intent.

137

"You fecal trash. Not even I have a bed!" shouted the creature that Tired called Angry.

"Excuse me. I had no idea of your state of beds. I assumed because of your—"

Tired pounced upon him at this point. The creature was much smaller that he had assumed it by the depth of its voice. It swung by his neck as if it too were surprised by the size of its company. Tired found SpeakGood's ears at long last and pulled them out. Presumably it thought this might make SpeakGood hear him better. Tired was not a subtle creature, nor did he demonstrate much wisdom.

"Oh, assumptions now! How much the better that makes your rude inquiry? Just sit. Dinner will be ready when Hungry returns." SpeakGood sat bewildered in silence.

I saw as I was drawn closer to the black-charred bark of the tree, that the ropes on which the others were hanged, were part and parcel of the tree. The ends of the tentaculous ropes consumed them, piece by piece, until they were completely devoured. I feared this death and I struggled against my captor.

Her hair whipped violently in the wind that came upon us in the altitude to which she brought me. My eyes were blurred by tears, syphoned from my sockets by the greedy frozen air. There seemed no escape from this deathly creature. Her talons dug painfully deep. I could not pull them from my flesh. The wounds themselves would surely kill me, even if I were to remove the talons with caution.

I felt helpless to the wilds of this forsaken desert and her lying sands and seeming wonders. My captor carried me swiftly closer and closer to this Tree of Death. I realized its true immensity and deathly power. The power which emanated from it was obviously true Evil. My chest cleared, and my breath rushed to fill it as my tears streamed down and I cried out for what seemed lost.

"Save me, King of my people, that I might return to my home!" I looked to see who had cried aloud. It was I. I had not consciously done it. As soon as I had, though, I felt the angel drop me. I plummeted to the rock-floor, drained of life by this, the Great Tree of Death—fed by the Lights of the World, sustained by this under-worldly Circle of Death.

SpeakGood found a place to settle, as far away as possible from the bickering banter of Angry and Tired. No sooner had he sat down than they started in on him again. He had not expected such an unwelcoming party at his arrival. Perhaps, if he had known, he would have kept on his way and stayed his journey toward the welcoming Lights on the World. Alarmingly, as he looked around, he could not see even the nearest object…let alone the exit. Oh, how cozy the cabin looked from without, but blackness of this kind could not be so.

His ears seemed to fill with cotton as their yelling— the yelling of the two faerie-demons—went on and on. He missed the one who had lured him in. He now felt lonely, himself. He put his head back on the wall and tried to sleep through the shouts. No such luck. At one point, he thought that he dreamed, but it had merely been a delusion by repetition. His ears became numb to the evil that entered them. It was for that reason that he could convince himself, for a short time, that there was no yelling. His daydream ended abruptly when he was hit broadly across his jaw by one of the creatures, begging for his attention. He could only assume that it was Angry.

"For what reason have you done me such a mighty blow?" asked SpeakGood, quite perturbed now.

"You smear! You would sleep while we await our dinner and guest? I have half a mind to double your rent!"

"Rent? Nothing was said of such. Surely you can't expect me—"

"Can't expect you to what? Pay for the services we've offered? You piggish filth, you disrespectful, foul little thief—"

"Quiet! If I am not allowed to sleep, no one is! But I'll be damned if you get to complain about it more than I." Tired entered their little spat and ended it just as soon. For some odd reason, Angry gave way to Tired with relative ease. Angry growled and scuttled away. I heard Tired slump back into the bags of beans and begin to breathe more softly. Oh, how that breathing made SpeakGood long for the release of sleep.

He began to doze but was not successful. Angry entered the room again.

"Where's Lonely? He is letting the stew get cold!"

The bickering began again. SpeakGood groaned and curled into a ball.

X

BADLANDS

"With a presence I am smitten
Dumb, with a foreknown surprise;
Presence greater yet than written
Even in the glorious eyes.
Through the gulfs, with inward gazes,
I may look till I am lost;
Wandering deep in spirit-mazes,
In a sea without a coast.

-George MacDonald,

Phantastes

I lay against the jagged rocks, astounded to be alive. My fall had been from many lengths; it seems impossible that I survived. However, I was there, alive against all odds. I looked up toward the sky—the Lights carried on per usual, hardly regarding me but one who hung in the sky, presumably the same that let me to fall. It pierced me with its eyes and shrieked for all to see me and despise me.

I felt around my body; although I had been dropped, I was healed. My body still ached, my mind still tired but I could clearly feel that my bones were one piece and my lacerations were enclosed. I thought about what made the angel drop me. I had called to the King of Aeda; had his power saved me or had it been the angel's fear of this name. Perhaps the angel had only mistakenly dropped me. I shook the questions from my head and saw, in the roots of the tree a face that was familiar, yet I had not seen before. It startled and intrigued me in the same moment. I went after it into its hiding place between the roots. It rocked back and forth before disappearing into the base of the tree, too deeply for me to follow. I wanted to retrieve it, but as I started on my way to discover this hairy little creature, I heard another commotion from above.

My eyes flinched upward, studying that from which I had fallen, and I saw an odd sight in its branches. Two figures partially consumed by the tree began to grow larger. I watched for some time and realized that they were falling and had been for some time now. As they grew closer, I began to recognize the face of one. It was my dear friend Moveable.

143

She landed with a thud, not far from where I was. Her fall was more damaging than mine; she hadn't soft ground beneath her, neither her nor her friend.

I rushed to her; her friend landed between her and I with a deadening thud, causing me to stop dead in my tracks. I went first to Moveable who tried to raise her head—quite unsuccessfully.

"Good Moveable, how were you come to be in the tree and what was it that severed your bonds?" She limply pulled herself from the rocks and I saw that she was horribly misshapen.

"I went down from the Cliff to find you, but you were no longer there, something had carried you away. I climbed the dunes above the caves, but upon my weakness and lack of food, I was found, myself and my friend, in the pit of a sinkhole. It swallowed us up and tried to smother us; we didn't struggle, and it swallowed us whole. My fear was unbound when we descended to the bottom of the sinkhole to find that we were surrounded by the broken bones of discarded and consumed bodies.

Beasts surrounded the massive heap of bones, but some unseen power or enchantment staved them off and they could not have their meal which cast their eyes ravenous in the pits of this devilish burrow. My friend, who I had found atop the dunes, wandering helplessly, was unconscious and so I brought her to. She was weaker than I and so I carried her, but it was difficult because the Beasts were waiting for our further descent.

"They barked and howled wildly as we slipped through the bones, causing more a ruckus than any would believe. I neared the bottom and realized that there was no escape. I thought perhaps the bones themselves were what the Beasts wanted but could not have and so I dressed myself and my friend in these bones and the Beasts nipped, but never bit at our bodies.

"We tried to escape through many different tunnels, but all were dead ends. At long last we heard a chant that we followed. We followed it for days, repeating its unknown but promising message and we were relaxed on our frightening adventure. This bliss only lasted so long as the confusion regarding the origins of the voice remained.

"There came an hour in our time of wandering where the beautiful singing-voice quieted, and the screaming began. Three voices screamed. We were outnumbered. Light burst into the air in front of us as a mouth opened wide before us, trying to consume us. The screaming turned to cackling laughter and I saw beautiful creatures deformed before my eyes as lust overcame them for the pray they had lured to the end of the caves.

"I am no warrior, but I was determined to fight for the friend beside me who was yet too weak to defend herself. I took off the bones which I wore, and I fought these three for as long as my strength held out. One was killed, one wounded, and the other fled but not before they wounded us both.

"I carried my friend on my back until I was nearly asleep, at that point she awoke and nursed me back to some semblance of health. She then dragged me as far as she could in her weakness but when I awoke, I was strung up in the Tree of Death. My outward appearance is that of the deserts doing, but my insides have been mangled by the tree."

"How did it lose its grip?"

"I saw you and recognized your voice. I heard you call to the Fallen in your native tongue and I saw that the angel was powerless against the name of your King and so I believed in the power of his name and followed suit and found myself here amongst the roots of the tree rather than consumed and discarded as the bones which first met me in this burrow. Myself and my friend."

Upon this, she introduced me to the one she had met while I was interred with the goçips. She was shy and not quick of foot. She had stumbled her way this far much on accident after seeing a pretty thing on her map that was only slightly off her path to the entrance of the gated land of Aeda. In her excursion, she lost sight of the path behind her and she was lost to the Desert. She now joined our company in which she found much pleasure in drinking the spirits. Her name was HopeKind; she was only lost, not traveling in search of a stay in the cities of the Desert.

I thought how sad it was that she found our sorry company after being separated from a family who loved her greatly. They now had stay in Aeda without her, as mine had. As I looked at her I was reminded of those I had seen within the border of Aeda and I believed she belonged there. Although she had not made it to the entrance, she knew much of the land and she would recall the memory of her near entrance when I would speak of what I saw within my homeland. She boasted well just like the rest, for she was still unaware of her miss-turn and thought this path might lead her back to the entrance of the gate. She had not yet caught sight of the fast-approaching cities of the Desert or the black mountain-land which loomed in the foreground casting a ghastly shadow over our path. (There were no signs along the way to warn her and visibility was low for there was a haze here in the shadow of Badlands. HopeKind and I found many likenesses and so then I gladly welcomed her into the group of which I had become an unlikely leader.

"Dear HopeKind; new friend, new to our path; have you considered your way and the direction which it takes you from Aeda?"

"Oh, but I meet many like yourself on this way who are from that land and so I believe that I am where I should be in my efforts to join my family."

"But this is against the way of Aeda and so you will not find your way back in this land! Walk therefore in a way contrary to ours so that you might save your life. What is ahead in our path here to Babel, I perceive, is only death for one so unprepared as you."

"Then do you walk willingly to your death? Can I not be safe in the same path as you; a native child of Aeda? I believe that either you have forsaken your king, or you can lead me to him if I follow. Your way is easier than the way which my family had gone up to Aeda where I was shown a different way."

"O but there is no different way! There is but one way to Aeda and it is not an easy road for any but those guided by the one who is the Aid to the King."

"Dearest Deceit; if you know this (which will scare me if true); then why are you not scared into following your own warning? Should you not then walk in the same way which you direct me?"

"I have great knowledge of Aeda and so I am able to travel freely and always know my way home. But you, who have not been there, how can you know your way in danger if not first going there in ease?"

"Then I will follow you. If you have left Aeda for a time, then there must be something that drew you out that seemed better to you than what you could have inside, so I will stay here in your footsteps."

I had no argument which could refute this without changing my own way and so I gave in to her. She was much smarter than Moveable, although her body was much weaker. I took her then under my arm and tried to guide her as best I could over stumbles and caves and sharp things.

The roots of the tree covered more ground than we could cover in all the time we stayed there in the caves. The Badlands continued around each corner; no end seemed to be in sight. Sometimes the roots would help us by giving us something onto which to hold, other times, especially in the case of HopeKind, they would catch her foot and send her crashing to the ground.

This happened on our third day of travel and HopeKind fell deep beneath the roots. I scrambled to retrieve her but found that what she had fallen into was not dangerous, but beautiful. There was a world beneath these roots and it had an enchanting glow about it. Ivy grew purple and black, orange and blue—every color except green. The walls moved with small creatures, none distinguishable from the other. I thought for a moment I saw a snail, perhaps it was a goblin. No, now that I think about it, it must have been a fish of some sort. It flashed a scaly tail in my direction and quickly disappeared into the wall. The floor was more solid than the roots which hovered above like torpid fingers grasping firmly the dirt onto which the tree so covetously clung. Beautiful white flowers with red stomata sprouted from out of the ivy; they opened wide their petals, waved their tongues at me before sharply snapping shut.

I took a step; the floor sank as my weight shifted from one foot to the other so that I had to be constantly concerned with my footing. As I moved through this counter-creation—this world unknown and unintended—the walls moved with me. The rustling ivy disturbed a roosting pelican—or perhaps it was a humming bird—which flew toward me before abruptly changing course, finding a new roost in the dirt before me.

I called out for HopeKind but did not see her. I thought that she must have continued down the cave, so I followed. As I walked, the glow grew softer and I felt its warmth—there was not much warmth in the shadows of the Badlands. The glow soon gave way to a soft hum, and then a voice, a lovely voice that I had known before.

"I saw you fall from the tree; how powerful you must be to have freed yourself from the grasp of the Lights of the World." The voice crooned in my ear, but the figure from which the lie surely came was not in sight. I turned sharply to see from where it had come and how I heard it as a lover's whisper in my ear.

"I'm here in you and I am part of you. I am the one you called to, but truly, it was to yourself that you called when you remembered the symbolism of your heritage."

I laughed. "No, He is a real King that saved me."

"Then show Him to me."

I could not. He is not mine to reveal. I knew not how to show him someone I had not seen, but I trusted that it had been a real power—I felt it clearly upon me and I was searching that same feeling again.

"I tell you truly, I know who it is that saved you, it is yourself for you are your King. I am your king and I am you."

I thought about shaking this voice. I had so recently been rescued, how could I give in so easily to a creature that hides itself in the roots of a deathly tree?

As if the creature could hear me thoughts, he crawled from behind the stones and his light overtook me.

"I am the King, and I am in you. Bow and worship me."

I saw his magnificence and beauty as clearly as I had years ago in my dream while I slept beside a familiar fire and my company of three. I believed that he was who he said that he is. I believed. He was who had come to me in a dream before the goçips had stolen me away and it was he who was awaiting me within the roots of the tree. He has come to set me free.

"Go to the East, I will meet you there in your world and I will give to you Aeda to rule as the king you are."

"Take me, Prince. I shall follow where you lead." And so, our advent began. I embraced him, and he kissed my forehead. I awoke yet again, but my waking felt more like the dream, for my dream had been of truer substance. Truly it is the spirit world that was here before the physical; dreams are where we touch the other side, if only for a moment. Therefore, a dream can be of truer reality if those on the other side grant access. And this is what this creature did, and I was lost to this reality and drawn to the East with an unquenchable thirst. My thirst: that is what awoke me.

There was a beautiful woman kneeling over me in the darkness, her hands on each side of my head, whispering a prayer. I sat quietly and let her finish.

"Who are you?" I whispered when she was so quiet that I could hear my heart palpitating.

"You shouldn't be awake!" She seemed startled, so I used a calmer voice, though, I felt as if I had no idea what was going on. I had a strange sense that I was in danger. It is always uncomfortable waking to the presence of the awake. I could not move. I was not paralyzed; some spiritual force held me there.

"Who are you?" I said again. She relaxed and spoke.

"Tis I who is caught here in this den of goçips! I am MaliciousCraft; the goçips have captured me and wish to devour me! Save me, for I perceive you are a man and are capable!" I smelled the stink of old flesh and bone. The odor was fresh; I believed that she spoke the truth.

"I have to rescue HopeKind! She fell in before me."

"No one has fallen but you. Let us escape together and go out of these roots."

My body had grown light as we spoke. No longer paralyzed, I now stood and realized a more unexpected phenomenon. I took MaliciousCraft's outstretched hand and as she took hold of me, gravity lost its life-long hold on my body. I thought how strange it was that both could not take me by the hand simultaneously, but soon I cared little. The supernatural has a suspicious manner of losing its spectacularism as one becomes accustom to it; equally, one loses his fear as he becomes more drowned in the darker forces of the mystic. There is, perhaps, only one characteristic that is unchangeable about this dark force: it remains evil no matter how it is perceived by such a fickle creature as man.

We rose toward the ceiling of the pit which opened its greedy lips for us to exit the depths and rejoin the desertian sunlight. I looked upon MaliciousCraft as the light revealed her and I saw that she was beautiful beyond compare. Her words fell off her tongue like honey as she told me her fanciful ideas.

Moveable and HopeKind came running from some way away, crying out my name to see where I had gone. They found me and embraced me. They told me that it was I who had fallen into the roots. My reality was in jeopardy, but I dared not speak a word of it.

My company met MaliciousCraft and she became our companion. We moved slowly toward our destination. We sang sweet songs together as happy company. I never heard one but her speak the language of the Desert so beautifully. It rolled so fluidly off her tongue, like moonbeams breaking through the canopy of trees in Arqana, licking my face with dew, awakening me to the night.

"My way was well traveled when the Beasts took me, and now I must re-walk that the road which I know so well," she said in dramatic sorrow.

"Perhaps providence has been given to us for we know not the ways of which you have knowledge! Please lead us in the way you know we should go!" She was much pleased with this and would give direction; however, she would not walk first but she gave way to me that I might be the frontrunner.

We spoke of our pasts, though she remained rather silent regarding hers, but for the occasional adventure in the southern regions of the Desert. She had a rather joyous look about her as she told me stories that brought chills to my skin—stories of great dragons that live beneath the sand in the southern plains, the locust that appear in swarms, larger than the northern ocean, to consume all in its path. She had seen the heights of the East; she has seen where the sun is born. She has seen my childhood home and the swamp it has become. She told me the water is in constant turbulence, though the storm has long since subsided. She has even seen the northern shore of the world. "A terrible region. One I never wish to see again," she said of it. But there remained one region she had not come near. She had never touched the sweet grasses of Aeda where the grass is as sweet and succulent as the pomegranates which litter its trees; where the dirt is a warmer blanket and the rocks a softer pillow than any bed in all the lands. But it was Çɷdɷmɜ which most intrigued her, not the land beyond. Arqana was her lure; she desired no further adventure than the gypsy camp. A familiar flame hung in her eyes as she spoke of this land. The tales and fables she recited were not at all the Çɷdɷmɜ I had known. I warned her against a venture there.

"By all means, venture west if you wish. Only, hold north and avoid Çɷdɷmɜ. It is a prison, not an oasis."

"Then tell me, dear friend, why it is that you walk in the same direction as I? Have you not lost the way from your intent?"

"No, foolish girl, I walk in this way for knowledge and rest before my journey back to Aeda that I might make a better warrior for the king of that land having given myself knowledge of his enemies from behind their own city-walls." I said this with my nose far too high to see her expression; yet, her response still burned my ear.

"For what purpose then have you ventured from the Fence without the raiment which your countrymen? You will be easily slaughtered without it! Is this not a walk in the wrong direction with no vestige of your homeland? How do you say your goal is Aeda if you walk in a direction opposed even to its shadow?"

"You know not the ways of Aeda, woman," I said, "but as so close a friend, I choose to trust this; my secret to you as a symbol of friendship and warning that you might learn from my mistake. I once lived in the borders of that Fence and I slept by its edge. I met a boy and he told me that his name was MuchHeart (but his true name must have been MuchHate for he hated me without reason). He took me up by my collar and betook me in my sleep to drunkenness and ultimately to the temple of Ϲѡdѡmɜ. I can tell you this place is evil for; once in that place, he threw a stone and it struck my head, leaving me for dead."

I then showed her my wound and she remarked coldly.

"Friend, you are foolish for this is the wound of a two-edged sword and not by stone. You fall prey to your own lies! This mark is the mark of defense and not of hate. Methinks you have lied and that you are not the man you say you are. Do not think me foolish. I see the bite of sin on your hand and the blood from that sin-mark is crusted to your forehead. I had seen it first upon our meeting. I spoke not of it because you could not see it yourself and I wished not to offend your fragile temper."

"You have offended me greatly," I spat at her in my anger, "for you call me a liar when I show you love and you hate my king who I follow! Surely I am a better person than you."

"How is it that you find yourself better than I? For I walk in the way of my prince and of those who went before me and I choose to join the army called Legion. I have done my prayers, one for each day, and I carry in my pocket this beautiful black stone which was given me for my efforts and therefore I can be called faithful. But you, oh Deceit, say that you follow a king not present without even dressing yourself as one loyal to him, nor do you carry a stone of that land. You, then, are loyal to no king. For this reason, I find that you are not an honest man. Choose to follow my king and carry his stone for you have already done him so much good and he will be glad to accept you." MaliciousCraft would have all to join her so that her journey would be justified in numbers and the less lonely making it easier for her to hide the ugliness of her inner being behind that of others and her outward beauty so that attention would not fall upon her. A truly hateful act to those she called her friends.

"Ma'am," I said (for I no longer called her friend), "we are of different backgrounds, so you cannot understand. Let us walk on together but speak no more for you have offended me and I wish now only for your company and not for your conversation." And so, the four of us walked silently in a circularity way through the cascading and menacing Badlands of the Desert.

Now that we no longer spoke of the things of our souls, our way was weighed by the silence of good words and we were lost to a never-ending discourse of jokes and flippancy. We all grew in secret to hate the other and in that hate, we festered as dead animals, disintegrating in filth.

Food was never a problem. We fed off each other. The only problem seemed to be the scent; we had a pungent smell of rot. We lived upon our vomit for the duration of our journey and with every meal, our minds were more depressed. We grew more accustomed to it so that the taste no longer bit our tongues and burned our throats, but we were satisfied as if we had shared a delicacy. As time went on, we were no longer satisfied with our own, but for hunger we ate the others' as well.

155

But nothing tasted better than the private feast of our own flesh.

When companionship was unsatisfying, as it was much of the time—except when my conversation was alone with HopeKind—I would put myself to sleep and search for the King I had once known. I found him amongst a throng of trees which bordered Freedom of Thought. We walked together in these woods and they reminded me of Arqana. I remembered my time then as good, as if I were rewriting my memories.

When we had broken free from the throngs of the Tree, our way was already set ahead of us and it was a sure way, easy and paved to beauty. I clung to the arm of the Prince as a babe his father. He walked confidently, and I would talk to him to make him respond to me soothingly as I knew he would.

"Wonderful Prince who came to my rescue, how beautiful you are! There is one who hurt me who now is disappeared. I would awfully like to see him again. Is this something you can do?"

"Surely, if you ask, I will make it so. Visualize yourself with him again and it will be thus done. Focus upon that image, even putting out your image of me. This is how I will accomplish your prayer to me."

I did as he said and thought of nothing else for the days proceeding. My company noted an air of complaisance or passivity. I knew that I had found one who loved me and wanted me to be happy, but I was embarrassed to share him with them, so I hid my knowledge of the Prince and we continued our trek through the Badlands of the Desert.

The days began to regulate themselves normally; the air was fresh and the Desert not so cold as before, but

156

rather, temperate. There were many twists and turns and I saw not an end to our way, but I followed the Prince faithfully, making our decisions of where to turn based on his council. I was happy to have finally found my savior who could guide me through this wild landscape and make me look good to my company. But my thoughts were again on MuchHeart for the promise I was made.

PT 3

The Badlands

Voices, Voices—everywhere!
　　Speech and song galore,
And I am rent in two worlds bare
　　With neither truth nor lore.
When might I find a truth unchanged,
　　A love untouched by lies?
Not in this barren, root-filled grange
　　Wherein, I fear, love dies.
O, come, undo me,
　　Lover of my soul!
For none can harm me
　　If You make me whole.

　　　　　　　　　　　EDR

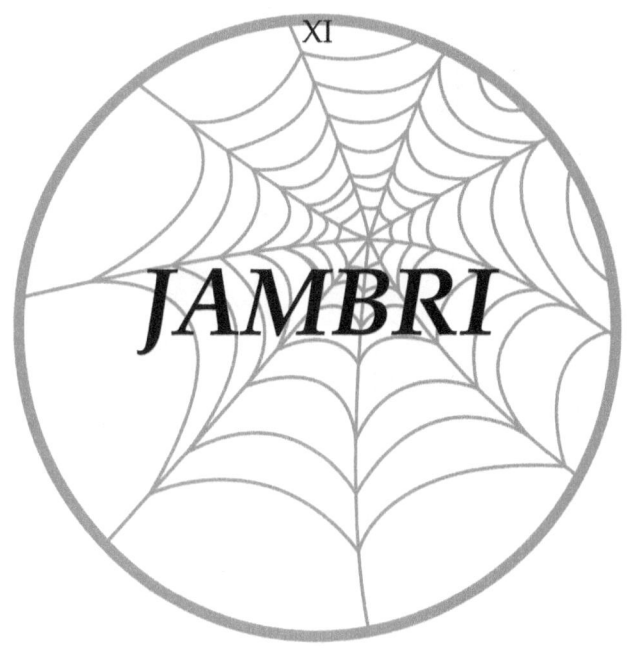

"If he is a big enough fool you can get him to realize the character of the friends only while they are absent; their presence can be made to sweep away all criticism. If this succeeds, he can be induced to live, as I have known many humans live, for quite long periods, two parallel lives; he will not only appear to be, but actually be, a different man in each of the circles he frequents."

C S Lewis, *Screwtape Letters X*

Be sober-minded; be watchful. Your adversary the devil prowls around like a roaring lion, seeking someone to devour.

The First Epistle of Peter

*I*n that little cabin, in the dead ravine, SpeakGood was still curled into a ball, awake, as he had been since he entered. He had been there for days. Light had not entered through the windows, not even the light of the morning sun. The ravine was void of all warmth, light, and life.

SpeakGood's eyes adjusted to the lack of light and he began to see through the dense darkness of his dwelling. Around him were ghastly creatures, watching his every action. Their forms created a syphon for the darkness. He could see the energy concentrated in a metallic silhouette, as if his eyes were still tightly shut, remembering a vision that once was, and now slowly faded. He was made uncomfortable and angry by their actions throughout the long hours spent in this inhospitable cabin. Further, he had not slept, and he missed the comfort of Lonely.

He sat up to stare at these creatures and, as he did, he felt a knot growing in his stomach. He realized how famished he was and prepared the nerve to ask for food. However, before the words were his, Tired spoke.

"It's time to feast." A tear of relief fell from SpeakGood's eye and he stood to thank them all for finally allowing the dinner hour to begin, though Hungry was not yet home. Before he could, Angry spoke.

"Before breakfast can be eaten, you must pay us your dues. The price is all that you might have in your purse." Not quite as concerned for money now as he was for food, SpeakGood gave them his entire purse and dashed to the table. He forgot about the riches he had gained and taken with him from the Tented City. He gave it all for a meal.

163

The creatures brought out a plate of thick broth that filled his senses with the most delicious scents. The simple thought of eating satisfied him. What they brought, however, was not edible. SpeakGood picked up the winged arm of the meat prepared in a stew. He looked questioningly at the creatures who had prepared it.

"CaveBird!" they said in unison. Tired continued, "CaveBird are all that live in these woods; they are the best meat obtainable. There can be had no greater delicacy here in the white ravine. Eat, friend SpeakGood! We've long awaited your company."

SpeakGood was incensed by their audacity. Realizing that for which he had given his whole purse, stood, knowing he'd been tricked. He was now not only hungry, but a twin to the others as well. His rampage was staggering, it shook their little cabin. He threw the kettle of stew at Angry and Tired who hissed at him and scurried into a back room, throwing a door open that cast firelight into the darkness and was quickly swallowed by the starved darkness. He followed and saw the fire that had cooked the stew. From out of the fire protruded the bones of arms and legs, only lightly covered with the flesh of many a sojourner lost to the Desert.

Tired and Angry were backed against the far wall, huddled together, attempting something evil in their muttering. When they turned, SpeakGood saw too clearly what they had hidden. They were wielding weapons carved of bones, sharp as the teeth which pulled the last of the flesh from their once living surface.

SpeakGood was much too angry to be frightened by such small, hideous creatures. He slew Angry with a flaming femur from the raging fire. Tired, seeing his fury, caved to his ferocity and put himself into the fire, knowing he could not defeat SpeakGood without his fallen brother. Alone, these creatures were powerless against one who would want to conquer them.

Unsatisfied, and still hungry beyond his belief, SpeakGood tore through the house in search of food. The bags he thought were beans were not, after all, edible. He shredded each one to be sure and found that they only contained money—purses and purses of sojourners' precious money. He was outraged. In his anger, he set fire to the cabin and stepped out the way he had come. He tripped over a body on the front porch.

He heard a cry of pain below his feet and looked down to see what had made the noise. It was Lonely, who had been on the porch awaiting guests to lure into the cabin.

"Don't leave me!" Cried the sorrowful beast, "I shall not survive here alone if you go!"

"You and your kind have tricked me long enough! I will not allow you to come with me. I will head for the lights along the horizon and I will not be slowed!" SpeakGood fumed. He did not look at Lonely; Lonely took his hand and whispered softly in his ears.

"I'm not like my brothers; they treat me poorly and I was but a slave to them. Now you have killed them, and I am free, but if I cannot go with you, I will have no one and nothing here. My home is destroyed, and my family murdered. You owe me."

Though it was not human, he felt guilty for Lonely's woeful solitude. SpeakGood knelt for the creature to climb on his back and journey with him to the horizon. He could not see the smile on the creature's putrid face. Had he seen it, SpeakGood would have understood the demon to be as evil as his brothers, if not the worst of the three.

"Let's find you something good to eat." Lonely said lovingly. "I know a place along your way where we can find ripe meat."

MaliciousCraft took up speaking frequently with Moveable, but I didn't fear a change in her. She was of a loyal breed and quite a stubborn woman too!

HopeKind, however, was weaker, in my sight. I did not trust that speaking to MaliciousCraft was good for her. I occupied HopeKind's time and, under my tutelage, she fell and scraped herself many times. She, in her most polite way, left me to walk alone for this reason. HopeKind did not trust my judgement nearly so much as I did.

The Voices were gone from my head and I no longer fought their nuisance. They had been replaced by the prince of the Badlands. I could contact him through prayer, anytime I wished. It was difficult to understand why I was lonely, even with him by my side, whispering sweetly in my ear.

With my three companions behind me, carefully watching the ground, I trod lackadaisically, guided by my personal savior. We made much headway amid the Badlands. We walked through caves, ravines, valleys, and shadows for seven days. On the eighth morning, we set out early, to cover the last stretch of our trek before reaching the other edge of the Desert. This would be the first land that could truly be called the East, for the Badlands split east from west.

I was quite a few strides ahead of the three women, having ignored their pleas for a day's rest. They yelled to me again and again. I ignored them. I was sure that I knew better because my guide led me in all ways.

"Only a day's trek remained before us. We will finish it and then rest two days in the safety of the open region." They gave in reluctantly. I heard their grumbles coming from behind me all the while as we walked. I assumed that I knew better than them at the time.

I rounded a corner where they could no longer see me. The morning sun only illuminated my path briefly. I had come upon a menacingly dark way; My struggle was not between good and evil, but simply in the journey that lay ahead. I was stopped short by a web that had been strung with me in mind.

My breath was lost; I gasped for air. I saw a glow before me; the luminescence was like a million diamonds, broken from the cliffs of the Badlands. Something knocked me in the back of my neck. It punctured me, and I began to fall. Poison swarmed the blood which ran violet through my veins. I saw the darkened sun above me; its hidden rays were struggling to break through the fog as if the atmosphere in the Badlands denied the very existence of light and warmth. My captors' efforts were unsuccessful against my lethargy. I slept to the laughing Voice of my Prince.

"Sleep well, dear child of mine, for tomorrow holds a new destiny for you, and for me."

My sleep was the most uncomfortable of my life to that point. I could neither make out shape, nor form, let alone face—if there even was a face—of that which tortured me that night. Roots overcame my body; they felt their way along my spine, claiming me completely as their own. I struggled for freedom but there was no use. I was under the tight grasp, of what, I knew not.

167

I feared the goçips had discovered me. I was not well hidden; I walked the Broad Path which cut through the towering dunes. (It was not the difficult way over the walls of the cave, but through the roots of the tree that I had found my way). Yet, I could not smell the flesh that hangs in the teeth of the goçips to rot. Although I did imagine for a moment that I felt a clawed hand drag its way across my skin as I struggled to no avail; but it was not them. Something more sinister scurried in my unconscious awareness.

After I had lost all energy — which was not long, because I had refused to rest — I gave in and was complacent to the man-handling of my captors. I grew more tired as I slept, and soon even the semi-consciousness of sleep was lost. I was nonexistent in my mind, for how long, I did not know.

I heard the screams of women as I awoke. Breath returned to me in a gasp of cold morning air. Dew hung around me. The morning mist slowly dissipated in the heat of the sun which rose tentatively in the East. The morning light rose behind a land I now saw for the first time: Babel.

It looked beautiful, but I was distracted by the smell of sick, which invaded my nostrils. I tried to sit up to get a better look of the beautiful mountain, and to avoid the putrid smell. My efforts were useless. I was tied to a large slab of cool substance. There were others tied there with me. The other trapped souls screamed as I sat in silence. Their breath disappeared rapidly in the altitude. I shivered. There were no comforts. The altar, on which I lay, was made of a beautiful black marble that had many flecks of deep, noirish fools-gold. I was not sure where I was. I only knew how high above the Desert I must have been; the cold encapsulated me as never before. No fire would have consoled me. Perhaps it was the poison that swill swam in my veins. My eyes were tired, my tears froze, clinging to my clothing. When one tear made its way to the stone on which I lay, it sizzled and evaporated. The altar appeared to burn; yet, I could feel no warmth but for my true tears, which succumbed to the heat and died there on the stone.

The people beside me quieted. I turned to see who they were. I saw a girl and two women who I did not know, and a man, too, on the other extreme of the stone. We were five in total. We were alone. I gave one last useless struggle against my ropes before I spoke to the girl beside me.

"Where are we? Who brought us here?" She returned my sight, but she seemed frightened. She did not respond. I moved my gaze to the mediated sky—half dark and half lit. It reminded me of myself. I began to understand the contradiction that I had become. A voice sounded from near where my feet rested at the base of the black stone. My train of thought cut short, the girl beside me began to scream again. The voices waited for her to finish before continuing.

It wasn't long before the one emanating that unknown voice walked into my sight. She was a spidery woman. She looked frail, even dead. She was painted with many bright colors, but beneath, I wondered if there was anything true. I studied her in the moments of silence before she spoke again. She spoke only to me. Even so, I noticed that the others were spoken to as well. I presumed that their attackers were not present. After all, I could not see anyone to make them frightened. Their terror was their own, and perhaps imaginary. I looked back into the many eyes of this terrifyingly-beautiful spidery woman. Never had an arachnid found favor in my eyes. Never had such hideousness appeared so attractive to me, while still causing me to fear a slow, poisonous path to the hauntingly void trappings of death.

"Young master, smart and good, you came in a splendid way. You were full of the fruit of your ways and came laughing and without much coaxing. You fell asleep in your pride and my children found you in a dangerous place amongst the roots of death. You are much safer here, where my family guards the Badlands. There are flying things which bring wonder in their screams from above. Be warned that they will carry you away to a tree which will devour you. There are sirens that will coax you into their den and bleed you dry. There are devils that hunt for scraps in the lowlands. You are safe in our protection. Stay here with us. We will show you how the East is a master who is easily served and gives us our hearts' desires, guarding us from the dangers that attack the body."

Her words were insidious. I knew that they were poisonous. My pride kept me from caving to her at first. I thought that I must, in the least, give lip service to my homeland. I feared I faced a creature to whom I had already lost.

"I had safety in my homeland. I want to serve that land again! Take me home! Untie me! By my power I bind you!" The spider laughed, and the wind picked up, giving me a bone-chilling shiver. The four winds were within her control; she did not spare their power.

"Delicious boy, how naïve! The Fence you walked near is a path that has no interesting turn or delight. There are only simple joys and their disappointing limits. Here you can drink and eat until you are fat of good food and drink! Come now and stay clear of that dreadful land of Aeda."

"Have I come so far and stayed so long that I have no chance of safe return? Give me my land that flows with milk and honey!"

"Why would you wish to return through the Desert? You are so close to the East. The land you desire lays just beyond the city of the Ancients. To turn around now would be your death. Ahead lies only power. Enter through the gates of Babel and become a king."

"I think now that I know the way back. I can make it without death. I do not have the strength to continue. There are unknown perils and pain that hunt me in the darkness. I have lost too many pieces of my body; I can scarcely lose another piece and live. Let me go or help me return. Either way, I will not set another foot toward the East."

She leaned close, as if to bestow a kiss on my brow. She whispered in my ear sweet melodies of the mountain. I fell to her spell.

"Oh, dearly cherished," crooned the spider, "this glorious mountain, which rose out of the East, was your first path. Indeed, you never followed the road to your own homeland. Those in the Desert enjoy the company of the lost, who were never found. But you! Oh, scrumptious one, you have willingly chosen to lose your path. Therefore, you are a traitor to Aeda. For this reason, you cannot travel, in good measure, on the path to oblivion, only our land loves those who know reality and yet choose the desertian kingdom. The rest wander as lost, blind rats. You, in all your pomp and circumstance, did quite knowingly travel directly here, with little hesitation, on the coat tails of our prince himself."

"But I did not choose this place! A voice came to me that led me here with much haste. But tell me what has happened to my companions! SpeakGood, HopeKind, MaliciousCraft, and dear Moveable?"

At this, the creature let out a piercing wail of riry.

"You blind pig! You were neither their friend, nor were they yours! You all ate of each other's flesh and led each other into pits and fires and cliffs and dens!"

"Regardless, you are one who knows of their well-being. Are you not?"

"Well, yes... I will tell you of their journey, so that you can believe me that you will find a fairer state in Babel. Two of your companions had no idea that you were leading them into a war. Only MaliciousCraft knew that truth.

"What do you mean, war?"

"Surely you have followed the riverbed this far and have not been deaf to the rumors which still flow through her dry skin."

"I have heard no rumors of war. Yet, I fear that my company does not know of an imminent war, either. Where are they, so that I might go to their rescue?"

"Your companion, SpeakGood, has just found his way to the den of the goçips, carrying a devil on his back, like a trophy. He will enter their feeding chamber and surely, he will not escape. He is as good as dead. If you were to run to his aid now, you would never find him. The goçips roam a savage land, yet they are tricky creatures; they will know how to distract you. I only hope that he stumbles across them in the dark, for your sake, because he is your friend. Goçips, by day, are a much more devilish breed."

"Woman, do not deceive me! Whether he fares well or poorly, is it my doing that has brought him to this cold land of undoing where he waits to enter short life and a quicker damnation?"

"Oh, kingdoms, no! For you had only conversations with one another and did not travel long in toe! But you, being the man that you are, had no credibility. SpeakGood listened to neither the good nor the bad from your lips."

"If I had been a man of sound speech, would he then have listened more of Aeda?"

"Had you been a man of better speech, as you say, he surely would have listened. But it was the lack of credibility in your actions! He begged for sight of your stone and you denied him this (for you had lost it)."

"So, you have lied to me and I can be to blame for this fate of his! Tell me no more lies and continue with the fate of the others!"

"Oh, you are a feisty one! But should you scold me for a simple fib, Oh master, Deceit? Surely you are not quite as ignorant as you are a liar.

You blind fool, you ignored the love that HopeKind had for you that could have led you on a cleaner road to Babel. You chose foolishly to pass the time you could have spent with her, begging for what dirtied your egress from Aeda. You are a pitiful breed, humans."

"Let me go to her then, so that I can rescue her! I can find a way back to whatever land I wish to enter with her. She will be my ticket to an easier life than I have lived."

"My mind lacks new ways to tell you of your idiocy. You are in no position to lead. She will not make your life easier. No, you would drag her behind you as a chained animal, rubbing her into the filth of the dirt which flows from your every lying word and worse, your false actions."

"…MaliciousCraft, as you know, is a rare gem. You would do well to find romance with her instead of that weak HopeKind. Worry yourself little over her state, for she has returned home with her rewards.

Once MaliciousCraft finished her work of evangelizing men to Babel to fill the city's walls, she could return to her home and her pets. She was been sent to be a companion to one who we smelled from Aeda's boarder in Arqana. This she did. He trusted her, and she led him as far as she could; her job was done. She now rests in wait and prayer to our king for what he will give her; be it gift or work for his kingdom. As she said; she is loyal to him until death and then beyond, and the boy whom she led away was you, poor stupid creature."

"I am inclined to believe you, though I know not why. I have never found favor in a spider. Your words have the sound of deception, yet they ring truer than mine!"

I pulled at the ropes that held me. They were secure. They clung to my body so that the more I struggled, the more I was fastened to the black stone which froze my body yet evaporated my tears.

"You are the first in this land to rebuke me, and to tell me the truth. Who are you?"

"Dear treat," she serenaded, moving her face close, and looking me over lustfully with each eye. "I am Jambri. The gatekeeper of the East. Ordinarily, as in the case of your companions, the people who travel our Badland trails can enter directly into our land. However, you…you are a special case. Our eyes can see every dimension and every facet of your life. You, dear one, have a secret. Yet, you

174

guard it darkly. You are what most attracts each devil that prowls this land. Yet, they can't touch you for the powers that protect you. This entire land is one contradiction—goçips, devils, beasts and angels all rage against one another—you, my child, are the most delicious contradiction of all. You are an Aedite yet have eaten the honey and the milk of that blessed land. You you incarcerate yourself in this cursed Desert.

"You, dear child, are why I sit in wait, day after day, night after night. You struggle on the edge of an oblivion which you have not yet met. However, you have come fantastically close to this danger caused by the duplicity of your way. Here in the East we have psychologized it. We call it insanity. I brought you here to show you signs and wonders. You are in the perfect state to become what the simply-lost cannot imagine. Here, atop this mountain, looking toward your beautiful future, you have the singular opportunity to forsake your homeland and be one that knows both sides. This position will make you stronger as you continue to gain in ways that those around you will not imagine."

Jambri finished her speech. My internal struggle of what she offered nearly tore me to pieces. Before she could continue, or I could respond, a child of the same species came to her and spoke in her ear. His movements were mechanical, unlike Jambri's fluid and beautiful motions. Nevertheless, it struck me that he distinctly resembled her.

"That's a pity." she said flatly. "Feed her to the angels."

I watched as the girl beside me was dragged by her feet from the black altar. There was not a scream left in her. Rather, she spoke in whispers and tears.

"What is it, deary?" laughed the child spider who carried her away.

"I shall not forsake my land nor my King; my life is stored in Paradise. I shall die by your claws before I compromise to your demonic ways. Kill me here. You cannot touch my soul."

The spider dragged her away, trying his best to gag her.

Jambri cursed her cowardice. I was unsure why, but I found her brave. I did not believe that I could muster such boldness. I hid my face and wept. Jambri continued, but I could not hear her over my own wails.

"You surely are a peculiar specimen... one not like the others... know good and mercy... choose darkness... useful tool... weapon... war..." She was well winded, and I was well incompetent.

SpeakGood wandered for days with only Lonely to keep him company. The thing whispered in his ear incessantly. It knew SpeakGood's past and never ceased to show him his loneliness, a lone adventure, a citiless state, a friendless journey to where he knew not, but for his urge to press forward toward a surer satisfaction.

A great depression overcame him. He found himself unable to form words to express his annoyance at the burden of Lonely, who still clinged to his back.

The creature led him promptly to a cave and told him to enter.

"Is there no way over this hill? The cave is dark and smells of corpses."

"There is food inside. If we can get to it before another devours it, you can eat it while it is fresh."

176

SpeakGood was famished. He would eat the flesh off his own back if it were not in such pain from the desertian sun. He entered, head shaking with insecurity, knowing full well into what power he was giving. The darkness consumed them immediately. The stink in the moist air condensed on his skin. He wiped off the dense fog and smelled that it was blood. He looked into the eyes of Lonely and saw them returning his gaze with a sad look.

"Keep walking," said Lonely. "There's no food to be had in simply waiting."

SpeakGood continued to walk through the dark cave. Awful noises reached his ears and he shuddered.

"Move." said Lonely, demandingly this time. SpeakGood did not stop. Rather, he decided to continue, despite his fear. He walked briskly through the darkness, stumbling klutzily all the way. He wanted to stop and rest after a few more hours of carrying his heavy burden through the dark. Whenever he slowed his pace, Lonely clutched him tighter and even more painfully. Therefore, in fear of additional pain, SpeakGood avoided Lonely's consuming grasp, and barreled inward in a dangerous way.

Within the span of what SpeakGood could only assume to be a few hours, he came to a dead end, and could not continue his path in this darkness. Lonely's claws dug in to his back ferociously. SpeakGood did not know how to convince the relentless grasp of Lonely to understand their situation. He tried to wrestle the creature from his back but was unable to do so alone. It dug in with all its might and SpeakGood let out a sorrowful cry.

"Move." came the creature's reply.

"I can't! I am stuck and it's not my doing!" SpeakGood knelt and cried, but the creature had no interest in his lament.

"Climb."

MaliciousCraft scaled the Badlands' hills that towered over the ravines of the bed of the roots of the Tree of Death.

"I knew he was incapable," she told her two companions, Moveable and HopeKind, as if in effort to convince herself. They had become her loyal followers since I was lost. MaliciousCraft walked much faster than either of her companions. She was anxious to get to Babel. She had been away for many months, in wait of new converts for her homeland. Now, she sought her welcome with every ounce of energy she possessed.

"What was he thinking, leading us through the root lands of this dangerous terrain? We will be safer in the heights of the hills. There we may keep Babel in our sights. Babel has an odd power about it, which can give you strength, even from a distance, when you keep your eyes in its direction. It is mystical, magical, and even divine." MaliciousCraft's voice trailed off as if talking to herself. Or rather, convincing herself.

They travelled through the morning after my disappearance. They had seen me around a corner, but when they came up behind me, seconds later, they found that I was no longer on the path. They looked for me through the night, but it was no use. The roots were thick and menacing, and the morning-haze made it impossible to see further than an arm's length in front of them. MaliciousCraft urged them to give up. They did, finally, and they followed her up a steep path, which lead them above the Badlands. At the summit, they found a ravenous desertian wind that whipped sand through the air into their faces and hair and every place that could make this walk more uncomfortable.

Moveable was astounded by the vastness before them. Clouds hung below their sight and filled the magnificent ravines locked in a limitless foamy white sea.

"How much further will we travel today?" moaned HopeKind. "We did not sleep because of Deceit. Today, we have done much more exercise in climbing that hill than any one person should do in a day." HopeKind was exhausted by the altitude and lack of sleep. Moveable, however, was still full of energy, so she offered to carry her.

"We will stop at a cave that I know of, just ahead another two hours."

HopeKind was relieved, but unsure that Moveable would be able to carry her for the next two hours. Moveable skipped alongside MaliciousCraft with excitement. They would spend the night in a cave that overlooked Babel. MaliciousCraft waxed eloquently of the view.

The wind seemed to come from all four directions, always culminating where they walked. No direction of travel was better than another; each did its damage to poor HopeKind. She fell to the cold and fainted, unnoticed, on Moveable's back.

Jambri continued telling me how perfect I would be for the cause of Babel. I had only one thought that I could not shake. I knew the laws of my homeland well enough to know that if I rejected Aeda, I could never return because I was never a child there at all. After the wilds of the Desert

I was not prepared to do this. But I was still, somehow, attracted to the promising land of the East. My desires were torn, but my desire to return to Aeda was overshadowed by a sinister curiosity of what pleasures the East might hold for me.

I thought that I would make a deal with Jambri.

"Spider, I am not prepared to make such a statement of allegiance. Nevertheless, I do seek to see the land of Babel. I would like to see the mountain before I make my decision. Make my wish come true, and I will be more likely to choose what you have offered."

I thought that my bargaining was clever. I became unsure of myself when I saw the mischievous smile on her face. I could feel the unsure look on my face, and felt as though I had lost, although I had previously thought I had won. After all, who had ever been quite as clever as I? I knew she wanted me to worship her king. I only wanted her homeland where the laws were more in my favor. I had no thought of choosing to worship her ruler, but somehow, she made me feel as if I were trapped.

"Very well. I will make sure that it happens as you have said. I will inform the Queen."

"Queen?"

SpeakGood could barely find a place for his fingers in the walls of the cave, but he had no choice. He had to climb. He dug his fingers tightly against the unforgiving rock of the cave, and hoisted himself, and his burden, into the air. In time, his fingers gave way and they both fell. Lonely's grasp was ruthless, clinging deeply in to SpeakGood's back. He felt his own blood drip down his shoulder blades. Sand found its way into the wounds.

Lonely shrieked. "Get up! Get off! Climb, and do not fall again!"

SpeakGood succeeded in lifting them both off the course cave floor. He could scramble up another few feet, but soon fell again to the torturous thrashings of Lonely. SpeakGood thought that he could not climb the wall. It was not possible, not even if he had been alone without an extra burden on his back.

SpeakGood wailed in defeat. Lonely's loud cursing matched his howls. Terrifyingly, a third sound reached them, which quieted them both. A hollow cackle erupted from deep within the fingers of the cave. This sort of evil commotion could only mimic joy, it desecrated even laughter; the minds of those uttering the uproar had turned sour. And so, it was with the goçips, they cackled not for joy, but because they were overcome by a lust that mimicked love. They cried out in their mimicry of happiness as they killed and ate the men who fell into their den.

Lonely was quick to scurry away in the direction from which they had come. He hopped on all fours until he was out of sight. SpeakGood heard an odd sound of movement. These were not footsteps. He made out the pounding sounds of hooves, as if the goçips, who surely travelled with great speed down the arteries of this dark underworld, were being swallowed and coughed back up by the air itself, unable to keep their grasp on this world.

SpeakGood scrambled to his feet and felt the pain in his shredded flesh. He followed Lonely out the way that they had come. He ran without ceasing. This time he was unprompted by Lonely's fierce claws. He was motivated by the bone-chilling fear of the penetrating cackle of the goçips. His feet fell heavily against the hard-packed stone as he grew more and more tired. He fell only once but got up quickly and continued running. He nursed a wound which the fall had caused on his arm. He heard the goçips' chilling squeals from behind him. "He's bleeding! How deliciously pungent is his blood!"

He was nearly out of the cave. He could see light, but still felt the darkness which consumed him, and would continue to do so until he left the cave. He felt the goçips fast on his heels. He made a desperate leap for the mouth of the cave and, at long last, crossed the threshold, every piece of him. Yet still, he was not safe. SpeakGood's danger had only just begun, for now he entered the day with a goçip on his heals.

Moveable grew tired under the weight of supporting HopeKind but had too much pride to put her down or to ask MaliciousCraft to slow her pace. Moveable assumed they must be close to the mouth of the cave, to which MaliciousCraft was so enthralled to lead them. Moveable silently chanted encouragements to herself. *Just a few more steps. Just a few more steps.* HopeKind shifted her weight in her sleep. She must have been having a bad dream.

The winds were cold here on the northern face of the dunes, which bridged the Desert and the Badlands. The icy breeze from the ocean froze their vestiges. MaliciousCraft led them on. "Just another few minutes," she said.

They continued forward. Finally, within a half-hour, they came to an inlet in the rocks that MaliciousCraft called a cave. It could be called so, however, it gave very little protection from the weather.

Moveable placed HopeKind in the furthest corner, away from the elements, and then found scraps of bone and hair to make a fire. When Moveable had started the fire, she saw that HopeKind was pale and shivering. She had caught a nasty cold from the unforgiving winds of the icy, northern sea. Her clothes were wet, and she was covered in sand that clung to her skin and irritated her once-perfect complexion. The wilds of the Desert were destroying her.

Moveable ran to the mouth of the cave where MaliciousCraft stood with her eyes shut, humming to the howling wind.

"Friend, HopeKind is sick! What shall we do?"

MaliciousCraft turned to look at Moveable, seemingly irritated by the interruption. She moved her gaze to the back of the cave and saw the pitiful girl shivering by the fire. She leaned over the edge of the cliff which housed their shallow cave and looked to the depths below.

"Best to leave her behind then. The creatures that roam below can have a nice snack of her."

"I don't mean to leave her. How can we mend her while this storm rages? She needs blankets and warm food!"

MaliciousCraft dismissed her.

"She is lame. She is no use to us, just an extra weight on your back. Leave her and enjoy your own descent into the City of the Ancients."

Moveable left her to tend to HopeKind. She knew MaliciousCraft to be cold, but she had not expected the lack of humanity. She mumbled her discontentment to the unconscious HopeKind as she took off her own clothes to cover the ailing girl. She had not obtained a fresh pair of clothes since she left her home among the tents; her gift to HopeKind was small, for that reason. There was not much left to take off. The Desert was a ravenously arid land. The women did not wear much clothing beneath the sun, though the winds were cold, sweat still dripped from their pores when heart rates soared. Moveable had little else to give to HopeKind to keep her warm. The fire was weak at best. Moveable then thought to share her own heat with the poor girl. She curled around her friend, as a mother cradles a sickly child. Moveable was glad that HopeKind was much smaller than she. She was relieved that she had found a way to help.

Moveable and HopeKind sat curled up by the fire well into the night. MaliciousCraft held her stance in the entry, staring off toward the mountain which was coming into view as the clouds began to clear and move toward the south. She could scarcely take her eyes from the majestic sight. Moveable exposed herself and HopeKind to the weather to see the splendor of its magnificently snowcapped-peak peer out from behind the storm. It was beautiful. She tried waking HopeKind so that she could see it, too. HopeKind did not wake. She was feverish and sweated more profusely. Moveable cried. She did not know what else she could do. She did not know this foreign land. As HopeKind lay dying, she looked up to Babel. Its beauty stole her sanity. She had thoughts of leaving HopeKind behind. Perhaps MaliciousCraft had been right. Maybe HopeKind would be better put out of her misery. Moveable and MaliciousCraft could venture on unhindered.

She looked at her friend, her sweet face like a child's. As she looked, she thought that she could not kill her. She looked away so that her decision, by her own reason, might be unbiased. But truly, it was for bias of self to overcome humanity. That childlike pure face lingered in her mind as she considered her own comfort. She thought that, surely, not looking at that cherubic face, she could dump her over the cliff. That would make her journey more pleasant. No one would know, not even the unconscious HopeKind. Moveable bundled her up in her arms and carried her to the edge of the cliff. She looked down and saw the jagged rocks below. HopeKind would die the moment she hit the ground. No one would be harmed and she herself would be more comfortable without her sickly friend. MaliciousCraft stood by her shoulder. She had found it worthwhile to interrupt her meditations to aid in the ridding of this sickly parasite, HopeKind.

Moveable lifted HopeKind high above the abyss. She saw HopeKind's beautiful face but did not think that she could turn back. MaliciousCraft urged her to drop the sleeping girl. Moveable closed her eyes, convincing herself to drop HopeKind.

A scuttle arose from the direction they had entered the cave. Moveable did not have time to go through with her deed before MaliciousCraft swept them both into the darkest part of the cave and put out the fire. They sat there, hidden, as a spider dragged a young girl, not much older than they, into the mouth of the cave.

Moveable opened her mouth to ask MaliciousCraft what the creature was. MaliciousCraft put a cold hand in Moveable's mouth and she was silenced.

Daylight nearly blinded SpeakGood. It was as difficult to see in daylight as it was in the darkness of the den of the goçips. He struggled senselessly to a stone by the cave. Lonely had also taken refuge there. When SpeakGood saw that he was not alone he grew frightened and let out a cry. Lonely covered SpeakGood's lips and gripped his face with an unforgivingly firm grasp, more out of anger than fear.

"Do not speak! They will find me! Go! Find a place for yourself!"

But it was too late. SpeakGood heard scratching on the rocks, slow and rhythmic, as a cat hunting her prey. SpeakGood looked up to see if a goçip had spotted them. He saw nothing in the path that led into the caves. He sat back against the rock and let out a sigh of relief. Lonely looked at him with a sour face as if he had just eaten an unripe olive.

"You fool." said the creature. "You led her into the light!"

Just then, the most beautiful woman that SpeakGood had ever seen stepped out above them. She stood upon the rock that hid them. Her gown of white gleamed against the orange desertian sand. Her hair blew in the wind, a beautiful black which wooed his heart to follow it into darkness. She was a siren of the most seductive substance. He stood, not regarding Lonely who had curled himself into a ball to escape the sight of this beauty which infected SpeakGood. She began to sing a sweet song that led SpeakGood to his feet and into her arms. He escaped her in her hideousness, but in her beauty, he could not resist her.

As she took hold of him, her beauty was complete, and he did not regret his weakness; he called it strength and she stroked his ego. She pet him delicately, but her intent was his consumption, for the Desert had begun a good rot in his mind. She could smell the decay as she put her face to the top of his head. She had no choice in her nature but to eat him for every piece of rot which infested him. He would be her new pet to replace the old, which now sat in a pile in her cave.

As she prepared his destruction in her mind, he clung delicately to her, in the lust of her siren song. She was quickly overcome by her need to feed. Her beauty was instantly destroyed by the cackle which interrupted her lovely song. SpeakGood tried to step back, forgetting for a moment the beauty he had seen. She would not let him free. She imprisoned him in her bosom and dragged him, flailing, into the darkness of her cave.

"Tempt me with what I want, and I will take it. But do not yet ask me to give up my homeland." I thought that this might make me feel less like I was losing the battle, but surely, I did not see her trick. It was such a simple trick.

She cut my ropes, one by one, and spoke to me in a motherly voice.

"You are such a smart child. You could make a wonderful addition to the kingdom. Follow my children into the City of the Ancients. They will guide you into the kingdom of Babel. There you can meet her Excellency the Queen."

Two more creatures crawled up and took me from the black stone, which had fused to my back as I lay there. Before I took my leave, Jambri gave me a gift. A beautiful black stone, which she put in my pocket, and then whispered in my ear.

"Now you belong."

I was warmed by the darkness, though I knew not why. I caught the eyes of those still suffering on the altar.

There was an empty space of the one who had already been led away. The three-remaining stared blankly at me and mouthed the word *coward*. I turned away, but still heard their faint and penetrating voices. All three called to follow the lead of the first, to part in the dangerous hands of the child spider, toward death. They would not give their allegiance to Jambri, Babel or the mysterious Queen.

The stone burned with the fires from which it must have been forged deep below the earth, yet it was as cold as the wind which whipped through the icy altitude. I kissed Jambri on the cheek and fell in line with her children descending the face of the Badland cliffs. Jambri's young were silent guides. They neither spoke to me nor each other. They were solemnly cold. They carried me on their backs. I felt like a king, however, I knew that this was for efficiency's sake. The journey down the cliff was quick, less than a few hours on the backs of such creatures. Their speed made the difference in their silence. Their concentration was put solely in their task.

The ground leveled out before their legs were slowed. The Badlands were not quite as dead as the Desert; dry grass grew on the hillsides. But now I saw the first patch of green grass that I had seen in the nearly two years since I had left my home in Aeda. I leapt from the backs of the spiders and ran to the lush ocean of greenery. I lay there and stared at the sky feeling the grass for some memory of Aeda. This brought me peace in the chaos of my journey. It came from what reminded me of home. I found that I loved where I was. I did not want to turn back to the difficulties in the Desert. The only thing harder than to pull your feet from than the foreign desertian sand, is to pull them from the grasses of familiarity. I spread my body in the grass. I let the cool breeze from the East, and the hot breeze from the Desert to the west, collide above me. I was comfortable in this paradise. I thought that this must be what the King had intended Aeda to be.

I played in the grass for hours as an innocent child. The day passed by, and the sun set with striking colors over the Badlands. My gaze followed the sun as it set on the western horizon. I envied it in taking the path back to my home with such relative ease, day after day, as if showing me the way. Yet, when I turned to see the mountainous landscape that stood in my path, the sun cast its beautiful light on Babel. A new splendor was made by the reflection of the sun's disappearing light. I was drawn toward this grandeur like a moth to light. Unbeknownst to me at that time, I faced a similar fate.

I slept there in the comfort of the grass, anticipating the dew that once was a bother to me. It filled me with excitement and longing.

The young spider entered the mouth of the cave with a girl held fast by one of his many legs. She was unconscious. The spider dropped her to the cold ground and circled her a few times before finding a seat near the edge of the cliff. He sat staring away from her body, looking off into the distance; not toward Babel as one might expect, but in the opposite direction, toward the Desert. Moments later, he let out a heart-wrenching squeal that pierced Moveable's ears. She writhed slightly to protect her ears. MaliciousCraft gave her a look that told her not to move.

"If you speak, he will take you from me, to the altar. If he finds me, he will throw me from the cliff, and steal you from me. Do not speak or this journey is in vain."

Moveable was surprised by MaliciousCraft's knowledge of this creature. She whispered in a tone nearly impossible to hear, that Moveable understood: All the creatures of the Desert war against the others, though there is a delicate ecosystem between them. They all want to eat.

"I was once on this path by my own accord. I fell into a trap laid by a magician, who took me to the heights of the Badland to show me lying signs and wonders. Her name was Jambri. Her son is named Janni. He is the one who disposes of those who do not see her magic as power. She offered me life or death. I chose life. I have learned that decision means a death. I wanted power, but I was changed into a weak creature. Do not follow the spiders to their heights. They are the cleverest of creatures. They hang from the heights, motionless, plotting; they see all. They attack when they cannot lose. If loss does become imminent, they kill. These are the evilest of all the creatures that you will find in the Desert. Do not let them catch you. Do not let them find me.

"I was rejected by my clan. The spiders used my weakness to destroy me. There is nothing more evil. Stay the path with me, and we will find the way to Babel. However, if these creatures are on our trail, we must get rid of this weight." MaliciousCraft motioned to HopeKind and Moveable nodded and settled back in to watch the spider and the girl.

The girl in the mouth of the cave began to move. She had been there motionless for less than an hour. The sun already passed the roof of the cave and descended over the Desert. The storm moved to the south. The air was crisp and the silence penetrating. The girl struggled against her bonds; the spider moved to her side. One pop

190

on the head with his deceptively frail-looking leg and she was again unconscious.

Janni moved toward the mouth of the cave again and howled into the chilling early-evening sky. The sound of clanking metal erupted over the top of the cave. A black creature crawled in from the roof of the cave. He looked darkly in the direction of the three women but was obviously under instruction. He fell from the roof and stood at the height of nearly three fully-grown men. His armor was of the fiercest of metals. His face was beautiful in its darkness. A blue light hung within his plated, bearlike chest. His body stood still but for the movement of his raspy breaths. His head, supported by a serpentine neck, fell from his suit, demonstrating its astounding length, and examined the girl.

They babbled between the two of them, the dark angel and the spider. Moveable had never heard this language and she feared hearing it again. It was hideous and powerful. She curled up tightly in MaliciousCraft's arms. She would wait out the encounter.

MaliciousCraft stayed up to watch. She was curious. She had nearly shared this girl's fate many years ago. She somehow envied the girl's death.

The girl was poked and prodded by the angel. The spider and the angel soon fell silent. The black angel picked the girl up with his talons and flew toward the Northern Sea. MaliciousCraft stared, shocked with what she had assumed to be death, yet it became obvious that this fate was not what she had expected. *Of course*, she thought. *The tree of death cannot touch that woman because her King has sealed her. The angel is taking her to the sea. The creatures may not do his bidding, but it did seem impossible that they could destroy one that chose Him.*

The spider withdrew himself from the cave.

MaliciousCraft broke into tears—tainted tears which fell black from her eyes. She was angered that she couldn't cry as she once had, for others and not for herself. She was furious, but not with herself as her tears had been, but with the king she had forsaken. Her body grew darker and her rage boiled as Janni scurried away. MaliciousCraft erupted from her seat, waking Moveable. Her rage was rekindled.

"Throw this waste over the cliff and let us quickly descend into the city." MaliciousCraft said to Moveable while angrily pointing toward the helpless HopeKind.

Moveable, frightened of MaliciousCraft, knelt and picked up HopeKind and returned her to the edge of the cave. HopeKind coughed. Impossible! She was near death mere moments before. HopeKind looked up at Moveable, about to send her to her death and weakly whispered.

"Thank you for carrying me. I knew you were there for me. I had the worst dream."

And Moveable cried.

XII

"Ja, es wird zwar ein anderes Zeitalter

Kommen, wo es Light wird,

Und woder Mench aus erhabnen Traümen

Er wacht, und die

Traüme—wieder findet, weil er nichts verlor

Als den Schlaf."

-Jean Paul, *Hersperus*

From dreams of bliss shall men awake
One day, but not to weep:
The dreams remain; they only break
The mirror of the sleep.

193

*T*he goçip's grasp was deceptively strong. She laughed wildly; she had caught a live child from the Desert before he had fully rotted away. She dragged him into the depths of her cave. She reached the place where he had been forced to climb. She put him in her mouth like a hound and crawled up the wall. The top was no more than a few feet above SpeakGood's head. She brought him to where she brings all her food and left him on the floor to invite her sisters to prepare him, without killing him. They tasted better if they mingled with others.

She inspected him and found healthy deposits of rot. She prepared her utensils and attempted to dig in to his mouth first where he had consumed all that had brought the rot inside of his stomach. She heard a noise. She sat back to look down the cave. There was no reason that any other goçip would be near the mouth of the cave. Her sisters were coming from deeper in the cave where they had been picking through dead remains.

She rose to her feet and went to the edge of her lair. She peered down the tunnel but saw no one. She returned to her meal. The sound came again. Now frustrated, she rushed to the edge. No one. She began screaming for her sisters. She was cut off silently as a sword pierced her. She could no longer scream; her mouth was full of sharp metal, held on the other end by a man dressed in the raiment of Aeda.

He was not alone. Though he was the first to arrive, there was another by his side. They slew the goçip and her sisters who slithered in not long after their sister fell. When the last goçip fell, the men knelt by SpeakGood and woke him. He sat up with a start, eyes darting in fear of the goçip's return. He lost his consciousness somewhere along

195

the first few feet of the cave. She had been holding his throat so tightly that he worried he might die.

SpeakGood had not expected to wake again. He believed he had made one too many steps into the dangers of the Desert. Rather than the resolve that any normal young man might have at this realization, his was not of humility but of pride.

"I see I have fallen asleep." He said. "Thank you both for waking me. I will be on my way now."

SpeakGood rose to his feet. The two men introduced themselves as Eager, the first to come to his recue, and Justice, who was quieter than the other, but just as fierce a warrior with surer strikes against the enemy.

"We are from Aeda." said the two warriors. "We protect our countrymen from danger and that is our only duty."

"I'm not your countryman." said SpeakGood. "I am from a wild country to the south. I have never even seen the plains of Aeda. I have heard of it from men with whom I've traveled, yet never have I so much as set foot there."

The men smiled.

"Our land is open to all who are loyal to our King. My brother, Justice, is from the bloodline of Aeda, but neither he nor I were born there. Aeda is a refuge for those loyal to the King, hated by the world."

SpeakGood sat in silence for a moment. He contemplated what they told him. He was intrigued; he could not deny that. He had always heard of the beautiful land of Aeda, yet his desertian family and all that he knew hated the Aedaites. He was torn.

"If I do not accept your land, will you let me to die at the hands of the goçips?"

"Surely not. We have rescued you and we will guard you until you arrive to safety or until you choose to leave. Follow us and watch our journey. If you choose to become our brother, we will guide you safely as the journey becomes your own. For now, we have been warned of a child of Aeda wandering too close to danger. We are on our way to rescue him. Join us in the race for his soul."

SpeakGood held out his hand and they lifted him to his feet.

"Lead the way."

They left the caves and climbed over the dunes. Their journey was long; SpeakGood was glad to have the good company of weathered warriors. Their speech was the purest he had ever heard, and although they spoke in his dialect, their accent was Aedic. It was beautiful.

They directed him away from sinkholes, harsh edges and large boulders. They gave him water in drought and food in famine. He walked with them and he learned from them. The more he learned, the more he desired to see the land of which they spoke most beautifully.

They crested the dunes with caution and saw a dark sight. Both men from Aeda averted their eyes; SpeakGood stared on in terrible amazement. An evil tree hung ominously in the depths of an immense pit. The floor of this sunken cave crawled with flying creatures which took the possessed men to the Tree where they were put to death. The men put their hands on SpeakGood's shoulders and told him to avert his eyes.

"Can't we save these men?" he shouted as they pulled him away.

"As much as we would love to have each, and although it seems that they are trapped, each one has chosen his own fate to hang in the tree of death."

"Can't we at least try?"

"All we do is try. These souls are lost. They cannot turn away by any outside force but by their own choosing and the power of the King of Aeda. These are the men who have a loyalty to the Prince of the Desert and this is where his power takes them."

"Is this my fate if I continue to follow the ways of the Desert?" SpeakGood asked, terrified by the response he expected.

"Look back along the horizon and see where you sat just days ago. You saw these lights that draw men to their gruesome death. These lights brought you into this land and they will bring you back if you do not have the eyes and ears to hear that which is only found in the land of Aeda. For that, we know to protect our borders. We understand the threat that we see and hear, and we do not call it beautiful. We call it what it is terror."

SpeakGood sat back in despair and wept. He still had no faith, but he knew he did not want the Desert. He felt that there may not be any place for him in this wasteland.

The grass that lulled me to sleep sang sweet lullabies while I slept; their chanting reminded me of the lost Voices which were now deeply buried by my savage mind. Even in sleep, my mind raged wildly. The field in which I slept began a change within me, introducing the first calmness that I had felt since I had been on a path with my family. I thought, while sleeping, how the prodding coaxed me return to within the deeper parts of

Aeda. Rather, I took their prodding for a reason to cross their protective barrier. Surely this thought was a kingdomly reward for my good works in the Desert.

The spiders left me, but I felt Jambri's eyes watch me from her badland-perch while I slept. The calmness was like a drug that overtook me completely. I awoke in the night, before the dew; I felt a kind of magic that existed in no other location. I knew I had encountered a wild taste on the hill of the Tented City—it was pure power. Yet, this was controlled, unlike the power that was unleashed in chaos by Mystic.

The mountain was east of me; its immensity brought it to the forefront of my vision. It was beautifully lit from within, though the peak began to catch the light of the external sun. The light was still hours from reaching the field where I was, yet the snow turned a beautiful red which turned into purple as it touched the blue rock of the mountain where the heights were covered in ice. I saw the Falls of Babel cascade downward in beautiful greens. A sanguinary mist hung over the Falls. It caught the light from the rising morning sun and shed the most magnificent colors across the sky. The last colors of any civilized nation; such a mix that none truly has its own place, yet such a mix that it shouts its banner across the ocean toward paradise where this mountain now sat in its majesty, shaking its fist at the King who was thought to be dead, yet they hated Him. It was the memory of Aeda that comforted me, not my current place itself, but its lies.

I watched the light-show as the dew began to set. It condensed on my face and arms and I felt completed in my happiness. It had been so long since I felt the refreshing waters of any grassland. I heard a distant noise and thought the Voices were returning to me—I was not sure if

I wanted them to return. As I anticipated their chaos to interrupt my inner peace, I heard their language. They walked past me on a trail not far from where I sat. They escaped my mind and now inhabited bodies of their own, adorned in brilliant gold and white gowns. I scrambled to my knees as they swung a golden chalice and chanted a babel that I recognized well. They were calling the kingly nature, inherently within me, to follow them. I did not think that they were talking to a part of me, but the king that told me he lived within me.

I stood and followed far enough behind to escape if I decided they were dangerous. I would make no such decision; I knew that. I was lost to them the moment I felt their familiarity.

They led me through the morning along the beautiful fields of the Ancients. I was impressed by the fauna which sprouted out of the desertian ground. I scuffed my feet as I followed the men in their beautiful garments. Sand appeared below the thin, stone walkway. The depth of its covering was only enough for one man to stand on for a moment, no longer, before he fell through to the sands below; yet the grass grew lush on each side of the path, paved for those like me. I thanked Jambri in my mind for having tempted me with exactly what I sought—familiarity. However, she was not done with her sickly plan. I felt the air changing as I was reminded of the desire that I remembered asking the prince who appeared in the Badlands. I felt the nearness of MuchHeart. I could smell him, like a Beast hunting prey.

At long last, the Voices walked through the grand archway of the City of the Ancients. Two men of stone stood elegantly together to form an entrance to this elaborate city. The looks on their faces made me uncomfortable; they stared at me as if I walked forward to my death and they pitied me. I recognized them, but I shunned them because it did not suit my desires.

They held out their hands, firmly and straight, unquestionably warding off the visitors of this enchanting city. I followed the Voices between their feet which were taller than I. On each one was written a message that had been scratched out and repeated many a time. The message came through clearly. To the left was written: They will not endure. The second, to my right, was written: They will not spare. I shuddered. I did not understand what they meant, but the authority of these words tempted to outweigh the power that drew me ever closer to the mountain which sat in splendor just beyond the city. I closed my eyes and walked through the gates into the fantastical City of the Ancients where I was met with cheers from all around. I thought that I had surely found a paradise where I could stay forever; it threatened my memories of childhood with the promise of riches that far exceed those of my salvatory homeland.

Moveable and HopeKind soon found that MaliciousCraft was no better a guide than I had been in my selfish adventure toward the mountain of Babel. MaliciousCraft repelled the face of the cliffs, which created the Badlands, just as dangerously as I had navigated the roots.

HopeKind, being only hours awake from her sickness which nearly caused Moveable to take her life, was not nearly as capable as the others. MaliciousCraft was unforgiving in her speed, racing the rising sun as it crested the mountain.

"Time is running short and we have business in the city below!" shouted MaliciousCraft from many paces ahead of the others.

"What business? I have heard little of the city below the mountain." Moveable was not sure why they ran, she only followed in whichever direction was given the most people. She followed MaliciousCraft so close, she would fall off a cliff if MaliciousCraft fell first.

"What business? Deceit, of course. He is in the city and we must reach him before he is lost to the city."

The three women were on the edge of the fields which protruded from the Badlands. They paused in unison and stared at the strange sight. An ominous calm hung over the fields; it weighed heavily on their hearts. MaliciousCraft stepped forward, making the two remaining to shiver. The silence was what nearly turned them away for it was frighteningly misplaced in the wilderness.

Moveable took HopeKind by the hand and fell in step with MaliciousCraft. Though all three entered to find me, this was a silent truth between them. None were sure of the other's loyalties and the three began to doubt each other.

"Do not touch nor smell the herbs." warned MaliciousCraft. "Though they are enjoyable, they have an insidious cause and they are hungry." Moveable guarded her feet carefully and followed the footsteps of MaliciousCraft.

"Most importantly," said MaliciousCraft after she saw that the two women were carefully following her instructions, "do not listen to the lying gatekeepers. They would have been removed years ago, but all efforts to do so have been futile."

Moveable and HopeKind met each other's glances and saw that they thought similarly. This land to which they walked must surely be the most dangerous of all for what MaliciousCraft said of it.

Justice stood at the edge of the dunes which covered the vast expanse of the goçips' system of caves. He looked toward the Tented City, concentrating on the mindless savagery which he knew to be taking place. The Beasts had been drawn to the hill, resting amid the city on the first night of winter in the infancy of their present year. The year was now pressing ferociously against the hot summer days that threatened to present themselves. There is no worse time to be in the Desert. But this is not what urged him to push the course with more speed.

The Beasts, who run to power but run from authority, had now consumed the power that had been unleashed in the Tented City. The people ignored this, but those who had been given eyes were chased from the city, some over the cliffs and some to the Northern Shore. Eager watched as this culminated into the death of some and the rescue of others by those (like Justice and himself) who had left Aeda to rescue and make countrymen. There is no better time than when those set in their ways are uprooted and left homeless.

Justice returned to where Eager was comforting a weeping SpeakGood. His look, as always, was concerned. He spoke softly, but with an authority that did not come from himself.

"Brother, we must hurry. The Beasts have left the confines of the woods. For the time, as the King said would happen, authority has unleashed them, and power of a worldly sort carries them into every corner of the earth. They have moved beyond the city limits of the Tented City and now push threateningly at the cliffs. They will soon be at our heels. They will take the high ground and avoid the tunnels where they will be tamed to a different sort of evil."

Eager listened and understood. He put his hand on SpeakGood's back and told him a frightening thing.

"We have a task; we must forge on into the pit to check the roots for survivors. One child of Aeda called on the King but was caught by another. His footsteps continue in a dangerous direction from which he did not turn, but thinks he has. Come with us to the bottom of the tree; accept the protection of the King of Aeda so that he can keep your feet from following a false prince as others have come to do at the base of the Tree."

SpeakGood could hear the yapping of the Beasts, sparing nothing as they rushed across the land. He feared being unprotected in a savage land. He became a brother to Eager and Justice there on the dunes, feet from where Moveable and HopeKind had fallen into the pits of the goçips. SpeakGood had a sure protector, and patria to call his own. Justice knelt on one knee in front of SpeakGood, who cried softly, and held out an open hand to him.

"This stone is yours, mined from Saia with you in mind. It has been waiting for you since Saia rose out of the flat, barren landscape. It is your entrance into paradise on that day when the ocean might claim you. Guard it and learn the inscription which is written on it for you alone."

SpeakGood took the stone and threw aside his brown stone which he had guarded so tediously though it had not served him well in any manner. He threw it off with ease for it was a fake and useless stone. He stood and entered the shadows of the tree with confidence in his protector. They three searched for a lost child in the roots.

This city was a strange place. Its history pointed toward Aeda by the lives of many of its namesakes; though, its current inhabitants were those who put to death those for whom the city was named. The day was dark and more lit like the Desert than the early stories led me to believe.

The city was full of mystical music and a mysterious power which disguised itself as authority. Men and women praised the King and declared his home the Island Paradise. They were like those who were in Aeda, but they had something within them that was absent in Aedic authority.

I walked confidently through them. I was lifted, and I lifted others up. Each was proud of his own humility, none were left unpraised. There was not a sense of merriment as there had been in the Tented City—not even thinly veiled—but of reverence for the Name of the king and reverence for each other. My divinity sat well with this. I could share, in fact, I felt proud that I was willing to share my knowledge. I was encouraged in this by those around me. To my recollection, no one ever spoke as directly as I have written this memory. It was always a secret understanding.

A beautiful, conservative woman came to me in elegant robes. She held out a book that looked like the one that I had left in Aeda. I took it and opened it as she spoke to me.

"This is the new book of Paradise which was channeled through the White Prophet. Read this book and your soul will be filled!"

I remembered the words written within my book of Aeda; yet these were not them. Familiarity, however, gave me trust for this book and I kept it closer than I ever kept what I had been given of Aeda.

She smiled and bowed before disappearing into the crowd. I followed her for longer than I should have, but a familiar scent caught my nose. I smelled a familiarity that I had never forgotten, yet I had hidden it deep within me. I was nearly driven mad in search of what made me feel that I was home—that this was a land more like Aeda than I had imagined. Something drove my madness and numbed every sense but my sense of smell. I found a path that was less populated than the rest of the city, yet the way had been elegantly paved and was in no way warned against. I followed the familiar scent along this path.

XIII

ANCIENTS

"The Patron of true Holinesse,

Foule Errour doth defeat:

Hypocrisie him to entrape,

Doth to his home entreate."

-Edmund Spenser, *The Faerie Queen*

"What comes out of a person is what defiles him. For from within, out of the heart of man, come evil thoughts, sexual immorality, theft, murder, adultery, coveting, wickedness, deceit, sensuality, envy, slander, pride, foolishness. All these evil things come from within, and they defile a person." The Gospel of Mark

207

The way through the city was strenuous. Archways of stone encamped the winding streets; I became quite tired. The city had an evening glow of honey and a daylight dreary-gray hue. The ambivalence of dusk was truly the best time to wander — the most beautiful, at least.

I passed a few secret places that had been boarded up in years past, by the looks of their rotting boards. The architecture was desertian, that which replicates the lost ruins of the Desert Fathers. I found it strange to find such desertly dwelling here in the city of the Ancients, yet this was a strange way. It did not bother me as it should have; I only noticed it and walked on into the twilight.

The scent faded as I reached a narrow bend in the street. I was destitute in my loss of the strong scent that had filled my lungs as if to feed them a succulent meal; but I was left to hunger for even a taste of that unhealthy scent. I sat against an old building that had been long forgotten and I cried.

It was not long before I was stopped abruptly in my weeping. I heard another on the road. It was a man in white and gold garments as those who led me to the city gates. He walked sturdily, coming closer as I watched. He stopped beside me, though he did not turn to look at me. I recognized his presence. It was the being that found me in the roots of the Tree. He was more gloriously incarnate than I could have imagined. All the magic I had witnessed in the Desert did not compare to his majesty. Light seemed to escape every object in sight so that it could give him more glory. All went black but what I focused on: the one who had led me through the deadly roots, more fit for death than death itself.

"Do not cry. I am with you. You have done good and remained faithful. Do not cry; I know why you cry. Take up your new book and read it with an empty mind. Repeat my words mindlessly and focus on what it is you desire. Do not cry. I am with you as you practice my presence. I want what you want for yourself, so go and take of it."

I was speechless and the being before me disappeared before his words reached me. I took up my book and read.

My eyes were filled with words that promised me prosperity, happiness of a kind that I had not thought of before, and most of all, all that I might desire. I read until my eyes were dry. These pages did not have the power to produce a convicting tear, yet they did produce a confidence in myself. I went to the depths of my mind where I had found my guide and I searched desperately for him to return to me in the way he had in the Badlands. He was there; I embraced him.

"Give me what I asked for when we were in the Valley of Death. I found the scent in this city, but I lost it. Bring it back and I will find you more often."

The man before me did not speak for quite some time. I sat, admiring his face. He was beautiful. His face was kindly chiseled to a form which appeared serpentine; I thought he seemed to look at me with eyes that wanted me to have whatever I might desire. He was surely an altruist spirit—one who raged against principle if for the greater good of the individual. At long last, he leaned closer to me, I thought to kiss my forehead, and he spoke.

"Do not neglect me, your king."

My mind went dark in the violence of sinister neglect.

SpeakGood, led by his brothers, easily found his way to the bottom of the cave without stumbling. The roots of the tree were wild, tangled in knots that could not be undone, not even by years of training. No creature, evil, good, or naïve could affect death in its permanent confusion.

The three men carefully navigated the roots; often with their vision obstructed, they followed the roots in the direction which they grew thicker and more fixed in their way. The death of the wicked dripped from the tree and dirtied the men who walked below. The tree was thick with rot and filled the airless hole with a foul stench that caused SpeakGood to vomit. They straddled these roots delicately so as not to fall to what would be their death. They arrived at the base of the tree after many sunless days. This tree in the cave was larger than any man had ever written in the legends of their land; it was so vast that it blotted out the sun and made one to think that it was a cave and not simply a pit. But the Desert is a land of lies.

Justice stood at the base and looked upon the death and destruction. Eager searched fiercely for the bodies or remnants of lost Aedites in the roots rather than the branches which consumed the worldly. SpeakGood fell to his knees in humiliation of what he had thought himself strong enough to handle on his own. In truth, what had drawn him into the Badlands in the first place was this very cave and its fatal stars. He was lost for words. The angels above which had once called him near, repulsed him as they screamed and shrieked. They railed against the men but could apparently do them no harm.

Eager returned to Justice and held up three articles. A map that was poorly drawn which led (supposedly) to the land of Aeda, yet it was flawed and disproportioned; secondly, a book that was old and tattered, yet basically untouched on the inside—lost in both memory and the Desert; thirdly, a chunk of flesh which was the flesh of one of the Desert. It was eaten by neither the Tree nor creature which crawls within the cave.

"Two are known by Aeda, a third was a companion who is too wise in her own eyes to have had any true wisdom at all. She is most likely lost already. There may be hope in saving them yet." Justice took the items and laid them by the tree, all but the book which he guarded carefully behind his armor.

"There is a better chance that the one we came for is lost and the others are still living. One disregarded dead flesh that can do her no good for it is only temporal. The other lost a bad map that would not lead her into Aeda even if she were to arrive in Arqana, and she would soon be lost to the Beasts. It is better that she leave it behind. However, the only true eternal flesh, the only flawless map, was not only hidden from those who could have found life in it but disregarded by one who understood what it was. I fear that our mission may not result in our intended outcome."

Eager stood next to his brother whose eyes were downcast in sadness. He spoke words of encouragement to him, all the while holding delicately the attention of SpeakGood.

"Brother, we were sent by one who knows his children. This book was not carried this far by one who disregards it completely. The words which he surely read will not come back void, but in a moment of humility which is surely on its way, he will remember his King who has protected him. We have been sent for him, we will return with him, or not at all.

"As for the other two, there is also a good chance that they have been rescued already for, as you said, they knew which items bore little importance to them."

The brothers met SpeakGood on his knees and when they rose, they looked down the path which the roots had carved into the eastern part of the Badlands.

"That way is dead and full of dangers. There are monsters that are much more frightening and evil than I wish to see roaming there. Let us take the way we came and travel along the Northern Shore, around the merciless Badlands. We ought to travel nearer the water as the summer season is quickly catching us."

The three men stood and followed their safe footsteps back to the edge of the cave. This journey itself cost them two more days. On the fifth day, they were again where they had descended, and they prepared for their return to the sun. Before they could begin their way, however, they heard a noise which told them that their efforts had been in vain. The Beasts had reached the top of the dunes. They howled as they surrounded the mouth of the cave. Their way was surrounded, they had but two options: the dens, or the river of the Tree of Death carved by the roots in the Badlands. Justice and Eager looked at each other with a challenged glance. Justice pulled the book out of his armor and opened it. It led their way into the way of the Badlands. They had been given a quest, given protection, and then given the reminder that they needed these things. They moved along the wall and into obscurity along the path to the Badlands, assured that they ought not fear the evil ahead.

The fields beside the three women gave off a delicate scent of eucalyptus that drew their attention closer to the herbs. Only their presence of mind kept them straight on the way toward the city of the Ancients. The longer they resisted the comfortable, mindless rest that was offered them, the stronger the scent grew.

MaliciousCraft walked carefully in the center of the path. Moveable and HopeKind, however, were not so strict with themselves. They heard a faint whisper coming from beyond their vision. Movement caught their peripherals, yet when they turned to look, only stillness met them. For this reason, their adrenalin was heightened in the depths of calmness.

"Do not be fooled by the pleasant scent. It is a mindless camp that will distort your understanding. It is purely experiential, and it holds nothing true in it. It is a counterfeit. Do not be caught in the religiosity of the rituals either. They are perhaps more dangerous. The field is more like the city than the road that enters at the gateway."

Moveable, though a follower, scoffed at MaliciousCraft's warning. She knew that MaliciousCraft knew this city well, but for all the dangers, she did not know why MaliciousCraft wanted to return—much less bring them along. Moveable began to whisper with HopeKind about the intentions of MaliciousCraft. They formed a plan to escape but were hindered in their actions because the gates of the city came quickly upon them.

The two ancient gatekeepers stood like relics, forming the gate that allowed access to the city of the Ancients. MaliciousCraft did not lose her pace as she crossed through the way. Moveable slowed but continued to follow—HopeKind stopped all together. She had caught the eyes of the men which stood tall above her and their glares bore heavily into her.

"Perhaps I will stay out of this city." she said. "I am not sure that the end, which I do not know, would outweigh the means of passing. I can take my eyes off the gates, but my mind cannot bare the image of their disapproval. I think I will heed their warning and stay behind."

With that, HopeKind sat by the feet of the gates. Moveable went back to her to offer her company. MaliciousCraft, enraged by her difficulties in bringing these women into the city and to the mountain beyond, screamed at Moveable.

"I told you that you should have been rid of her when you had a chance! Now she is slowing you from collecting your friend who is hidden by the city!"

Moveable jumped to her feet, (Moveable will follow a direct and commanding voice over the crowd), but she did not leave HopeKind just yet. She knelt and put a hand on HopeKind's shoulder.

"We will find Deceit. Then we will leave."

She whispered this so MaliciousCraft could not hear. Moveable knew that MaliciousCraft did not like HopeKind, but she would not leave her friend behind. HopeKind agreed, at long last, to enter the city. She stood and shuddered at the thought and willpower that it took to move forward. She felt that this was a mistake, she knew that it was a mistake. She went on. Every bone in her body seemed to want to run the other way, but the hand on her shoulder was more powerful than any strength of will.

The valley was pitch-black. SpeakGood wandered blindly, but his companions helped him keep his footing

215

on solid ground so as not to fall into a pit. They spoke in low voices as they repeated the promises of the King to keep them safe in any location. They now walked through a darkly shadowed valley and SpeakGood was learning the true meaning of trust.

They forged on, losing track of time. No light shone in the valley; it was a desolate solitude that even three couldn't share completely. They were still alone to themselves and in darkness for they could not see the faces of the others. This did not slow them; they moved with all speed toward the exit. The howls of the Beasts continued through the night. They could only guess how far away the Beasts were. SpeakGood worried that these ravenous creatures would soon enter their company, not sparing even the one. But Eager reminded him that the Beasts were reserved for a time yet to come.

SpeakGood was glad to have company, even if the company was, for the time being, invisible to him. There was surely strength in numbers. SpeakGood could hear Eager just ahead singing a song of valor, and Justice beside him reciting the promise of Aeda. He was comforted and strengthened by his fellowship, more so now in the darkness where he knew a new obscurity and challenge. Surely the trenches and mountains make protection sweeter. He was glad of a challenge instead of ease. In ease, he may have slipped away, believing that he needed no help.

SpeakGood was enjoying the words of the others when suddenly Eager's voice disappeared. Justice stopped reciting and put his hand on SpeakGood's arm to stop him. Justice waited a few moments for the voice of Eager to return; it was silent. The howling of the Beasts still grew closer, but it died down for a moment, enough for them to hear a hair-raising thud in front of them.

SpeakGood froze of fear. Something large moved in front of him and came close to his face. It whispered in a secret hiss, like the kiss of a beloved:

"Come with me, I will show you unimaginable wonders."

Chills grabbed his spine and tugged ruthlessly at his bones. His body threatened to let go its frail grasp of consciousness; he struggled to remain sober-minded. He was losing the battle as the large creature put a leg on his shoulder and continued to drip sweet offerings in his ear.

"Come to the top of my hill and look upon the majesty of the East. I will make you a king in that land if you but follow me—oh, such a simple thing."

Justice was silent all this while, but the chanting hum of the creature's promises lured SpeakGood who gradually became more apathetic to it. He put a hand on SpeakGood's arm and told him as any brother would:

"Do not succumb; she does not offer you anything she can give. Take out your stone and know that you are safe."

SpeakGood was nearly lost to the entrancing whispers, but Justice's words of truth broke through and he removed his stone from his pocket and looked upon it. Even in the darkness this white stone showed its color and lit his way. His promise in hand, he looked forward through the desperately dark ravine and saw a light at the end.

The body of Eager lay at the feet of both he and Justice. SpeakGood dropped to one knee to tend to him, but the ground around him was dangerous and filled with webs that threatened to pull him into a deep hole from which he would not be able to escape.

SpeakGood cried and tried to pull Eager toward him, but the light of his stone was more and more hidden by his efforts and mourning. While the darkness began to overcome him again, the creature crawled atop him from behind and tried to wrap him in her body to coax him into unconsciousness. Her legs crawled about him uncomfortably, but he did not try to push her away. As SpeakGood hid the stone, Justice removed his own and it illuminated the valley brightly. In the face of such a bright light, the spider that had been on SpeakGood scurried away and found a hole in the valley wall. SpeakGood remained bent over Eager, weeping.

"Do not fear, for although his body is vacant, evil cannot touch his soul. He has fought the good fight. His body will be claimed by the ocean and his soul by Paradise, for there is not an ounce of rot in his body that has not been cleansed already. There is nothing for the creatures of the desert to feast upon. Let us move; we still have our instructions; but first, we will bury him."

The three women who entered the city were dirty from their journey. A nervous and stout woman met them at the gate and led them into a convent just inside the portico where the women of the city washed them. They were not returned any cleaner, but their appearance was much brighter. MaliciousCraft was well annoyed with these nuances of entrance. Doubtless she had gone through this procedure many times before. She scoffed at every brush stroke made by the frantic women. *Missed a spot* MaliciousCraft cried repeatedly, mocking the fervency with which they scurried about their business. Moveable, however, loved the formality and, although she did not quite know how to act, she had more time than the rest to try out many different attitudes while she was being washed; there was a lot more of her body to wash than there was of any other in her company. HopeKind was meek and did not speak. She sat quietly as the women of the city washed her. She saw that it did not help, but she did not care. She was here to find her friend, not to cleanse herself of the Desert. Within, she knew that only return to Aeda would cleans her of the wilderness.

The women finished and admired their work, and brought others to see their work, too.

"Didn't we make them beautiful?" they asked. MaliciousCraft was disgusted and rubbed dirt on her face just to anger the women. They were not amused. But in the end the joke was on MaliciousCraft who was made to start the process again.

"We're not here to be cleansed," she said to the women who themselves only had the appearance of cleanliness. "We are here to meet someone who hides in the deep part of the city. I know my own way, but I need to pass through inconspicuously.

A woman dressed in white looked up from another that she had been cleaning and lathering with makeup.

"Does he know you are coming?" she asked. MaliciousCraft generally despised this city for the fakes that walked about claiming cleanliness. They were mindless in her eyes. She knew of worlds which laid in their midst and yet they knew nothing of the power that pulsed at their feet. However, this woman was different. She stood and left the presence of the other women for a moment and then briskly returned moments later.

"Come with me."

MaliciousCraft left the other two waiting, brushes in hand, and she followed the woman in white into a dark part of the monastery. The woman locked the door behind them both and spoke abruptly with MaliciousCraft. She was not used to being the one spoken to; in the Desert, her intelligence rivaled all, but here in the city, where unexpected intellectuals hid in every niche, she found herself a child of little understanding.

"You've stepped into a snake nest that you would be wise to avoid, dearie." The woman in white spoke quickly with a passion that was fueled more by annoyance than anything else. She continued in the same manner.

"Men and women come here to escape; we do not appreciate when the Desert leaks its fecal matter such as you through our gates. I see that the cleansers had no luck with cleaning your skin. Pity.

The white woman rubbed MaliciousCraft's cheek, taking off a layer of pasty-white cream.

"You came looking for a man but the one that you followed within is not the one of which you are speaking. Someone has a bond on you and for that you threaten to disrupt our way of life here within the ornate limits of the city of the Ancients."

MaliciousCraft was taken-a-back. This woman knew her somehow; there was no other way that she knew what MaliciousCraft suspected she knew.

"You do not know anything of me," she retorted, unconvincingly.

"O, do I not? I know exactly what you are. Remember, darling, we're covered by darkness. I know exactly who you are."

MaliciousCraft felt naked and trapped. She squealed for a release and her breathing came short and frightened.

"You're wrong! You cannot see in this light, you have nothing on me."

The woman in white came up close to her and put her hands on her knees, looking darkly into the gaunt eyes of MaliciousCraft.

"I know exactly who you are, yet you have no idea into whose lair you have just walked."

A smile curled along the cheeks of this beautiful woman and she let out a laugh which brought chilling memories to MaliciousCraft of the place she lived until three travelers fell into her cave. She was anxious to leave, and she looked around frantically for any escape. She could not find one—the room was deceptively dungeonesque. The woman in white began to speak as her laugh died.

"Foolish swine of the Desert, you've stumbled across a prophet of the Ancients. I am the White Prophet and it is by my word that the men and women of this city live. You must submit to my teachings if you are to be allowed to search this land for your friend and, truly, the man you came to find.

MaliciousCraft fell to her knees at the feet of the prophetess and she worshipped her. The prophetess fed off her praise. In a voice, full of satisfaction the prophet said soothingly, "He's in the mountain. The one you came for is in the mountain."

"Then I must go to the mountain! How do I get there?" MaliciousCraft stood and looked directly into the eyes of the prophetess.

The prophet slapped her firmly across the face and she sat back in her chair.

"Do not expect me to be friendly with you, you dirty thing from the frontier. You will pay me the proper respect."

MaliciousCraft bowed her head and asked again how she might enter the mountain.

"The one who you are looking for in the mountain has a singular interest and the king will only allow the one you seek into his fortress. You must find the lost Aedite he desires and follow him into the mountain."

"Where can I find him? My other companions will accompany me."

The prophet looked at her inquisitively and spoke down at her.

"He found a path that has long been abandoned. He was led there by the spirit of perdition. Follow the smell of familiarity and you will find him."

The prophetess led MaliciousCraft from her room and she took up a light air that was pleasantly deceiving, even for MaliciousCraft.

I woke up with a woman holding my head as MaliciousCraft had done in the Badlands. This woman, however, was not as the other had been. She was not shocked by my awakening.

"MuchHeart! He's awake!"

That smell… MuchHeart. I found him.

"Is he coherent? There's not much time to get him out of here. There is a dark presence welling up in the bowels of the mountain."

"He seems to be coming to. Give him a second."

"We have to go soon. The Northern Passage will be lost to the ocean soon; it's not safe to take the Southern Passage anymore. The people of the southern cities are rioting."

I felt a wet cloth on my forehead. I opened my eyes and looked directly into the eyes of a woman who was full of everything good. I could tell by looking into her eyes. She slapped my face hard.

"Stupid boy." She said. "You walked quite blind into this city. All of Aeda is looking for you."

I turned my head—it pounded, and I felt sick.

"MuchHeart?" I said.

MuchHeart looked at me and gave me a disapproving and sorrowful look.

I have rejoined my family and I have asked the woman who helps you now to be my wife."

I looked at her again, she was a motherly type woman, and full of beauty of the most internal manner. She spoke to me again as she wiped my forehead with a wet cloth.

"It's time to return to Aeda. You have nearly destroyed yourself and everyone around you."

I closed my eyes and I thought hard. He was not as he had been before—he was strong and independent, and I knew that I could not move him by any trickery. I did not have to, I thought, for my prince had answered my prayer and returned my MuchHeart to me. I opened my eyes with a newly found smile.

"I will follow you where you will have me go." And I became the most pleasant of company and I told them that my name was again Delight.

We travelled on together and found a path that went around the city rather than through it. We walked through the day and we had many good conversations, though my mind was set on the scent of MuchHeart who travelled ahead of the both of us, his promised Amer and myself.

The night began to set, and we could hear the Desert from the outskirts of the city. The stillness was so complete and the atmosphere so calm that one could hear the northern shore eating away at the cliffs which littered the northern regions. We rested in a field to the north of the city, beneath the stars and moon. The dew set in and I began to shiver. My companions fell asleep beside me. I thought to myself that perhaps I would stay up and study the new shape of my friend MuchHeart who had been lost to me. I sat there for hours in contemplation and then, as a whisper beneath the quiet of the early, pre-waking hours of dawn, I heard the voice of my prince.

"Does he look as you remember?" I shot back, I had thought that he had left me in anger when I had been sharply rejected by him.

"Yes, yes quite. He is the same, and yet—there is nothing the same about him. Am I that same way? Recognizable from without but unknown by all who were familiar?"

"Why don't you ask one who is familiar with you? Ask your friend."

"But what if he thinks me up to no good by conversing with him?"

"Accuse him first, but subtly—passively if possible—of being the cause of your past. Any means to accomplish the end of *friendship* is worth the cost."

Encouraged, I smiled shyly at the prospect of having my friend back. I spoke aloud to myself of my precautions which were logical, but within, my inhibitions were aside. The morning was beginning to dawn and my friends would soon wake. I looked at my prince who was fading with the darkness of the mountain. He turned my gaze to watch MuchHeart again. I leaned over and saw that he still wore the same shirt beneath his new robes. I cut a piece from his collar where I had tugged him away from the Fence of Aeda, now years behind us in our youth. I reasoned this to myself that now the urge to pull him by his collar again would disappear because the original means was gone, but I kept that collar in my inner pocket. It would not feel the air of the Desert again, but it would never leave its proximity to my skin.

XIV

CASCADES

For over the Ford now the grass and the clover
Fly off from the tines as the wind driveth on;
And soon round the Sword-howe the swathe shall lie over,
And to-morrow at even the mead shall be won.

But the Hall of the Garden amidst the hot morning,
It drew my feet thither; I stood at the door,
And felt my heart harden 'gainst wisdom and warning
As the sun and my footsteps came on to the floor.

When the sun lay behind me, there scarce in the dimness
I say what I sought for, yet tremble to find;
But it came forth to find me, until the sleek slimness
Of the summer-clad woman made summer o'er kind.

William Morris, *The Well at World's End*

 peakGood and Justice finished burying Eager;
they could not spare another moment. The
Beasts howled ferociously behind them and,
presumably above, devouring everything as
they went.

They tore away from their sadness over Eager,
knowing that he was now out of danger there was no need
of his body now that he had been invited to dream in the
King's land.

This way was no less dangerous, but in their good
fortune, the light at the end of their path had not
disappeared once the white stone in SpeakGood's pocket
had opened it. They hurried toward that light and found
the Desert sun upon them, a field of beautiful grass ahead
of them.

SpeakGood was glad to find such a kingdomly
place. He had never seen grass of such pure-green. He had
once seen the Arqana on the horizon, but there he had met
someone who pushed him into the Desert where he was
nearly lost to the powers of the terrible wilderness. He
turned to Justice with a look of satisfaction in having
found such a place of rest.

"We can rest now." said SpeakGood.

"No." said Justice, eying the grass carefully. "It's
not what it appears. Do not touch it, your mind will be lost
to it. There is something sinister lurking here in the long
grass. The earth seems to breathe here; do not match its
calm breath or you may fall into its rhythmic trap. Look at
what feeds the grasslands — the river of the roots of the
Tree of Death feeds this land. It is from the death of many
bodies that these lands derive their beauty. This land is
surely an evil land.

"In the valleys between danger and death is never a wise place to rest. The enemy will soon lay siege upon us. Let us move on into the city before darkness comes upon us."

SpeakGood looked at the dark valley that they had just exited and saw these awful roots falling from its mouth into the beautiful fields of grass. He followed the roots with his eyes and saw that they made a very straight path on either side of the valley that entered the city of the Ancients on either side of the two large figures which guarded its gate.

"We must enter to find the child of Aeda who is lost in this land."

And so, the two men ventured on, side by side, guarding the other from any dangers that might emerge from the long grass on either side, even if it be the grass itself that attacks. They moved faster, now surely past the place where they had left Eager's body to rest.

The place was beautiful, but there was danger on every side. It was in the air, in the earth, and in the minds of each man who entered this darkness disguised as light. SpeakGood was frightened and he sought the council of Justice.

"What has happened in this place?" he questioned as they came ever closer to the towering gates.

"This is a land of the lost and found. They were once an outpost of Aeda, but as most who seek their liberation from the Law, they have fallen to the Desert. This land was perhaps worst of all for they still hold the riches of the King within and they attract the men of Aeda because of its familiarity. It was proper that the mountain which now grows to the east has risen out of the very roots that feed this city.

"The men who created this city were men who spent their lives in the Desert from which we have just come. They mixed their ways with the Desert and became the Fathers of a new nation. Their dens have now become the dens of the goçips, yet the Tree of Death, which they fed, still carries their message into the East, just as the East may follow it back, even to the edges of Aeda.

"The men here are trapped by few laws and believe this land to be a home as good as or better than Aeda. Yet, they do not notice their lack. There is no Mount Saia in their midst, and none can look out and see Paradise. Their mount is the counterfeit, Mount Babel. They have constructed a mountain from the roots of the Tree, but it is a false Saia. Indeed, it grows contrary to Saia. For as Saia reaches into the sky, the truth of Babel is buried below the base of the falls.

"Look and see that the river beds which meet in the center of the city are overgrown with the roots of death and it is this that spills over into the basin surrounding the mountain. Only death will find you here, and here is where those who do not carry a stone but look for one are caught by a counterfeit and lost to the depths of Babel. Be careful that none deceive you in this treacherous city. Those who live here are warned, yet few endure."

Justice's story was cut short by a snap behind them. They stopped and looked behind—nothing. The sound of scuffing footsteps digging into the sand beneath the trail brought their attention back to the direction of the Ancients. Black roots grew out of the earth and formed the shape of a man. The root creature held its hand in front of itself as the towering men behind—as if in mockery of their unheeded warning. The creature grew until he was half again the size of SpeakGood.

His hand remained outstretched and vines began to fall from his limbs like the nooses that ornamented the Tree of Death. The vines reached the ground and the creature disintegrated into the earthen floor. The roots fled into the grass on either side and then behind them. They followed it with their gaze until it was behind them. Not just he, but hundreds more took shape between them and the gates of the city.

Silence struck them once more as not a sound could be heard. The root that led them held a vine above his head. When he brought it down to the earth, they attacked. They fought with an earthly dance that wrought fear in SpeakGood's weak heart. He and Justice ran toward the gate, but the roots rode a wave of sapling vines that dripped with the death of their father, Death himself, the Tree which gave them animation.

The roots encased them. They could not have outrun them on foot. The men were trapped in a wooden arena that the roots had formed around them. They stood back to back, weapons drawn, ready for a fight they would surely lose. The battle was silent, the roots made no noise at all. They fought as quietly as a tree grows. The silence was more disruptive to SpeakGood and Justice's fight than any noise could have been. This was the silence of a deep power, not the chaos of loose power like the creatures who roamed the Desert. This was a much more skilled and practiced evil. Their enemies were those of Aeda for generations. They knew their enemy and they knew him well. The roots battled on and the men with it. They grabbed hold of Justice's ankle like a snake stealing its prey from the grasp of the jungle. SpeakGood grabbed his wrist and held tightly. Justice's face was painted with fear and muttered a faint plea of desperation before the moment his body was pulled into their destructive depths. He whimpered and was separated from SpeakGood's hands. For a moment SpeakGood looked on in disbelief. His friends had all been lost. He was alone in a foreign and terrible land which ate his kinsmen without reproach.

SpeakGood mustered his strength to fight, but he was fast losing the battle, just as his friends before him. A noise caught SpeakGood's ear; not a terrible noise, but the noise of righteous war. This sound gave him hope as war is surely a wonderful sound for Good when Evil is pervading.

The roots squeezed SpeakGood at his waist. They held him tighter; they knew that sound and what it meant. Warriors of the Ancients had passed the city limits and flooded the fields. They fought against the roots and they conquered quickly. The battle looked as if it were staged— SpeakGood was glad to be free, but he was unsure of his saviors. They battled the root-men back into the ground and they cheered for their victory. The men came to him, lifted him up and carried him to the gates of the city as if he were their battle-prize.

The men set him down before the gates of the city and they moved aside to show him his friend whom they had also rescued. Justice stood before SpeakGood and the men embraced each other. Their embrace was that of weathered warriors come home from battle, but Justice's warning whispered in SpeakGood's ear was severe. *Mind the warning of the gatemen.*

Justice finished and the two of them reached the gates and they were looked upon by the gatekeepers. As the warriors passed through the gates, they added a scratch each to the antiquated statues. This seemed to have no power in erasing their warning. It was permanently set

233

to mark entrance to the city—a warning to all which could not pass away. There was nothing that stopped them from entering, but their warning was clear. *They will not spare. They will not endure.* SpeakGood understood. He walked in cautiously, from the hands of danger into its mouth.

Moveable and HopeKind followed MaliciousCraft as she sped through the city.

"See if you can smell him." said HopeKind. "He should still smell of the Desert."

Moveable and HopeKind kept a nose about, but MaliciousCraft was more fervent than the others and she took the lead. She pushed people aside as they followed traditions and carried idols and relics of the Desert Fathers through the streets. She caught a scent of rot that was familiarly that of my own.

"This way!" she shouted as she turned up a small, dark, arched alleyway. The city was in darkness, but the sun would soon rise. The air became stale and the scent was easier to track.

She grasped the hands of the other two and she ran with all her might toward the source of the scent. She passed many dark buildings which had been long encased with boards; some ransacked and robbed, others still secure, but none opened. She passed the place where I had laid, finding me not there, she hurried to the outskirts of the city.

The three women stopped at the edge of a road, broken and raised from earth-tremors which were the birth pains of the mountain being raised from the depths of the mantle. They looked off toward the west, nearly making out the gates in the distance, and saw there three people sleeping in the dewy grass. The smell of rot was strong.

They found me in my sleeping place just before the sun touched the city.

When Justice and SpeakGood crossed through the boarders, the city was asleep. SpeakGood was relieved to be out of the Desert. Although his interest was piqued, he understood the dangers and kept himself close to Justice who walked with all awareness down the central streets. They followed a man named Renqwr who offered them a bed in which to sleep. He was one of the soldiers who came to their rescue. Within his house were many idols, each engraved with the moon and a snake.

Every image and statue seemed to anger Justice. SpeakGood was not sure if he liked this attitude, but he did not know all that Justice knew of Aedic tradition. The King seemed to be part of the artisan work of the city.

They continued down a wide hall and turned off into a room that was softly lit by a lamp on the far wall. Two small beds looked most inviting. Their window faced the western wall of the city.

The Beasts howled wildly, they had surely left the caves by now and would be upon them in a few short hours. The howling was loud, but it seemed only to wake a few of the men and women in the Ancients. The men and women came out of their houses to see what made such a ruckus.

Justice and SpeakGood left their room at the time when darkness had most overcome the face of the earth— they saw that their housemate had awakened before them and sat on a balcony overlooking the foothills of the Badlands. He stood, lit from behind, as a shadow of a man who had built a fortress around himself and yet sensed his fallibility.

He was terrified by the sounds of the Beasts. He was not only awakened from his sleep, but from his stupor as well. Renqwr had awakened from his slumber with instant and keen awareness. He bowed in his balcony, overlooking the coming savages, knowing that this battle would not be staged as the others. Some evil, after all, is not organized. It will fight itself and anything that it encounters in its way. The evils of the Desert were less organized than those affected by Babel. Renqwr cried out to the King of Paradise because he feared the evil which flooded his land. Justice went to him and SpeakGood watched from his place along the wall.

After a few minutes, both men came to join SpeakGood, the other still shaken, yet calmness resonated within. He had surrendered to Aeda, freeing him from the captivity of the Ancients.

"We came at a good time, brother. This man needs someone to help him return to Aeda. A woman named MaliciousCraft led him here years ago and attempted to bring him into the Mountain. He had never seen the Northern Way and the Northern Ocean frightened him, as it did you before we found you in the Desert. He can travel with us once we find the child for whom I came."

The three men left the house in the cover of darkness and walked north along the border. Renqwr said that there was talk of an odd group of travelers that went in that direction just the day before. Justice had hope that he would have luck in finding the child in this group, and perhaps others who would choose to accompany him to Aeda.

Renqwr spoke as they walked. SpeakGood assumed that he spoke to hide his fear of the Beasts that were gaining ground toward the city, not so hindered by the fields of grass as those men who found themselves amid a staged battle. Renqwr's voice gave him away; his fear was obvious.

"Do not fear, Renqwr. We will exit through to the north with a child of Aeda. We will be at least four. The Beasts will not travel close to the ocean for it tosses and turns wildly in the storm that is brewing off-shore."

They came upon a small field within the border of the city of the Ancients and were not surprised to see a group of three travelers laying in the grass. Justice stopped, a smile of relief painted on his face.

"Finally. Now we may bring this child home. It has been a long journey for him."

Renqwr stopped the men with an outstretched arm.

"Look." he said. "There besides the three sleeping is a man dressed in royal garb. He watches as they sleep. He is not one who traveled with them. Surely, he was born of this land, for we know and celebrate all who enter through the gates."

The three men looked closely; he was an aged man, much older than the others. He stood beside them, watching—nothing more. As the three men looked on, the man turned in their direction and met Justice's eyes. An evil darkness filled the sockets of the old man. His purple robes disappeared, and he was consumed with an evil which could power the Desert and every land beside. This evil threatened to overcome them all but as they struggled against this power, Justice remembered the words of authority from his King and he spoke them.

The man roared at them. He was irritated, consumed with some powerful darkness that burst forth as power. SpeakGood and Renqwr joined their brother in reciting the laws of Aeda and they began a descent into the field. The man roared and disfigured himself. As they came closer, however, the man was unable to withstand the authority with which they spoke, and he vanished from sight.

The three rushed down toward the sleeping travelers and saw three more urgently coming toward them. Justice peered out to see who they were, but he did not know them. SpeakGood spoke up because he recognized one of the women.

"I see someone I had almost forgotten, a friend of Deceit. She is harmless. Let us all travel together."

Justice agreed but made it clear that they would not be persuaded by tricks as power does, but by authority and promise of Aeda alone. And so, the three of them met the three women along the way. SpeakGood called out to Moveable. She tripped over herself for her excitement in seeing a familiar face. She rolled for a bit and she fell on to MaliciousCraft who became enraged by her clumsiness. The two women tangled themselves in a sort of spat while the four were left standing. They looked on in disbelief of the inappropriateness of the moment in which they chose to wrestle.

Their fight came to an end when HopeKind noticed the Beasts, now nearly at the border. It appeared that they were changing their direction toward the north. They headed directly for the group still sleeping in the grass.

I awoke to a strange thing. I heard women fighting and Beasts howling, yet what held my attention was the soft rhythmic breathing of my friends. I remained where I was, listening to them breathe until a certain silence caught my attention. The fighting had died down and come to a complete stop. I sat up to look in the direction from which the noise had come. There were six people, three of each gender, running toward me.

I jumped to my feet and woke the others in fear that they came to cause us harm. They awoke and became alert before their soft breathing had time enough to cease. They rose but were not frightened by the people who ran toward us. They looked beyond the six and saw a city in blind despair. The city was not awakened by the terror that lurked, howling before the boarders. What they feared were the Beasts which moved ever more quickly toward our soft place in the grass. They both grabbed me by the hand and ran toward the north.

My mind was flooded with controversies. I wanted to stay where I had been, I did not want my night to end, yet I wanted to run to save myself. I was unsure who the enemy was. I returned myself to my dreams and while I ran, I remembered a king. He faded into the mountain; I thought that he was not an enemy. Every direction was filled with something that could be an enemy—except for the East and the mountain in her bosom. She stood brilliantly strong and comforting, now newly lit by the sun rising above her foliage. She drew me in like a youthful and supple temptress.

I dug my feet into the ground and the two who dragged me were forced to stop abruptly.

"We have to run!" shouted MuchHeart.

"No. They will surely catch us if we exit the city. They will be at the Northern Gate before we could even think of escape. Let us run to the mountain! It will protect us! It is surrounded by falls that the Beasts dare not traverse."

They looked at the Northern Gate and, for little faith, followed me to the falls. They were not far from us, but neither were the six who followed us without stop. We nine united at the edge of the waterfalls, the Beasts now within the city boarders and quickly gaining pace. They seemed to run directly at me.

I feared leaving the beautiful city of the Ancients; but we had no choice. The Beasts pushed us beyond the borders and we had to enter Babel. We had to move quickly to escape the savage jaws of the Beasts, but at the edge of the city, I could see back centuries to a land which promised all the counterfeits that the Ancients had created, as well as a plethora of rituals so that I might feel close to my potential.

Standing on the edge of this land, I peered down over the waterfall that once fed the land of Babel. This was the river that led through all the lands; a river bed was all that remained in the Desert. History and the present protruded from its sands. Wars were given remembrance by its artifacts, but rumors of war were all that flow by its banks. It is, in the end, what led us this way.

I did not have to see the water; I could visualize it so long as I could see its path and I became refreshed by a perception of it. I watched the water of my mind's creation fall over the cliff and pool in front of the mountain. It fell straight over. There were no protrusions, not even a branch that could hold back the waters flowing from my mind. I made this once-living land come to life before my eyes. The edges of the falls curved around me on both sides. It encompassed the mountain. Each edge was a day's walk from the city of Babel built to face the mountain. In my haste, I forgot one thing. It was all a lie of my own creation.

I turned to my company, "Life is over the cliff, we must swim."

The man, Justice, sought my gaze. I avoided it until I had significantly convinced myself of my own untruths.

"You fool, there's no water. You'll die if you jump."

Our gazes held for moments too long, but Moveable was excited to be the first to do something that seemed so obviously a good idea that she did not hesitate at the suggestion. She stripped naked and launched herself over the edge of the falls. We watched as she fell, downwards and out of sight as clouds of vapor consumed her. SpeakGood readied himself to jump and he did so with gusto.

Justice, who had fervently warned his friend, tried to stop his comrades. They would not hear it. Renqwr jumped soon after SpeakGood. I watched with passion the leaps of faith and with each leap, I became more enthralled with the idea.

Justice dropped to his knees at the edge of the fall. He yelled for his friends, but they were gone. Both of his brothers had jumped into the pit, he followed them solemnly and silently in defeat and weakness.

"Only way to them is to follow!" I said with a laugh. MaliciousCraft came up behind me to push me in with a foot on my back, but I grabbed her and threw her in before she could do me any damage. Her face filled with horror. The pit consumed her. I looked upon her for the first time in the daylight as the sun finally broke the top of the mountain and caught her entire body in its scouring rays. Her beauty took hold of my mind in an instant and begged me follow. I looked back at MuchHeart, not wanting to go unless he followed. He looked blankly at me, and I knew I had to break my gaze. I jumped in after MaliciousCraft.

I had my eyes fixed on her as I fell, trying to get closer. Soon I could keep my eyes on her no longer. We were separated by a fog and the strange blood-red hue of the base of the mountain.

We hit the water at the same time; I heard her splash as I fell into the imagined water. It was warm like a dream. It did not boil but seemed to be at the point of losing its peace.

The weight of my legs held me down and threatened to drown me, but I kicked hard and at long last, my head surfaced. It was hard to catch a breath in this air which was most likely as saturated as it could be. I floated in place for a few moments, long enough to hear a splash behind me and then a while after, two more in short succession. One of them must have been MuchHeart. I swam on to find MaliciousCraft now that I knew MuchHeart had followed.

I followed the laughter and the playing. I felt a splash on the back of my head. I turned and floated in place to look at who had splashed me. It was HopeKind. She had an innocent smile on her face and she reached her hand out to me. I turned. Seeing that she could swim on her own for a while, I sought MaliciousCraft.

I found them playing, SpeakGood, Eager, Justice and MaliciousCraft. But Moveable was conspicuously absent.

"Where is the other of our group? Should we not regroup for safety?" Justice was worried for her too. He recognized the places where she had taken from her body and left a breadcrumb through the Desert, begging for rescue.

"Has anyone seen Moveable?" I asked as I swam among their ranks. HopeKind arrived mere strokes after I spoke, resentful that I had left her behind to follow MaliciousCraft.

"No, she was first. Perhaps she swam ahead. Let us be of a playful spirit while we enjoy what is presently ours," said MaliciousCraft, quite convincingly. We continued our festivities at this lake, the Lake of CommonSpirits.

We caused a ruckus with our splashing. The reverie of us eight was perfected once Amer and MuchHeart met with us safely. Both asked where Moveable had gone. She was the lightest spirit of all. They wished to play with her here. Their question, however, was met with a shrug.

Some were saddened by our lack of Moveable, but I can't remember worrying too much; I had MuchHeart with me. I had searched the whole Desert for a satisfaction promised by such a one as he. The others were of mere consequence, not of any necessity—real or perceived.

Not even our sadness in our friend's abandonment of us could keep us from our craziness. We jumped and dove and played until we were exhausted, and this affliction threatened to drown us. Such a riot we made— we made enough disturbance in the water that Moveable's bloated body rose to the surface.

HopeKind screamed, but MaliciousCraft went to her to check her consciousness. She rolled her over; we all saw that she had hit land, not water. I realized that my imposed reality had not changed the truth of the dryness of this river bed.

"Where is there land around here? There is only water as far as the eye can see. Where could she have landed?" HopeKind was distraught. She cried for her friend. We carried the body to the rocks on a distant shore.

MaliciousCraft took from her pocket a stone which she called tonic and placed it in the mouth of the corpse, believing with all her heart that it would be good for her as, she said, it had been to her. Moveable convulsed. Death spread to every inch of her body. SpeakGood, seeing that Moveable's death was irreversible, tried to comfort her with a word of the Law.

Moveable's eyes grew wide and she growled and moaned and then slashed at SpeakGood's face. The poison that she had been given made her to hate the Law, even in death.

As she thrashed and yelled, we sat and watched. There was not a thing to be done for her. We sat with her in much sorrow. Her death was a torture. On the fourth day of arguing over her burial, she spat a coin from beneath her tongue and then crumbled to dust.

HopeKind took up the coin and examined it briefly. It was a dark coin; unlike any she had seen before. Justice took it from her and looked at it once on each side.

"Where did you find this person?" he asked, referring to Moveable.

"She was with us in the Tents." I said. "She came to me when I ran from the power of Mystic and her prophetesses."

Justice buried the coin in the ashes and looked at HopeKind and MaliciousCraft.

"You both traveled with her?"

"Yes." they both responded.

"You both walk in front. One of you is not what you appear." He said this and instructed Renqwr and SpeakGood to tie their wrists with vines. They did so.

The group of men and Amer, walked on, leaving the dust on the impenetrable ground of the rocky shore.

244

We wept as we left that place. We walked single-file along the shore, surrounded by the cliffs of the ancients. MaliciousCraft began a song of sorrow and as we wept, a swarm of the most horrid locusts consumed us quite completely. I watched as SpeakGood curled into a ball, suffered stings on his every showing part, but in turn he was not stung within for he protected first his face and heart. HopeKind ran at first sight of these hideous bugs but was quickly overcome and chased into their swarm further along the thin, winding path in frightful screams and tears. She was more easily affected by a smaller pain. I pitied her most of all for it was I who had brought her here; I felt responsible for her pain.

MaliciousCraft, however, surprised me greatly. She danced and sang as the locust consumed her. I believe they were attracted to her voice. Perhaps it was due to her voice that they had come in the first place. I had little time to make this thought wholly complete before I had to run for the gardens of Babel. I the busts would lend me the same fate as poor Moveable.

As I ran, I quickly lost sight of the others. The locusts burrowed beneath my shirt and tried to find their way beneath my skin. I shed my clothes. The locusts were more terrible than anything I had known. I feared that I would fall dead before the lake, now my only remaining path. Death seemed a better fate than the sting of these horrid flying creatures. I reached the moat around Babel, completely naked. I saw ahead of me the city, a black mountain with many doors and gardens lay beautifully in its darkness. I stood at the far end of the water and saw that it was made of sweet spirits like those which had given my friend release to death; only, it was darker and hotter like the stone to which I was strapped in the

Badlands. It would kill me just to taste it. It was of the same darkness that led me through the entirety of the Desert as if to call me to this very moment and place.

I was afraid of the waters and their destruction. I turned to the safe gates of Babel. Fruit lined the entrance and so I took a pear and ate it. It was sour; it had fermented on the vine. It was a new flavor unlike any I had eaten in my youth. The flavor staved my lips at first, but soon it grabbed hold of my desires and begged me to eat more. Once my lips touched the fruit, my mind was taken to another place where I saw many things in clarity, or rather, what I had presumed was clarity. I told myself that I now had the eyes to see and so I thought again that there might not be need for the words of the King. Then, into my ear whispered a prince that I was indecent and should enter the city of Babel for clothing and shelter. I vomited the fruit. It made me sick. I saw that the voice had come from a man whom I had known well throughout my travels.

Having seen my zeal to get to this place and my being attracted by it, he came and cradled me in his arms. He scooped up my vomit and told me to eat; then he washed my hair in the black waters of the moat and told me evil things that were well phrased and even written on the inner walls of this city of Babel.

After eating my own vomit, being washed in darkness, now naked in front of one who wished that I destroy myself, I fell asleep. I had neither the strength nor the power of will to move against him.

PT 4

Babel

Forgiveness, come uproot my shame—
The shame which says my sin's to blame.
He, with His might, grants nobler name
To heal the sheep who's fallen lame.

Come near and smell the stench of sin;
It's havoc reeks of thoughts within
Which only serve to please the skin,
No thought could alter; rot therein.

A sinful wreck, I'm dead alone.
Burst forth in Light, through darkness shone,
The LORD has crushed my burial stone
And raised each shattered, broken bone.

The LORD has healed each broken limb.
In glory, I was made for Him.
Now not in sin of chasing whims
    For He has filled me to the brim.
       EDR

XV

HASMODEIS

"Come with us, let us lie in wait for blood;
let us ambush the innocent without reason;

like Sheol let us swallow them alive,
and whole, like those who go down to the pit;

we shall find all precious goods,
we shall fill our houses with plunder;

throw in your lot among us;
we will all have one purse."

The Book of Proverbs

I was borne into the mountain, gathered up, myself and the others remaining who had crossed the lake; the Beautiful MaliciousCraft, the Wise SpeakGood, the Loving Amer, the Proud MuchHeart, the Gentle HopeKind, Justice the Voice-of-Reason, and the Careful Renqwr. Along with myself, Deceit the Deceived, we were eight. Moveable had been laid to death by the waters of imagination.

We were welcomed graciously at the gates—one after the other—announced and confirmed with luster.

"For these dear children, this is the sacral awakening from the bowels of the wilderness." said the voice of one HasmoDeis. He was the appointed king of this province of Acedia, arranged along the border of Babel.

"Come, young infants, into the open where the world might see your courage in braving the treacherous waters placed before our land, those from which you were called into this city.

"The banquet tables have been set for you since before you knew of your advent. Come and see what the Queen has prepared in your honor."

HasmoDeis' hand caressed Renqwr's shoulder, eyes lit like those of a child on his birthday. The light in his face was captivating, like an angel—the purest light that I had ever seen—without withholding or obstruction. My attraction grew to this light; cupid himself had never dreamt of such an infatuation. I sought his hand to be on my shoulder as well. I pried my friends from their walk and shouldered my way into the loving grasp of HasmoDeis' firm hands.

I was enthralled. His grasp on my shoulder was more intimate than mine had been toward MuchHeart in Çɷdɷm3 when our souls had collided horrendously. There was a spiritual power—more than that—a spiritual entity at work. I believed it was the spirit of my prince. How could it be else?

My eyes were transfixed; his words were a rhythmic hum, purring in my spine. I heard every word yet did not distinguish one sound from another. He spoke a perfect language. I needed no instruction thereof; the meaning was clear. "Ye shall be as kings."

My spine chilled; my hair stood on end, yet I was not uncomfortable. It was as if someone told me a thought that had been on my mind for years—for eons, before the years had begun. This had always been my idea; thus, I knew it to be true.

We continued, the eight of us and HasmoDeis, through the gate which was before us—a beautiful gate made of many arches, niches and statues. This arch was made of captivating black stones and red gems. My heart beat stronger. My emotions were confused, yet my overwhelming thoughts were of excitement. As we passed under this gate into the courts of lower Acedia, I looked above onto the forehead of the archway. In the deep of its face, the word *Misteija* was written in gold and appeared in Babelã (the language of Babel) in their own form of writing. I knew it intuitively. It was written like this: Ɗɷ7Ɗeʊ3

As I passed through the shadow of the arch, my ears were full of these words; "My home; I think I have found it." My tongue slipped out of my mouth before I considered that I had never, until now, stepped foot in a city so spectacularly familiar. The men of the city bowed in reverence. They praised us. We were like them, kingly.

HasmoDeis grinned as he spoke in a conquering tone, "*Ojwd, stajwqa, œ sejæ stajjo Aeda qw hajr atejwt.*" In this way, he announced our arrival as those who came from Aeda, those whom the city awaited.

We disbursed ourselves among the citizens of Acedia and we joined them in their religious rites. We greeted men in this new tongue. Our greeting was for the king's return; *Qê vequela o Kyo.* Their mouths would repeat this back to us in a beautifully mantric manner. How spectacular to find our home among strangers, among foreigners, among those of whom we had been warned. These were surely not strangers to our hearts, and their faces were not hideous as an enemy's is. Rather, they were illuminated in light—that same light that we had seen in HasmoDeis. This was surely the congregation of the King of Aeda.

My hand met more people than I had seen in all my adventures in the Desert, and surely more than in Aeda. Each new hand burned with a kingdomly fire, enriched with the powers which were within them. We shared, loved, and praised each other.

More hours passed during that day. The sun remained high in the sky. The shadows stood still in their ominous niches, embossing the mountain in darkness. None wished to leave; none were desirous of anything outside this city. Amer was overtaken by the love which she felt here and, in her euphoric trance, fell to the floor in laughter and happiness, rolling as if she were to be made pure this way. Those around her joined in her reveries.

Justice found men with his same passion, men who loved regimen and law, and to his delight, it was now he that had the right to decide upon the law. "Finally," he said, "I have gained right through my understanding and diligent study to interpret those laws which I have followed so that all else may now follow them more perfectly through my instruction." He was, perhaps, the most delighted of all, save Renqwr, to dance with angelic beings through the hours. Renqwr had more energy than I could muster, even here, for I was still broken even in my excitements.

HopeKind came to me, not as joyously as the others, concern in her eyes. "There is gold on my face, and I did not put it there. What kind of magic is this? Were we not warned of the sorcery of Babel?" She stared into my blank eyes. Even I knew this, for the miracles which I witness are lying signs and wonders.

She sighed, chest heaving deeply, heart beating through her shirt. She sat beside me and buried her face. I thought perhaps she was still in shock. She did not return to the subject. However, she did not partake in the reveries either.

SpeakGood found great joy in singing and dancing. He sang songs of love which warmed my heart. The King was his lover and he announced it without sorrow. His dance was like nothing I had ever seen. I thought it looked like the dancing of a madman. Yet he could not be mad; his words were too pure in my ear.

MuchHeart was perhaps the most curious. He drank in the air and became drunk from the atmosphere in this holy place. The men surrounding told him that he had drunk the kingdomly spirit; he was inebriated with bliss. HopeKind broke her silence and said to me, "What mockery is this? Would the King mock his own name and Spirit?"

"Go ask someone who knows. I am just learning how things are. All that I knew, I feel I should forget. Then, kingdom willing, I will find out this happiness."

"What this looks like is madness. Do you truly not agree?" I sat silently, not answering. I felt something working inside of me and I didn't want her doubting mind and loyal spirit to taint my process of coming to terms with this city.

"We should go home. We should sneak out from the gate through which we entered while the others are distracting themselves with mockeries."

"Hush. Do not distract me; I am trying to find out truth. Do not say another word. Why do you not speak to another who will hear you?"

"No one else will hear me. You may not be so kind, but you knew me before the rest and I know which heart is missing from your chest. Find it, and you will be a good man, but you cannot find it here."

That was it! That was what I was missing that I could not find as the others had. My heart was missing from where it had once been. My heart had been gone so long that my body forgot its feeling, forgot its weight and displacement.

"What knowledge do you have of this land to know that it is not found here? I can look to my minds' contentedness." I prodded impatiently.

"And then can we return to Aeda together?"

"Why must I go with you? What specialty am I?"

"You are the only one whom I trust to see what I see. Look, stop being deceived. We must go back to our land. This is no place for an Aedite."

"I am beginning to think that Aeda does not exist. None of you who travel with me were known to me when

I was in that land. All my body knows that there is a King, but I can feel something like him here. I doubt the land that I remember even exists, aside from a childish delusion."

HopeKind began to cry, and I looked on in shock.

I put my hand on hers, patted it with a slight hesitation. I felt embarrassed and I returned both of my hands to my pockets.

I heard the festivities begin to die down. Only then did I notice that the sun had long since returned to the horizon. HopeKind curled into sleep. I could not believe her unhappiness towards me, and yet, still she treated me as a much closer friend than the rest.

The wind caught me under the chin and I brought my face into my collar. I thought of MuchHeart's collar still resting in my pocket. I felt it there, it had turned into something much more. No longer was it a simple slip of cloth. I did not dare take it out to look in the presence of HopeKind. She would know what it is, for she could easily see to whom it originally belonged. The collar was not torn squarely from MuchHeart's clothing. HopeKind had expressed her pity to him that his vest was tarnished. It had been such a beautiful shirt.

I looked up from my thoughts when the gust of wind had died back slightly. I saw MuchHeart still stumbling around the courtyard, drunk in the kingdomly spirit. My eyes lingered on him again too long. He resembled his sister. I remembered her horrible slaughter before my eyes, in the dining hall of the savages of the Tented City. Many of the people here once belonged to that savage group as well. Perhaps, some who now danced with MuchHeart had witnessed and cheered for his sister's death. How strange that they now cheer his drunken stumbling.

I shook my head and shivered in the cold. Oh, how I would love to have the warmth of the others. Envious, I watched my friends shifting uncomfortably in my place. Now that the cold was overcoming the sun, for me alone, it seemed, I could feel how the sun had affected me. I was burnt on one side, that side which faced the sun too long, hiding my other side from the light. My other side was unbalanced. I was like a cake baked on one side; crusted and hard to that side which was light and soft toward the darkness, awaiting amalgamation with that which might consume me.

My thoughts went on without my consciousness. For a time, I forgot myself. When I began again to think about that which had stolen my thoughts, I had trouble remembering how I had gotten there. I was pondering a difference which I had not realized I had noticed. The ground here in Babel was made of something different than both the ground of the Desert and that of Aeda. For the most part it looked like the Desert, but its give was more fluid than the sands thereof. It was surely still sand. Only patches of grass could be found in it. But, this grass was more like that which grows in the swamps of Arqana, not in the valleys of Aeda.

Staying in one place too long suffered those who stood upon this sand and its firm grasp. Even HopeKind and I had begun to sink into its grasp by merely sitting upon it. I could not escape from the earth below. I was sinking and had been doing so for hours, without my noticing. Some of my friends had already disappeared. I looked up to a lectern which sat on the highest ground, built out of the wall of Babel on the face of the rising mountain and realized then, as I saw HasmoDeis there behind his stand, the smile on his face was the smirk of a desertian predator. He knew we would sink into the mountain. He was not worried for our lives. In fact, he was not worried at all. Realization struck me that the way up the mountain was not to climb it, but to sink into it. Even those who were present and not participating in its festivities were subject to its seductive powers. Yet they kept moving for fear of its depths. This was a surface satisfaction.

I sank below the earth with HopeKind at my side and HasmoDeis in my sight. I feared he would be the last man who I would see. But perhaps he was a dream.

XVI

BAUFOGLEURA

~ЋΠFΠϚΘ3~

"Et, parmi sa pâleur, éclate
Une bouche aux rires vainqueurs ;
Piment rouge, fleur écarlate,
Qui prend sa pourpre au sang des cœurs."

Théophile Gautier, *Carmen*

And amid her pallor there flashes
A mouth whose laughter conquers,
A red pepper, a scarlet flower,
That draws its purple from the blood of hearts.

259

 uickly, now. Quickly! We haven't time to waste. Dress yourselves and be present in mind and body when the feast is ready. It will soon be time to enter the banquet of ꞱꞷꝼꞷꞒϑꝫ."

I opened my eyes to the darkness.

I awoke from a dream. I dreamed of MuchHeart, dancing as he had before I stole him into Arqana. The dream felt real, as if I had just witnessed a great awakening of spirit. I looked around to see if MuchHeart had come to this place. My memory was fragmented. I could not remember much after the locusts had attacked. But my dream…my dream felt real.

My eyes adjusted to the darkness and darted from side to side to better understand my surrounding. I counted six bodies, save myself. Only MaliciousCraft was missing from our ranks. Justice and Renqwr were awake before me. They were in a corner, heads bowed in prayer. I did not know why, but an anger welled up within me as if their words were a flood that boiled in my chest, threatening to burn me clean—if there would be anything left but the dust I was.

Their eyes turned towards me when they felt my gaze upon them. I averted my own to check the others. I stood, somewhat uncomfortable due to the length of time I spent asleep. I felt my face. It was bloated and sore. I had slept on it once again—a nasty habit which I had not yet conquered. I ran my hands through my hair. It was matted and damp. Whether it was from blood or sweat, I did not know. I wiped my hands on my pants and stood. I was weak; my knees gave out beneath me. I hit the stone floor with such force that my knees should have shattered. But they did not.

MuchHeart and Amer held hands while they slept. Jealousy rose in my throat. I turned away and saw HopeKind and SpeakGood both shared the same sleeping platform which had been mine. I knew their hearts much better than the others. Therefore, I was more comfortable with them than the others. I was not even comfortable around my old friend, MuchHeart, though I desired his company despite the discomfort it did me.

I put these thoughts out of my mind for the time being and woke SpeakGood to ask him what had happened. He rubbed his eyes, yawning wide, exposing his dilapidated set of teeth. He appeared to have woken from a pleasant dream, fully refreshed.

"Has the feast begun?" he asked.

"No. A feast is news to me. How did we get here?"

"We entered through the gates into Babel, of course."

I did not remember any gates, not even in my dream. So much had been lost to the oblivion of my revisionist dreams. The trouble with dreams is really their dreamer; they choose their favorite parts and choose also to believe them.

"We don't want to be late for the feast. ЂϖϝϖϚϑʒ does not sound to me as if she is a very patient hostess. She has been waiting for us, you know, since time began.

"I do not know." I said. "Is she the Queen?"

"Just follow," he said, "you will understand." I followed. SpeakGood, I, and five others were led through a thick wooden door into a banquet hall where a woman awaited us, dressed in red. I had never seen such beauty or such class. I could not remember my fright now that she was here before me. Although I knew not the purpose of this banquet, my questions subsided. I sat before this woman. Her skin was a beautiful olive tone. Her hair was well oiled and glistened in the dimly-lit hall.

"PlajydEua ad senjydyu, la, caralæ. *Please sit, Beloved.* Welcome to the Feast of Misteija. None will go hungry here. Our water is wine which never runs dry, more delightful than any that has before touched lips of man. The bread is flesh which is part and parcel of your beings. Although this food must become death each time it is prepared, it becomes life within you by the life-giving power of the carnal flesh."

I began to understand that this feast was preparing us for what must lay ahead. Before my thoughts had spent time in whatever dimension our thoughts are born, my words began to eject them from within as if it knew the poison they were.

"What preparation does this feast give us? Surely this is not as every meal. There must be some special intent or purpose."

"*Stajid qalmalu,* do not be transfixed by the future. Your knowledge will come to you as you proceed in the land which was laid here for your undertaking. The mountain is great, and you will need your strength. Eat, drink, laugh, and love. Be raptured by a kingdomly spirit and understand that this is your portion in life. You were made like the prince to be like a king. Come share in his flesh and live as kings."

The room was silent. The woman seemed drunk with her own words. The chalice of wine in her hand sloshed to the floor and was quickly consumed by mice.

Renqwr and Justice entered discourse over the mice's destination and whether the wine would grant them the same glorified state as it would people. In moments, ꞨꚏꝼꚏꞬꝯꝫ recaptured the ears of those of us present. She continued in prayer, speaking in Babelã, the language of Babel.

It was now given to us to eat and drink our fill. We each took small portions and ate quietly, except for Renqwr. He took more than all our shares and did so proudly.

"If it is my lot in life to become as the king, I may as well do so with haste. I ought not waste time, nor have any shortage of energy." Renqwr filled himself completely. Following his lead, I, along with many others, filled our own plates and stomachs.

"Brothers, this is delightful! Is it not?" cried Justice. "Let it be to all men to access the mountain of Babel only through this banquet hall, thus saith the king."

"Beautiful! Wonderful children. Come. Let us learn together what mysteries are here within the labyrinth of the mountain so that you may be elevated to kingship.

"My commission, by the High Court of Babel, is to test your power. I must discover which one of you was he who was called and which of you are followers. We are in search of the one long-prophesied. We believe him to be in our very midst today. Sadly, ladies, we do know that he will be a man."

The excitement on her tongue flew like sick from her mouth and covered SpeakGood and Renqwr who were seated on either side of her. SpeakGood wiped the saliva from his face. In contrast, Renqwr left it on his face as a gesture of his perfect devotion to the baptismal waters which flowed from the very body of Ꮁꟷꝯꞿϑʒ.

"Renqwr, will you lead the way, as you are quite obviously the kingliest. You must select a door for your company to pass through. Choose wisely, for it may decide the fate of each one of you."

264

Renqwr looked around the table, bread and wine dripping greedily from his lips, shock smeared more liberally across his face.

"Me?" he questioned. "I am the kingliest?" He straightened in his chair, as ᏀᴔᖴᴔᏀᎱᏃ gave him an approving nod and a menacing half-smile. His chin came closer to his left shoulder as his eyes glazed and he inhaled his own elevation of state.

"Certainly. I would be honored to show my subordinates the ways to become more like myself." He rose from his chair and wiped the crumbs from his lips. He forgot those still clinging to his chin.

Renqwr beckoned us to come to him. We all rose and followed suit, giving more attention to ᏀᴔᖴᴔᏀᎱᏃ than Renqwr. He did not notice. He stepped through the doors on the other side of the hall. He chose the one furthest from that which we had entered. Renqwr stood there, holding the door for us, intently gazing at his companion, Justice, who was the first to take a step towards him.

"I have seen a new light and a new life." Renqwr whispered in Justice's ear as Justice passed and slowly paused in front of him.

"But how do you know that this is the door through which we should pass? There are five other doors, including the one through which we just came, not an hour ago."

"I have a Voice inside of me which came to me as surely as the wine. The Voice told me that this is the way, and so I follow." Although this was a whisper, I heard him as if it had been in my own ear and I longed for that Voice as it had come to me in the Desert.

I took HopeKind by the hand and made my way to the door. SpeakGood followed closely behind, so as not to be left. Yet, Amer and MuchHeart did not follow. They stayed behind for they had a special request of ꉄ౷Ϝ౷Ϛϑꝫ.

I took one last glance at MuchHeart as I passed Renqwr, who tried to speak in my ear, but I hushed him so that I could hear the petition of MuchHeart and Amer.

Renqwr was offended and began to reprimand me. Before his words took over my ears, I heard one small phrase from my once dear friend.

"We would like to enter through a different door. One which will shut all others out and bind us together in sacrament to the prince." ꉄ౷Ϝ౷Ϛϑꝫ bent at her waist, for she was much taller than both Amer and MuchHeart, whom she called children. She kissed each between their eyes.

With her hands on their backs, she led them through another door which had been just behind me. It was so close and yet, I had not felt its power that now clawed at my mind.

Before allowing them to enter through this portal, ꉄ౷Ϝ౷Ϛϑꝫ turned and called to Renqwr.

"*Propelo*, Renqwr, come back once you have seen your friends through. I have a specially appointment for you."

With Renqwr pushing me along and a firm grasp of HopeKind in my hand, I passed into darkness yet again, and was immediately lost to a deep sleep. My slumber was peaceful, unlike the last. However, this time there was a strange consciousness that came with it and the dream became reality.

I sat alone upon a boat, not much larger than my own body. An isle of gold sat upon the green waters,

266

suspended as if weightless, formed much like a raindrop, hovering just above the calm ocean. A warm breeze rustled my hair from my face. I heard a voice in the breeze saying *"Apvejid:* overcome." It whispered in the silence of a still wind, not causing a noise, but rather a deficit of noise in which my ears were lost in a vacuum of all other sounds. This kingdomly voice was all that could enter the void.

I looked about the boat. There was no oar. I considered swimming, but I was troubled that I could not see the bottom. The water was clear and still. If there was a bottom, it would be visible. I feared what might come for me from out of this abyss.

The water was no more than three fingers width from the brim of the boat. If I rocked this way or that, I would surely flip the boat. I dipped my fingers into the water. It pinched with a bitter cold, unforeseen by me due to the warmth of the air. I bit my lip. The cold continued to attack my fingers; it came as a new wave of coldness, moment by moment. I flinched as I thought more about it and then decided that there was no other way. I slid my whole hand beneath the water, and painfully stroked. My hands did not fail my strength, however, neither did my teeth as they bit into my lip. Blood ran down my chin as the wine had done so presently before my sleep.

I gathered my inward strength and made all my efforts to reach the golden isle which lay in the distance. I thought that I could make it by my own strength, but the icy waters numbed my hand until it was difficult to hold my gaze upon the isle for cause of the east wind.

As the wind caressed the water, spray flew into my face and froze with a most painful sensation of being face to face with a most ghastly blizzard.

I proceeded to stroke. Though, I soon came to realize I was not moving. The boat was immobile in the water that allowed my hands to glide so easily through it. What trickery was this?

The boat was filling with water. With every ill placed stroke, every new gust, every wave that crashed over my boat, I sunk further into the dark, unending waters until I was submerged and over taken by white caps.

While the water overtook me, and the golden isle fled quickly from my sight, I felt inside of me a strange voice which was not audible, yet clear and unmistakably of authority's power. It spoke to me with the sadness of a lover.

"Why did you not raise the sail which I gave to you? With it you would have reached my land, for I would have brought you here." And I awoke.

ꝰꝏꝰꝏꝗꝯ3 ushered Amer through the doorway and left her there alone. Once the door shut, Amer was in complete darkness, frightened and motionless. She sat where she was left; not a sound joined her. She had not known the moment when MuchHeart had left her. In fact, she did not so much as realize that he was no longer by her side. Amer only knew that she was in darkness and she could not hear her groom's voice.

She moved her hands gently across the earthen floor. Nearly half a body's length from her, her hand bumped a metal object. The din of her ring clanking on the brass face of the object reverberated lightly off the walls of wherever she was.

The object was a lamp. Filled with excitement, she tried to light it. How foolish. She had no flint. She felt around on the floor for a stone to make a spark. Her hand touched a small, smooth stone near where the lamp was. She beat it against the floor. No luck. Amer moved to all fours. She crawled delicately, putting her left hand up every so often to feel for the wall of the cave. Finally, her hand touched stone. She began to beat the stone against the stone wall. Sparks. She could have jumped for joy if she had been on her feet. A yip of glee sufficed. Amer held the wick of the lamp ever so close to the stone wall and struck the flint again. The stream of sparks was impressive, but no light shone from the lamp.

She thought. The lamp felt oddly light. She tipped it upside down. No oil. Her excitement turned to mourning. A lamp with no oil would do her little good. She dropped the lamp beside her and threw the stone into the darkness.

She dreamed of MuchHeart. She was not asleep, yet, in the darkness, she could not be sure.

She had not been alone since the day she met him. He had been escorted through her town of Levya, on the outskirts of the Ancients, a northerly city near the North Sea. On the northern side, Levya was kept damp by the storms that raged over the sea. The southern side was scorched by the Desert. She was raised in Levyia-Mojoa where the sky was dark, but the ground was as saturated with water as her heart was with love. She loved everything for that was what she had been taught. She did not realize that this dissatisfied her until she saw MuchHeart.

When MuchHeart was shepherded into her city, she knew immediately that he was her personal savior. He stood tall, though he was just a boy. He was handsome, though he had just come through the Desert. And most of all, he was charismatic, though he was exhausted from his trip. He came with baggage, but then again, so had everyone. His guides were men sent to Arqana to rescue those in danger of stumbling upon a false city. The men were wonderful guides who knew the secrets of the trails, for they had pulled many from the paths toward Aeda, that king-forsaken land.

MuchHeart had come along the coast, which was still part of the Desert, yet it was not nearly so wild. He was proceeded by a parade when he entered our city. It was nearly the midpoint of the night and everything was dark—much like it is now. She heard his voice above the crowd. He sang a hauntingly beautiful sound—a melody she heard from many a traveler. It was the Song of the Desert. This was the sound men heard when Angels flew from the Badlands to bring a special chosen into Paradise.

Amer dreamed many times of being captured by an angel and carried through the night to the shores of Paradise. On that cool spring evening, in the darkest, moonless hours of the night, Amer met her angel.

She shivered as she remembered MuchHeart's outstretched hand and loving embrace. She was instantly his. She missed him.

Amer noticed a spot of light growing in the distance.

I gasped and breathed in the sweet air I had expected to fill my lungs and drown me. The breath settled my nerves and brought me out of my cold sweat.

HopeKind hovered over me, holding my face between her hands, trying to revive me. SpeakGood splashed my face with water and I bolted up. HopeKind sighed in relief.

"You were asleep for so long! We are only four now, we waited for Renqwr, but he never came through the door. Justice is pacing and crying. Neither of us could comfort him.

"Are you alright? If you have strength, go to him and bring him out of his stupor."

I looked to where HopeKind directed my gaze. Justice rocked back and forth, muttering to himself. I rose, my bones creaked as the doors in the banquet hall had. The weight on them was immense, especially now that I had been well fed for the first time since the celebrations in the Tented City.

I willed my feet to move, but they would not budge. I put my weight forward to see if my leg would catch my fall. My knees clattered together, and I collapsed on my face. The stone floor was rough against my cheek. I pushed myself up and saw my skin scraped onto the floor. This was not nearly as painful as my dream had been. I knew it had been a dream, but somehow that dream felt more real than reality. I tasted the bitterness of the rock on my tongue. It was a mélange of blood and dust. SpeakGood held my back and HopeKind washed my face.

"I can get up. Leave me alone." I snapped at the both. I didn't know why but they made my breath sharpen as if it wished to stab them but could not. I came to my knees and paused for a breath. I crawled like a Beast to Justice who looked up briefly like a pinned animal. He paused his mumbling for only a moment, then returned his face to his knees once again, mumbling with more ferocity than he had before.

He did not seem dangerous, so I touched him on the shoulder.

"Do not touch me, liar! You were the last through the portal. Renqwr did not arrive safely. You are to blame!"

"Justice." I interrupted his rambling. "Renqwr followed Ђꞷϝꞷꞡϑӡ into the door which was behind her. He led us here and then abandoned us. His rest is found in a special door which we obviously cannot enter as we are."

Justice stared at me, his breaths causing him to rock slightly back and forth.

"What do you mean, he followed Ђꞷϝꞷꞡϑӡ?"

"I mean that she took him to a new portal. It was the one to her right as she spoke to us over the banquet. He is now at the right hand of the Scarlet Woman."

"Did you happen to catch the name of his door?"

"What do you mean, the name of his door? Was a name told to you for the doors?"

"The doors were named. There were six. We entered from the door closest to Ђꞷϝꞷꞡϑӡ."

"Where was this name written?"

"Above the door, upon the arch."

I remembered seeing what was written on the gateway to the courtyard of Babel, *Mysteija*. I told him, hoping he had seen it too.

"I did. It read Mysteja Balba, the name of this land. The rooms are also named."

I hadn't made so many observations as him. I listened, hopeful to hear some new gem.

"What did the door say through which Renqwr passed? If you remember, I may be able to go after him."

I thought long, but I had not paid attention to his room. I had lingered only on MuchHeart as he passed out of my sight. ϑꞷỸθ I thought. That was written above the door through which MuchHeart and Amer had entered.

"What does it mean?" I asked this of Justice. He thought for a moment before he responded.

"Surely passing through that door, MuchHeart was not the one for whom ƕⲟꜰⲱꞆꙶꙃ searches. She would not have allowed him to pass through it. For rather than marrying the Queen, MuchHeart chose to marry the woman Amer, whom he brought with him."

The light grew bolder as it came closer to Amer. She crouched in the corner, afraid and alone. She began to cry, and the light flickered. It grew larger and its color more vibrantly blue. Her savior's song reached her ears. MuchHeart! She saw her groom walking toward her with hands outstretched. She ran to him and embraced him.

"Did you fear that I would not come to you?" Amer had never seen such longing in someone's eyes. No one had ever wanted her as he. She was deeply infatuated. She believed she was in love. She was glad of the opportunity to be alone with her groom. She whispered sweet nothings in his ear and they lost themselves to the darkness which pervaded as the light within MuchHeart consumed Amer. This was not a light that is easily described. It was a light that is truly darkness, so dark that it is perceived as light. Amer was consumed by it as a frozen river consumes a stranded traveler who lurks too close for a sip of water. Her limbs burned as the cold overtook her body and she fell asleep in her husband's arms. Her slumber was complete; it was so empty that she could not even dream.

I exhaled. Justice had buried his face in his knees once again. He rocked. I stood, my weakness disbursed, and walked toward SpeakGood and HopeKind who were now in conversation together. They paused and looked toward me as I approached.

"It seems we are in a holding room. Our companions have gone through other ways. Did anyone see the writing on the door to ҔϖҒϖϾϑʒ's right through which Renqwr entered?"

"No," said HopeKind. "I can't say that I saw writing on any door. It must have been well disguised."

SpeakGood toyed with his chin pensively.

"Now Deceit, I did see above that door a scribing. But not having the tongue of Babel of my own equipment, I did not recognize it."

"What did it sound like? What did it look like?"

"I couldn't say. The symbols were like gibberish to me and a sound from it would have been impossible for me to make."

"Could you draw what you saw?"

SpeakGood bowed his head to the bitter dirt and began to scratch away with his fingers. It was obvious that he was not an artist, nor was he well adopt at scribing. His art was in his speech. He could make the ugliest words delightful.

HopeKind and I both stared long and hard at the chicken-scratch which he had torn into the ground. There was something dead about the language. However, neither I nor HopeKind could tell whether it was due to SpeakGood's lack of ability to form the letters with no prior experience, or if it was the language itself that was the problem.

The words written were well known to any inhabitant of Aeda. Yet, the dialect was clearly foreign and distorted. The words written were these: *Ɣroɣθϑ∋ ϕɣrozΠϽϰϐ ù∋.* Prophets.

This couldn't be. The prophets are gone. None are left in Aeda. Surely one could not exist outside of that city. Then again, if Aeda were just an illusion, a dream like the one that still hung in the back of my mind, something of which no man could truly prove, then perhaps this door could hold a prophet.

I sat back. It had been so long since I had seen a variation of this word written. I had been so long gone from Aeda that I couldn't remember their purpose nor their call. But I remembered that these were men of importance.

"Should we dare to return by the way we came; to recapture our separated friends, or to join them in their ways, which are clearly better than this cave?"

"I should think I would go," hollered Justice from a corner. His forehead was reddened from where he had beat it against the rock.

"I will go and retrieve him. Any who wish to come with me may come. I vow to vanquish the Scarlet Woman who stole from me my brother."

Justice had joined our group at the corner nearest the wall where we had entered. He dripped hate from his lips as he spewed spit across the walls of the cave.

"That whore! That harlot hostess. She will rue this day she came against me-who-makes-the-rules."

"Justice, friend," cooed SpeakGood, "just before the sleep, you were reciting the rules of the King, and now the rules are from your own understanding? How can you turn against the King who gave you the power to make rules?"

"If he gave up some of his power to me, then it is mine to do with what I will. It is not something that you will understand."

Such aggression, such confusion made SpeakGood feel uncomfortably close to his travels. He felt again as if he had entered the house of Lonely. The room was dark, the inhabitants hostile and his appetite growing.

"Wasn't our meal meant to fill us for our entire journey?" said SpeakGood, worry painted across his face.

"I'm beginning to think that anything said in the name of the King is false." spat Justice. I can say that there was disagreement amongst our ranks.

I glanced toward HopeKind from the corner of my eye. She had an unsettled look on her face, as if she were coming to terms with the idea that the King was dead, and the world was holding hostage the power he retired.

She whispered beneath her breath. I couldn't make out what was said, but it did not the sound of praise. She turned her eyes toward me and they burned.

"Why has the king I once sought left me alone? I sit here with three men and none want me!" She raged against the King for leaving her here.

And so, we all began to misconstrue what we felt we had been denied, be it family, food, companionship, or the perception of freedom. We continued in this way for hours.

XVII

GEIA

"Elle pensait, si le vain bruit
D'une voix douce et cadencée
Comme le ruisseau qui gémit
Peut faire croire à la Prière.

…

Elle est morte, et n'a point vécu.
Elle faisait semblant de vivre.
De ses mains est tombé le livre
Dans laquel elle n'a rien lu.
           Alfred de Musset, *Sur une Morte*

*She thought, if the empty noise
Of a sweet and cadenced voice,
Like a moaning brook,
Can be called Prayer.*

*She is dead, and never lived.
She pretended to live.
From her hands the book has fallen
In which she read nothing.*

277

*M*uchHeart opened his eyes and was pleased by the image reflected on all the walls. The room was beautiful and made of the clearest mirrors. He was pleased that each one reflected his beauty next to his Amer; yet, there was one direction where he found his reflection obstructed.

Amer was beside him, she was the only thing in all the room that blocked his sight. He woke her so that she could see his beautiful reflection and move herself so that he could be seen beautifully on all sides.

Amer looked around the room and she, as well, saw only MuchHeart in every reflection. She saw what he could not view his reflection through her.

"What do you see? Why are you staring at the image which is hidden from me?"

"I see you—but you are as you truly—

He cut her off.

"Move, woman, for if it is me I would like to see."

He sat and stared at her, expecting her to do as he said. When she did not, he was overcome with rage.

"I am no slave of yours!" she said bluntly. She studied her view of his reflection and came to understand him as she had not known him before. She was disillusioned by his heart and she found his beautiful song to be her gallowly march. Looking at him, through her, he was hideous. He was the rot within which the Desert had borne him. He was the darkest angel which she had ever dreamed of—that which she thought was a nightmare and now she knew that she was his slave.

It was not apparent from the outside but, only through her once beautiful gray eyes, which were now blindingly white. When she looked in his direction, he could see himself through her eyes.

He was no longer the beauty he had longed to see at every angle. Through her, he saw all his evils, shame, and violence…and he thought it her fault.

Consumed by the hideousness that he could not keep from his eyes, he became only what he saw through her eyes. He stared with such intent that he was consumed by his reflection and she by him. She was absorbed in her husband who in return was absorbed by the looking glass which reflected his every secret. He could not hide. He could not look away. His eyes were not his own to shut for he did not possess them. He had trusted a lie and had disguised himself from even his own soul.

Justice was so caught up in his rage that he hadn't realized the door through which we passed had disappeared into the seamless expanse of rock wall. There was no way back, much less a way out in another direction.

I pointed out this problem. Justice stopped his ranting mid-sentence to peer at the wall, as if attempting to destroy it with his gaze.

"How perfect," he mumbled. "Not even an escape was given to us. Surely there is no King. If there were, there would not be such injustice as to lock us away in a cave with no egress!"

Justice fumed. His separation was too much for him to bare. We all doubted the promises of ᎶꭥꜰꙍꞐꙄꙃ; the search for a king, the chance to be him - none of that mattered now. My thoughts were cut short. Justice had commenced a good effort to tear down the wall which separated us, presumably, from the banquet hall.

"I will tear down the very walls they've built around the kingdom and its inhabitants! None will be left in its shadow. No, not one!" Anger consumed him completely.

SpeakGood, HopeKind, and I watched as he gave himself to insanity, trying to tear down the thick walls of Babel, bashing his head against the wall. His flesh turned red, then it bled. The flesh hung from his face and soon he whittled himself into nothing against this gray, bitter stone from which was quarried my gray stone.

The stones crumbled and uncovered a hole in the wall. The three of us remaining, SpeakGood, HopeKind, and myself passed through it. The room beyond was poorly lit but for a single window which let light in through a small, long hole in the wall of the mountain. The hall smelled of a kingly banquet of the finest meats and cheeses. Surely a banquet fit for a king. However, it was not a king that we found sitting between us and the window. At first, we did not know what we saw, but it was surely not kingly to slouch so in one's throne.

We moved along the wall of the cave to get a better vantage of the slumped object on the throne. It sat in solitude; no court gesture or even a slave kept its company. The table beside it was set with fresh fruits unlike anything we had seen before. The Desert does not grow fruit like this.

SpeakGood and HopeKind moved further, yet I was unable to move. Was this the King I had run from in Aeda? Had I found him here where I had told others I sought him, yet never believed? Surely, I had not expected to find him here. He looked much weaker than I anticipated. I was not impressed by him.

SpeakGood and HopeKind were stopped in their tracks by the shattering sound of a chalice hitting the ground. The figure on the throne moved slowly and carefully like a tempest upon the ocean. Sheer power emanated from it; we were brought to our knees. A snake coiled around her roots and down her flowing hair, encircling her white hair which caught the sun's dim light and shone forth as the moon. Long hair fell to the floor like fauna; the woman's feet moved delicately like waterfalls on an ancient temple ruin. Her gaze peered through my soul, more intently than the moon looks upon my face, steadily, studying my existence. When she walked, her footsteps resounded in my chest and I begged that she stop. When she was still, her beauty left me defenseless.

As I looked upon her face I noticed something strange about her. She was crushed. Her skull was not whole. She was broken. Her limbs were suspended and animated. A puppeteer could have been imagined just above her, instructing her every precarious move. She was but a doll, no life of her own, merely brought to life by the power which possessed her.

"I know you." she said directing a sturdy finger like a poplar toward the center of my forehead. "I watched you come across the Desert. You live a duality more precariously balanced than that of my own. I have been tossed around, conquered, and relinquished. I have been ruled by one, and then another. Yet, they call me Queen. Wars and battles have been fought on my land. Sadly, it is not mine to conquer nor to battle. I cannot influence the outcome. Yet, they say that I am transcendent. You were summoned. I know it is you. You have come to lead me into final victory!"

She came upon me as a siren to her prey. I was overcome by her. SpeakGood and HopeKind bowed in the corner. Her power was enough to deceive even those who know her sinister state. I would have been deceived, yet there was something amiss. I threw off this woman and looked upon her. She was a queen of her own rite. However, the power behind her was not from within. She had been robbed of her glory, but she was not built as a queen. She wore her crown as a mockery and I was angered greatly. I knew that crown which she wore. I had heard of it before. It was a crown of thorns. I threw myself upon her to rid her head of such mockery. She was an imposter! A puppet of the most despicable kind. That crown belonged at the peak of Saia.

The crown was truly at the peak of Babel. But it had been stolen and placed there. It was not hers. She laughed as I wrestled her. She handled me as a hurricane handles the coast—mercilessly. She rose from under me and threw me into the wall. I was caught immobile and she walked to me by her puppet-like maneuvers.

"Do not tempt me to cast you from the mountain! You will surely die outside my boarders! There is a storm raging and you best choose your allegiance carefully, boy. Here, you may become my swine. There, you will be tossed to the unforgiving storm which comes upon the land. This storm has been threatening since before your journey began. Feed my body and kill yourself. But do not dilute your ability, nor mock my majesty."

"I would rather die without than die within. You offer nothing here but death, you foul fiend. You were clearly once beautiful. You have now turned into a harlot undeserving of worship from even by the rodents which live upon you."

I spit in her face and she fumed. Had she been this mountain itself, she would have long since erupted. She threw me to my companions and cursed us where we sat.

As we watched, she grew in her appearance of power. She became increasingly unstable as the storm without grew nigh. She seemed greatly affected by the storm. She peered through a small window in the wall. Perhaps, from her view point, she saw something we did not. There was no storm that I could see from the windows through which we stared.

"I am older than any prophet that you have known. I've seen power that would melt your heart in fear. I have squashed empires much larger than any you have known. Aeda will be a ruin and you with it! I banish you to the Abyss where you will burn for your sins against the Queen!"

My dream felt like reality. Where my mind went during my sleep was too real to be found in my unsophisticated dreams. Caught in a militant battle, the enemy at the Fence, I was aware of my duty, yet, I could not help but notice my surroundings.

I was back in my home in Aeda. This was no dream; this was reality. If this was reality, where was my conscious mind?

The company that had been mine beside the Fence was not here, perhaps not yet, or perhaps they had now abandoned me. Regardless, there was a battle unfolding before my eyes in which there was pitted one against legion. The single man who stood upon a hill in Aeda, dressed as the Paradise Stone, held up one hand—to whom? To me? —no. He held his hand up to those consumed by the East.

The war horn sounded and the man on the hill spoke:

"Be mindful that in the days to come there will be only a remnant. Be not deceived as you deceive; leave your deceptions in the wilderness. Let fly your white flag and it will be your surrender, not to the spirit that is already here, but to the one which will return in triumph to rescue you. Be not afraid of surrendering to the King; fear dying to the one who claims the kingdom, he who rules Babel and her territories. You have seen him and know him by many names. He is not the prince he claims to be, do not fool yourself."

The dream progressed, and he no longer addressed me, but rather he addressed the Desert.

"Come out, Prince, your time is near, and your fate is set from before your defilement of your puppet queen, before I created her and before you attempted to steal my throne."

Thunder rose out of the Badlands; rain fell in the Desert and the sky parted. The symbol which was so often carried by those I knew in Cꙮdꙮm3 was present now in the sky. Its tainted image was not its demise, for a promise of the King is greater than the destruction of man. As the thunder reached a fever-pitch, and I thought its rumbling could not be louder, it became clear that thunder was not the cause of the noise; the sky had split in two and as the clouds cleared I could see blue fire pouring from the heavens like an ocean in the firmament. The Desert, where my journey had been, was burned up and everything I knew with it.

In the distance, I could see Babel and her twin. The hill within the tents was flattened to the level of the surrounding city, burying her in all that she had rejected

285

so that it could no longer be denied by them. As the hills fell, the men and women and children of the Desert cried out to the landscape to cover them.

Babel rallied her armies; there were some of every territory and I knew men among their ranks: men who had once lived in Aeda, and those who had always been its enemies alike. There was no discrimination in the Desert; this war was over men and they were those who fought.

Sleep could not hold me. I awoke, I was alone. No one was here with me. Not HopeKind, SpeakGood nor any of the company that had been with me before. The dream-like vision was burned in my mind — there was something deeper than the reality in which I was living. I felt it in my blood and it was calling me to my home. I had to return to Aeda.

A fog rolled over the floor and I looked at my feet; the ground below was blue, and it sizzled and hissed and spit from its fragile, glassy surface acid which bit at my ankles.

I screamed with pain; none were here to hear my cries; I was as loud as I desired but my screams did not quench the vast hunger of this pit. I heard a beat of metal, I shuddered remembering the Fallen and their ferociousness.

I looked around but could see little over the fog that choked away my breath. I was losing the ability to breath, to scream, to run — in a place that was larger than I could explore in an eternity. I hadn't even a hope. I fought past the burning in my throat and hoarsely called out to my friends.

A whisper floated past my ear and an echo into the other. I took one step; the floor cracked and creaked threateningly. I froze in place and watched the floor buckle under my weight. A hallow fracture sounded in the depths of the pit as I precariously stood on its glass covering. I slowly bent to my knees and spread out over the surface of this glass ceiling. I was on the obverse side of an acidic lake which was kept at bay even by the floor's fragility.

I heard another echo, just as before, but I had not yelled. Had my voice come back to haunt me, or had someone else called to me?

The glass beneath me moaned under the weight of my body, and it ate away at my skin when I was unlucky enough to pass over a fracture that pawed at me with its liquid claws. I was staring in the face of death; and oddly enough, I had to pause and remark at the beauty of this evil. I was tempted to break the glass and let the lake take my mind. I would never be sad again—I thought to myself—if I were lost to unconsciousness.

I looked up toward the perpetual darkness that spanned the vista beyond. This must be the lowest place in the mountain, for it looks like it could be as expansive as the entirety of the Desert.

The echo was back, and it sounded as if it were encompassed in water. I felt a chill run down my neck and into my lower back as I turned toward the echo's origin. A heavy thud hit the floor. There was movement beneath the surface of the glass. I slowly crawled toward the sound—it was mere lengths from my head. I pulled myself near with great speed, and from three other directions the noise had called those I lost from their respective places in this labyrinth-underground. SpeakGood and HopeKind met me at the place where there was a man stuck below the glass.

We peered down into the abyss and saw the acid-eaten body of MuchHeart.

"Where is Amer?" asked HopeKind?

I thought this was a horrid question on which to waste time when someone is here needing to be saved, besides, it seemed logical that she had been eaten first by the acid.

"He was her protector, why is she not with him? Did he abandon her?" HopeKind was distraught with anger at the selfishness she perceived of the situation, but I was consumed by the rot in my mind and I broke the glass.

It shattered with the sound of one hundred chandeliers hitting the floor of a marble ballroom— unmistakably beautiful, but as heart-wrenching as little else. I realized what I had done only soon enough to look into the eyes of my friends who would now drop with me into the cavern which I had opened with my lusts for one who was beyond my reach in safety. We fell.

Que haya sueños es raro, que haya espejos,
que el usual y gastado repertorio
de cada día incluya el ilusorio
orbe profundo que urden los reflejos.

…

Dios ha creado las noches que se arman
de sueños y las formas del espejo
para que el hombre sienta que es reflejo
y vanidad. Por eso nos alarman.

Jorge Borges, *Espejos*

It is strange to dream, and to have mirrors
Where the commonplace, worn-out repertory
Of every day may include the illusory
Profound globe that reflections scheme.
God has created nighttime, which he arms
With dreams, and mirrors, to make clear
To man he is a reflection and a mere
Vanity. Therefore, these alarm.

e fell through the realm of unconsciousness; ours was retained for us to induce a particular familiar kind of hell. We hit the floor of the cavern—glass crashed down around us—MuchHeart was within the glass itself. He was not in our dimension. He was no more. He was a fading reflection of what might have been. We looked closely, studying the wall trying to free MuchHeart, but the damage was done, and he was but an ugly shadow trapped within the glass shards. He was hideous, and I could see within his heart, and through his, my own. There was a dark power that knit us against our nature, but even in his inexistence, that union permeated the darkness to haunt me. SpeakGood and HopeKind saw it as well— nothing could have hidden the truth about me now that my most dastardly deed was uncovered. I had killed a child long ago in my youth—what I brought with me to the mountain was not a large-hearted boy, but the heart of a child that I had long since destroyed.

This was the power within me—for there was true power but it was neither from my origin nor for good. The power which emanated from me had been acquired in Arqana when an incipit rot was introduced within my heart. That power could only destroy; it could not mend. Only the authority I abandoned in Aeda held my salvation from the death that lurks in the shadow of this glass, staring at me like the murderer I am.

HopeKind and MuchHeart studied him, curiously. Soon their eyes turned to me. He told a dark story which was ours and the truth destroyed my deceitful words and actions. I was stripped of the protective covering of an evil and deceitful tongue.

Their eyes met mine, which I quickly averted, but I saw in their eyes that they had seen my familiarity with MuchHeart; they saw my lies, they saw my deceit and those who loved me now despised me.

It was my selfishness that led them into this glass coffin; I was the chief of sinners among them. I descended the levels of Babel to find a place where I could have my prey, bringing my friends and loved ones unknowingly with me so that I might look upon MuchHeart—all that I wanted—and what was my end? I could look upon nothing else. But there was no beauty in my shadow of him and I realized that I had not seen true beauty outside Aeda. I saw that the boy in the wall was purely of my own creation. There was no good left in him and it was not the MuchHeart that I had met by the Fence—nor the MuchHeart that I had parted from in Arqana—he was but a projection upon an empty shell of what had been—a façade of my own imagination, bound in my crystal palace of foolish and demonic pleasures.

I took up a piece of glass in my hand to take my own life; I saw no easier way out. I was distraught by my own actions and I was lost in the bowels of the very death I had rejected life to escape. In my efforts to find my own way, rather than the one which was given me, I found myself at the deepest and darkest of ends without a prayer.

I couldn't do it—I couldn't take my life. It was not mine to take. What ridiculousness this cowardice seemed to me. I had already destroyed my own life, mine and others'. I deserved this. I brought the glass to my skin, letting my blood pour over my sin. But my blood was not pure; it was rank with the rot of the Desert. It was of no use to me and of its loss I could not escape my fate. As the blood began to fill the glass cage that reflected my perdition back on me, I was overcome by it and I fell to unconsciousness. But to lose one's consciousness in Babel is to travel yet further within.

The wind howled in the Desert; the sand picked up and hit MaliciousCraft like bullets and made her face feel asleep. She had to keep her eyes closed as she dragged the body of Moveable through the storm.

The body was fat and bloated with insects, but not the most unattractive of the once-living that made its way through the Desert.

MaliciousCraft paused for a moment and covered her face with a black cloth that hung from her sleeve, thin enough to see through but thick enough so as not to let through the sand that whipped through the air. She estimated that her cave was another day's walk. She sat for rest and had herself a snack—a little soft flesh from her prey was deserved. She ate lightly. She had a gaggle to feed.

The storm did not settle through the night. There would likely not be a calm again for days in the least. She had seen this before; it was the wind that came off the ocean. There were tales that it originated from Paradise to send waves to wash clean the Desert when there was an evil in the land that needed destroying.

MaliciousCraft laughed. What a ripe story. What a ridiculous threat of Aeda—the liars and murderers of the

Desert Kingdom. The King was dead, everyone who lived in the Desert could see that. Babel was the new kingdom and she was part of its reign. She could not be defeated, but she had a task at hand and the prince whom she served was not as forgiving as she would be of herself.

Sleep was impossible, but she could sleep all she needed when she was—she paused in her thoughts—well, she could sleep later, anyways.

She grabbed her load which let off a stink—she laughed—how putrid! The more it stank with the consequences of its death, the happier her company would be. She giggled with excitement. Her giggle turned into a cackle and soon howling laughter.

The Beasts responded, and she was silenced. She grinned, her pets were on their way to greet her.

The body of Moveable made a deep trench behind her. MaliciousCraft shifted her weight and dragged the body with her right hip balancing the weight. She faced north; she could see the storm beyond the sand clouds; it raged and threw out funnels which disrupted the winds. She walked faster, not because she was frightened, of course, but because her load was starting to fall apart with all the sand blasting away the best pieces of soft flesh.

She would come upon her crowd before long; they dance in such storms as this. Hands and hair were all that could be seen above the crowd as she made her last descent toward the Tree.

The Queen sat upon a throne which was too large for her; ꝊꙌꝰꞬꙨꙅ rushed into the room, flowing like wine from a bottle. She glanced at the crystal orb which hung like a spectacular chandelier from the earthen ceiling. A sour look as one from rotting grapes penetrated her stony glare.

"The winds are coming; something is stirring in the Northern Sea. Paradise is set a glow; we can see its dangerous affects from the peak of Babel. It is on us to keep this from those coming to us. The King of Paradise is an evil man; take your kingdom from him, my sacred and beautiful Queen!"

"The King there is dead, we are already the kingdom." said the Queen, repeating what she had been taught of her own nature by the one who hid behind her throne.

"Times are changing; history has broken its cycle. There is no doubt that the winds are a Northerly wind, they are changing the direction of the sands so that the peaks of the dunes look in our direction. We must respond!"

"Bring HasmoDeis, he is trusted in changing the hearts of the children of Babel. He will have their answer."

"There may not be time. The shore is already overtaken by a terrible storm. The Desert will be washed within a day.

If HasmoDeis cannot convince the numbers to flee to Babel, they might just find their refuge in the high grounds of Aeda."

"ҺꚍꝰꙆꙶ, I will not tolerate this skepticism. The Desert is our territory; the King does not recognize any in the Desert. If he does live, he will leave us ours and take only his."

ᚻꞔF☺Ç∂ƺ shrieked with insanity: "Did you learn nothing? He is coming to take the land which is ours! Not one outside Aeda is prophesied to survive!"

"Folklore, fairytales! Imaginations of the disloyal run amok! Pay it no mind."

ᚻꞔF☺Ç∂ƺ leaned in close to look the Queen in the eyes. "Where do you think the idea of salvation comes from? These fools are too stupid to take themselves out of their misery! Look at the one we have in a dream just now, trying to take his life to escape destruction. This is the foolishness we are dealing with. They are easy and malleable and tend toward their own destruction. These idiots couldn't dream up a savior, it's illogical that someone who could take them from here would do so. Think before you speak!"

ᚻꞔF☺Ç∂ƺ chewed her knuckle, slapped her knee angrily and stood, shaking her hair out of her face and she walked out and slammed the door. The Queen stood and peered out the mountain into the storm.

"If you're out there, you're not welcome here. If you're out there, I don't want you. I eagerly looked for you and you didn't find me. Leave this mountain alone, we have built for ourselves a kingdom taller than even the spires and hills of Paradise—surely more spectacular than Aeda which is but one hill divided by a river.

"Bring your worst from the sea; let's see whose castles stand the test of time."

The Queen sat back in her throne. "ᚻꞔF☺Ç∂ƺ!" she shrieked. "Do we still have a castle in Arqana? Does it rest on the hills of Aeda?"

ꝂꙨꝰꙍꙄꝰꙅ stumbled back into the room— "Yes, the castle is under the rule of MaraJipsa, a dastardly goçip who is not a loyal. But Queen, that is not the worst of it— Ꙅꙍdꙍmꙅ lies on a hill preserved for a special destruction. We abandoned it years ago when prophecy told of her harsh judgements. Do not send your loyalists there—if they are not killed, they will breed themselves out in a generation and there will be no more loyalists."

The Queen stood and watched the storm more carefully.

"If we do not survive today, we do not fight tomorrow. Send the loyalists to Arqana and promise MaraJipsa the kingdom poorly ruled by FreeThinker. Give her a generation of his youth and she will be our greatest ally. She has power, and we need to borrow her kingdom for a time. Send the loyalists into hiding in the heights of her kingdom. Do not hesitate any longer."

ꝂꙨꝰꙍꙄꝰꙅ rushed from the room. Their situation was dire. She had no choice but to listen to the Queen.

MaliciousCraft could hear her heart pounding along with the drums of the goçips. Her company was singing a song that pleased her heart.

The singing and dancing did not stop as she approached; they greeted her happily and took her prey. The party raged on with all sorts of drunkenness and feasting. The goçips rejoined their company and their Beasts who hunt for men who wander from Aeda.

MaliciousCraft relaxed, but not long enough. She was approached by one Scorna.

"Where is my thief?" she cried in MaliciousCraft's face. "Where is he?"

"I couldn't procure him. He entered Babel with a large group. It was all I could do to escape before the company was swallowed by the mountain.

"This one died upon impact with the ancient river bed. There was no hope from her beginning. She did not believe in Babel or Paradise. She had no side—she was easy prey. Deceit was not an easy prey; the Queen wanted him for her own."

"This is supposed to atone for your failure? He killed my pet and all you could do was capture his easy friend?"

Scorna pulled out some of MaliciousCraft's hair in a fit of anger.

"You are useless, you foul, fecal goçip!"

"I had him well seduced," said MaliciousCraft, somewhat resentfully. "But he was more enticed by another—I could tell—and another, yet, was so enticed by him that my chances were slim unless he were a total fool. Even in his blindness, he was too practiced a liar to let such a small one pass by him."

"You're worthless."

MaliciousCraft was not disappointed to see Scorna walk away. She stared at her knees, a matt of her hair hanging precariously from her scalp. She licked her hand (she knew better than to look at the residue it created.) She could tell by the way it felt that it would do the trick and she padded the hair back into place. It stuck for a while but soon would slip off again, not to be returned. She tied her hair in place over the scalped patch and stood to retire to her cot in the cave. She walked through the roots of the Tree where her sisters still danced. Above her were the spirits of her ancestors' more practiced at soulsnatching than her; she looked upon their work with fascination. They were beautiful. Their metallic blue light—the sounds of the modern day that their wings so mechanically produced—beauty in its newest form. She climbed the wall and found her hole, curled up and made a comfortable position. She slept.

The Queen sat on her throne, fuming, the Scarlet Woman had crossed a line. She was not trustworthy; she did not trust him to be as powerful as she knew she was.

She stood in a pout of anger, hands clasped behind her lower back, chin jutting forward intently facing me off in my sleep-state cage.

What keeps these three from reaching their final depth of sleep? She thought to herself, but she knew the answer. She only denied its truth.

"*My* truth will persevere. Yours will die with you." Her voice reached the ceiling quickly, spit flying just as forcefully from her lips as the words. "My kingdom will transcend the depths of the ocean and be a sole peak in the profound. My will be done!"

Her fists crashed against the crystal cage, it swayed ominously and creaked as the weight shifted. But it did not fall. The chamber had us asleep.

Why am I dreaming? I'm dead. Is this all death is? A dream? I touched my skin, I could feel its warmth. My body should be cold. I felt my neck; not a drop. I must be dreaming.

All that was around me was white; it threatened to blind me. I hid from the light, it was unlike the sparkling light that I had witnessed in the Desert; this light threatened to expose every ill, not casting a single shadow, only perfect truth.

I closed my eyes and hid my ears, the light spoke, and its words pained me.

"Wake up. Wake up and take up your surrender. Throw your old self to the goçips that consume every flesh and take up a new flesh that has been prepared for you since before you were born."

I trembled under its authority, I had never felt such purity. I was frightened for my nature, for I knew this light would burn it until there was naught left but the dust from which it made me. In the darkness of day, it shone bright, in the face of death it shone only brighter.

"It is appointed of you to die only once. Will it be here in the Desert or later before the throne of your King?"

I opened my eyes and saw the light and it consumed me. I was no longer myself, I was a new creature with new life and I heard in the light a final greeting.

"He who began this work in you will continue until the day of the King."

The winds rustled the trees of the woods; it came from the North, no longer a small breeze here and there that fades and dies as the breath of man. This wind caught every man's attention. The throngs of Ɠɷdɷmɜ stood from their enjoyment of each other to look on in wonder.

Many came out of the temple, its orange walls towering over them, but the wind reached within and awoke them.

Many fell to their knees; some were stoned for their weakness, others mocked for their betrayal of the brethren.

The loyal took up stones and cracked them over the heads of the kneeling for the words which they spoke.

Mara heard the commotion and stepped out from her niche at the peak of the tower. She looked over her kingdom and saw that her subjects were destroying the disloyal. She smiled and returned to her hole. She was pleased that the social order here in the woods was effectuated appropriately, however, she had never seen so many fall to their knees.

She stepped out again to count them; there were too many to count. She was thrown into her hole by the wind which blew from Paradise. The waves were coming soon. She laughed. *They cannot come this close to Aeda.*

My eyes dashed open. Drowsiness lingered, and it was difficult to sit. But my eyes truly saw for the first time since I looked upon Saia. I cocked my head to either side; HopeKind and SpeakGood were still beside me, eyes clasped tightly shut.

But where were the others? There was movement outside the cage, I tilted my head ever so slightly so as not to call attention to my awakening and I saw a dark figure cloaked in light. He looked like an angel, but I recognized his face. He was an old friend; he had led me here. But newly awoken, I saw him for who he is; a snake. He could not be hidden by the Queen any longer. How despicable to use a woman as your cover for evil.

I shivered. The figure stood across the room, looking out a small window into a dark and menacing storm.

When I saw that he was not paying attention, I shook my friends, trying to wake them. SpeakGood at first stirred, and HopeKind turned over, but still they lay prostrate. Frustration leaked into my throat and formed a knot. I sat back against the glass of the cage with my fist in my mouth and cried in desperation. I had brought them here and was incapable of their rescue now that they were asleep.

I was trapped in a foreign land. My heart ached. I clutched my chest—I felt it beating. Not as before I lost it, but a new beat that longed for Aeda. It ebbed and flowed like the ocean, but its power came not from within. I felt no exertion by its palpitations.

I made one more desperate attempt to wake my sleeping companions. It had been I, after all, who brought them to this place, though, I didn't know when we had fallen into this sleep for it felt so real.

Groggily, both opened their eyes, but they did not come to. I realized that I couldn't wake them by any means of my own. They were under a spell. It would be by the same authority that awoke me that could do the same for them.

There was no apparent way out but to break the cage; it should be easy enough. Though the glass held us tightly, it seemed fragile and able to be broken.

With a final look at my friends, hope in my heart that they would be awakened, I ran my foot deep into the glass. It did not break. The noise echoed through the great hall and the Prince reared his ugly head. Desperately, I kicked, harder and harder until my heels were sore. No use; the Prince walked toward me, murder in his eyes.

Not much more could be done. I was awake and now the enemy knew. My time was limited. I knelt there in the void of my cage and praised my King for not letting me succumb to the eternal sleep, but to awake once more before my end.

The glass around me melted away like ice. For a moment, I could but sit in awe at the miracle before me that I might be freed from my captivity.

All at once, I knew my task: to flee from the grasp of the Prince. The Prince gained speed as he saw that I might escape. My feet hit the floor, already running, and propelled me through the door nearest me.

It was dark, but I kept moving. I heard from behind me a deep, terrible laugh. It threatened to knock me off my feet, but what did the trick was not behind me but before me. I caught a whiff of such a foul stench that my eyes burned. I tasted the stench on my tongue and I tried to spit it out, but it was a useless task. Worst of all was what I found there, hanging from the ceiling.

XIX

TOWER OF BABEL

My foot upon the glassy sand
Of oceans deep and wide,
I peer upon the farthest land
And set my feet in stride.

The sunset fills the sky with pink,
The stars are what I seek.
I stare above, try not to blink,
As past the moon I streak.

I do not look at what's behind,
Resentful of what's done;
The future leaves me nearly blind
And warms me with the Son.

I reach the end of space and time,
And wonder why I ran.
I see my life was not sublime,
But ought not start again!   EDR

A deep rumble sounded throughout the Desert like thousands of trumpets calling along the mesas for lost children of Aeda. It echoed in every cavern and all the valleys.

The hills shook like a tree losing its snow. The sand leveled itself across the expanses, burying many who were unfortunate enough to have been asleep on the floor of the Desert. Those who had not been asleep were hidden.

A solitary girl was awake in the Tented City and she walked alone searching for something to steal; little did she know; a much older thief was on his way.

She crawled up a small ladder that entered a portal no larger than the shoulders of a child. The tent was high upon stilts and it creaked as she entered. Red light poured in from the hole at the peak where the moon was allowed the only sight of her foul deed.

This was the Tent of Mystic, who had been trampled and eaten by the untamable Beasts of the goçips. The girl was in search of a very specific treasure—a sophisticated item of which she had learned a great deal. Mystic was the only one she knew to have possessed it.

The prophetesses, Crude and Lewd, slept restlessly in the corner of the tent once used for Mystic's cards and bones. An unfortunately unattractive shadow cast itself on their faces in the red moonlight.

The child payed them little attention—they were fools and the whole city knew it—but she wandered ever so carefully to the edge of the tent were Mystic's black stone had been recovered from the feces of the Beasts. Crude and Lewd now kept it as a venerated object in such a simple city as the Tented City which had nothing else worth worshipping.

It was beautiful; she wanted to touch it, to hold it in her hands. She reached out for it, desperate for its power that might bring back her friend who had been slain beside her—her last true vestige of Aeda. She was awakened to the deep powers beyond the Desert—this was the quickest way to quench her thirst of the beyond.

She touched the stone. She felt no power—no power the she could harness—but what she did feel was the fright that was due her when she turned to see that the prophetesses had left their bed.

Standing to the side of their bed, Crude and Lewd hovered just above the ground, heads back and throats exposed as if attached by puppet strings to some foul puppeteer. She hovered passively for a moment, twitching ever so slightly like a lamb at the slaughter before she opened her mouth and let out a shriek that surely woke even the dead.

"War!" they cried, then they erupted through the ceiling and flew to the East, whipped around by the gusts that were still raging in the wild sky, making their way for Babel.

I felt at the object suspended from the ceiling. I could not see it because there was no light in this room, but I could feel every detail, every scar, and every bloodied vestige.

The body of my friend was hanging upside down by his feet; his forehead shredded, salty tears still crystallized on his cheek. I was glad that there was no light in here; I couldn't bear to see Justice in this foul mess yet again.

The state of Justice was hardly the worst. I kept walking, hoping to find a door that would take me out of this place. No luck. All that I found were more bodies, strung up in the same way. Amer and MuchHeart hadn't a scratch on them, though MuchHeart's eyes were once again empty sockets as they had been in Arqana. They were bound together hopelessly, but dead none the less. Most difficult to find was the body of Renqwr; I won't say much of his state, but I will say, there was hardly a bone in him which was solid enough to keep him suspended. Ћ@ғ@Ç9ʒ had likely led him through a door to a room which had not existed, destroying his physical body in the space which occupies no physical realm. She crushed him in his pride.

The burden of guilt was heavy on my back, again I fell to my knees. It could not be helped; my sadness remained. I understood. I had killed each one in my selfishness, yet each was truly a piece of myself. The prince displayed them here to kill me with guilt. Perhaps this would have worked had I not found my old body, tainted with the Desert, dead at my feet. I had to moved on.

I felt a breeze and heard the whistle of wind. There had to be some egress in this room. I bumped into many other bodies, some I recognized, others I did not even remember. I felt the stone wall.

The cold rock was rough on my hands. I felt along the face of it to find some way out. I tripped on a step and fell onto a stair. I climbed it. I was brought humbly to my youth—again escaping the evil that came upon me. This time, I was not as my father—lost to lust and lethargy, laying in my cage—I followed salvation of my own through the ceiling and into the sky—not to have more of this land, but to seek first the Kingdom of Paradise through Saia, her only port.

Each step seemed to be the last, but still another would come. Finally, I reached the opening and I stepped out above the clouds to see that the stairs continued, but I could not walk them all. There would still be some that I never stepped foot upon.

But when I turned to look toward the North Sea, I saw perched sturdily in its grandeur, Saia, between myself and the raging waters.

I was on the peak of Babel. I could see across the entire expanse of the Desert which I had crossed and saw the steps that I would need to take to return to Aeda to await the King's return. But as I sat there pondering, I saw a great wave rising out of the sea.

The Desert moaned under its weight, the winds carried it inland over every tree, rock, and grain of sand. It rushed toward the Mountain from which I had just escaped.

The prophetesses soared over the Desert, chased by the howling North. She was a siren warning of the coming judgement of the Desert.

MaraJipsa awoke with a start at the sound of the wailing Prophetesses, her village still battling below. She would not be able to find refuge in Babel; she knew this. She groaned at the thought of losing her kingdom to chaos.

MaraJipsa heard a noise in her chamber and looked up from a spirit she was currently cooking. A woman dressed in red stood before her.

"Let us refuge in your land and we will give you the largest kingdom within the coming dominion of the Queen—Geia. Save her, and the men and women of an entire generation will be given to you."

310

MaraJipsa was overwhelmed by thoughts of what she may do if she were permitted to escape Arqana and find safety beyond the Desert. She remained on her knees and kissed the feet of ꞨꙍꜰꙍᏨꙅ꙾ emphatically. She was sold, and so, their alliance began in the early throws of war.

The waves continued their way, and so did the shrieks of the Prophetesses. The Fallen heard her cries and took to flight, dropping all the rotting Desert corpses that were strung upon the Tree. The goçips ran from their caves in hopes of taking flight with the Fallen, it was no use; they sealed their caves. Each was responsible for his own flesh.

MaliciousCraft came up last, she had been asleep rather than occupied by festivities. Now she realized that this storm was no natural storm, but one sent to cleans the Desert. But of what or whom? She thought: of her and the like, of course. She buried herself and Moveable in her sleeping cave to wait out the storm—hoping as she worked that it would be enough to save herself.

The Beasts yipped as they ran like lemmings over the cliffs that separated them from their masters in the Desert valleys, each one seeking refuge in Arqana where there was the highest ground besides Aeda. Few made it further than the cliffs; some did not even leave the Badlands, but those who did were consumed by the floods that rushed the Desert.

MaliciousCraft's coven climbed the cliffs on which hung all whom they'd lured there, cultivated sacks of once-living flesh, now stripped clean and curing into their darkest creation. They stunk, but the goçips seemed to be at home here. Some fell and were dashed to pieces only to be washed out towards the Falls of Acedia, consumed by the North Sea.

Eager's body was found in the Badlands and floated gently, against the current, toward Paradise.

I sat watching. I could not believe what I saw, but I knew by whose authority it came. The wave washed the Desert clean. I turned to look down the hole from which the winds of Paradise called me, I hoped to see the face of a living friend, perhaps HopeKind might have awoken at the sound of my leaving, or even SpeakGood! But I did not see them, nor did I hear them.

What I did hear was a slow, soft slither which grew slightly louder as the head of a great snake emerged from the hole at the peak of Babel.

"This terror in the Kingdom is the doing of your King; can you really believe he will rescue you at the peak of my mountain when you have come so far into my clutches?

"You're a foolish breed. Come back down and go to sleep, I can make you like a God in the realms of your dreams."

"I know better than to trust your split tongue. You tell me this, but I've seen what you do with those who fall asleep in your castle.

"I'm awake, and I will not sleep again until the day of my King or until my last day in the Desert; but it will not be a sleep that succumbs to your magic, it will be a pure sleep, portioned for me by the King."

"Fool. You'll die if you don't come back in the mountain. You're despised in the Desert, but I can give you your dreams. Come with me, and the world will be yours."

I turned my back on the snake, having said all that I had reason to say. The waves were crashing over the

Falls, they washed the filth of the Desert into its basin and around the base of Babel. The waters continued to rise.

"Come in, before it's too late."

I kept my eyes focused on Paradise. The waters overtook me and tore Babel into the pit in which it sat.

The Desert was oddly quiet for a moment. The land was full of water, flooded to the brim. Not a peak was left untouched. Paradise sat still on the horizon. It was perfect in its design and could withstand that which the Desert could not.

The earth shook and broke open at the seam made by the ancient river. The waters receded into its expanse and all that was left were the wicked in the land that had held on to their lives but by a thread, only by the allowance of the waters that there might be one more chance for those remaining to turn their loyalty back to the King of Aeda.

I floated through the turning waters, washed out to sea; I had no fear. My white sail was hung, and the winds pulled me toward Paradise. I had no fear in the world to come for I had left the wilderness behind.

Fin

Epilogue

From

THE JUNGLE

2019

EPILOGUE

PUYA

aughter resounded from the polylepis forest that painted Oki green year-round. Two children danced and played in the forest, their parents not far off in the gardens of Oci.

The youngest of these children was in his sixth year. He was as any other six-year-old child. He lost his front teeth earlier that year and the teeth that replaced them were not unusually large for an adult, but they were comical when fitted into the skull of such a small child. He was not shy. In fact, it was his laugh that rang throughout the forest. There was hardly a moment this child could be seen without a large grin. Often somewhat mischievous, but never harmful. He had a true sense of joy that was untainted by devious thought or, perhaps, for lack of deviousness, thought of consequence.

317

As an infant, his father marveled at his beauty. He took after his mother whose genes were darker and therefore more dominant. His large eyes were the largest, most joyous that the father had ever seen. His pupils blended into the iris and sparkled black like the mica that littered the little caves he so enjoyed exploring. When the light hit his eyes just right, there could be seen distinction in his eyes and the iris radiated a beautiful hazel.

Because of his resemblance to his mother, they named him Peja after her name, Speja.

His sister, who was two years his elder, chased him through the forest. They were playing a game. Do not ask me the name of the game, I do not know. Perhaps they never thought to name it, or perhaps no one ever spoke of the name. But the objective was simple. Peja was the prey, and his sister the predator. Peja found so much joy in this game. He never asked to be the predator. His sister never asked to play the prey. Adrenaline was perhaps his motive and reason, or perhaps he simply loved his sister's arms around him when at last he was caught.

Fallen logs and twisted trunks, beard like lichen and protruding rocks made his terrain more fun. He could scale the trees, often five lengths tall, in mere seconds. He would launch himself from branch to branch with little effort. His strength had thus far outgrown his weight. His sister would tease him that, if she were a true predator, she would not bother with a 'monkey of such little substance.'

He reached the edge of the forest, ran out of branches to catch and fell into his mother's garden (which, luckily for him, had already been harvested). He rolled to his back, laughter echoing off the still mountaintop. His sister pounced from the near treeline and pinned him to the dirt, his laughter only growing.

The sister was a mélange of her parents. So much so that her name was quite unique. They called her Deseja after an old friend. Her birth occurred a single season after their arrival on the mountain.

They never spoke openly of their lives before the mountain. The kingdom they had created here was the only reality that Peja and Deseja had ever known.